what the fuck

The Avant-porn Anthology

D1722216

what the fuck:

the avant-porn anthology

compiled & mixed by

Michael Hemmingson

a.k.a. DJ Avant-Pop

Soft Skull Press 2000

What The Fuck:The Avant-Porn Anthology
ISBN: 1887128-61-1
© 2000 by

Michael Hemmingson, William T. Vollmann, Kim Addonizio, Vivienne Wood, Larry McCaffery, Robert Coover, Jimmy Jazz, Alan Mills, A.L. Reed , Ian Grey, Don Webb, Tamar Perla, Harold Jaffe, Thom Metzger, Jasmine Sailing, Nikki Dillon, Tasaurah Litzky, L.A. Ruocco.

edited by Michael Hemmingson
cover art by Norman Conquest
interior art by Norman Conquest *and* Rene Farkass
design by David Janik

PRINTED IN CANADA

Soft Skull Press, Inc
100 suffolk st.
new york, ny 10002
www.softskull.com

Contents

Acknowledgements

First, Larry McCaffery, for handing the project over to me and letting it grow my way, as well as being an inspiration for the vocation of the anthologist. Maxim Jakubowski, another anthologist of inspiration. Marti Hohmann, wherever you are, whatever job you have this month. Some may say Al Gore invented Avant-Porn and Ralph Nader took it away from him, but I really think it was Derek Pell. The Fritz Theater, for the use of office space in the darkest days and the wee hours of 1998-99—R.I.P., dudes. Karin Williams: "no comment." Christine Doyle, R.I.P. (in Hell.) Lords of Acid, aural inspiration. And Michele King, R.I.P. (in Heaven.) Crescent Media, but they'll never know why. FedEx! Gordon Lish!—for not wanting to be in this book. And DJs Danny Tenagila and Paul Oakenfold, aural inspiration. David Mannis, for giving me a newspaper to run, and then screwing it up in the name of censorship and a fear of politicians and advertisers—anyone who says "there is no freedom of the press here" shouldn't be a newspaper publisher. So: R.I.P. *San Diego Downtown News*. Marilyn and Wayne Lewis, for graciously playing hosts on my trips into New York. Karla Zounek and Jim Fitzgerald, for believing in my work on other fronts. And, oh, *oh*—my colleagues and antagonists whom I didn't include in this volume...next time, dudes. And finally, yes, Sander Hicks and Nick Mamatas, for knowing a good thing when they saw it and giving this book a home—and everyone else at the Soft Skull Press family for strong dedication and hard work, injecting much needed fresh blood into the weird world of book publishing.

M.H.

Information

Dust Devil

A Preface

Larry Mc Caffery

If you've spent as much time pounding the experimental
literary pavements as I have, you get used to deadlines;
knowing that some illiterate managing editor goon type is
breathing down your neck threatening to postpone the publication of some project you or one of your Private Editorial
buddies have spent months or even years assembling
unless you deliver the prefatory goods has always had a way
of focusing my concentration.

This being a preface, I suppose I'm supposed to supply a
little background about how the anthology came to happen,
toss in a few catchy phrases, supply a narrative that helps
explain why this particular collection is so new, so "now," so
much better than all the other similar anthologies. But since
this preface has to be handed over to Hemmingson in the
next six hours—and since *not* handing it over to him is likely to have consequence far more serious than just delaying
the publication of this anthology—let's dispense with the
usual prefatory clichés and cut to the chase.

I was just deciding to call it quits late yesterday afternoon. Outside my office, an enormous dust storm was raging out in the Borrego badlands. It was the kind of desert
night that Paul Bowles might have used as the backdrop to
torture one of his naive fools into a deeper appreciation of
the ways of the world.

Literary clients being as scarce in late July out here as an
oasis with bikini-clad teenage girls lounging around in the
sun and shading themselves under looming palm trees, I
was passing the time yesterday afternoon trying to finish up
the porn novel I hoped to peddle to Grove—quality stuff,

mind you, not the usual wham-bam-thank-me-m'am formula, with two dimensional characters eagerly thrusting Tab A or B into tab C, D, E, or F—but something with serious literary ambitions (and if this penetrating tome didn't work for Grove, I could always try Blue Moon). On this particular afternoon, I'd asked my secretary, Lyna, to help me out with a certain scene that was giving me trouble. I find I always work best when I'm writing out of my own personal experience—not that my work is autobiographical, mind you, but sometimes my imagination needs a kick in the pants. Lyna was, as always, a lot of help—she was a twenty-something Greek bombshell graduate student who'd shown up at my doorstep several weeks earlier asking for help doing research on her cyberpunk thesis at UCSD. A quick glance at her c.v. and reference letters—and a more careful perusal of her tanned legs, perky tits, rich dark hair, and pouty, *pouty* mouth—I quickly determined we could come to some sort of arrangement that would suit both our needs. As an exchange for providing her with research tips about cyberpunk, she agreed to handle my secretarial chores during the summer, plus provide tutoring lessons in ancient Greek (a recent passion). I found her bright and eager to please, in addition to taking masterful dictation; she had all the secretarial skills a Private Editor could ask.

And she was an incredible fuck.

Anyway, when this whole thing got started, Lyna and I were working up a kind of re-enactment of a scene from my Grove Press hopeful. Having already spent the afternoon wading through all that drearily predictable anthology crap, I was anxious to develop something in my own work that was genuinely transgressive. That's where Lyna came into the picture—or rather into the video camera, which I'd set up on a tripod to provide a record of our transgressions.

"And...action!" I said, pushing the video cam's remote button to RECORD.

"I absolutely love to fuck,"[1] Lyna was saying, as I worked my fingers into her warm wet pussy. Her thick Greek accent,

---

[1] "Erotic language approves the actions of the body. approval is encouragement, and sexual encouragement is the point of all aphrodisiacs...Those who are completely satisfied sexually by language alone, like those who are satisfied by voyeurism or flaggelation, are certainly abnormal, possibly psychotic, that is, some psychic way dissociated from their total being. But it may also be, and this is no contradiction, that an intense use of dirty words is a lyrical celebration, primitiveness being at the very heart of lyricism, of the release of animality." Peter Michelsen, Speaking the Unspeakable. Boulder: University of Colorado Press, p.51.

so full of Mediterranean smells and sensual mysteries, charmingly transformed her opening lines into something that sounded like "eye apsoulootly luff to fok." Lyna was lying spread eagle on my desk, her skirt bunched up near her tits, her panties dangling on one ankle. I was just starting to push the tip of my throbbing dick into the wet darkness of her thick brown bush when Lyna broke character.

"Just a second, Mac, " she gasped, "I don't understand my motivation in this scene. I thought I was supposed to be a sexually inexperienced babysitter you were trying to seduce one night while your wife was on vacation. So why would I be saying something like this?" I always get a little irritated when my concentration is broken, and began taking it out on Lyna by biting her big brown nipples. Evidently she didn't take the hint, because she cried out, "Oh, what does this mean?!"

"Goddamn it, haven't we gone over this a thousand times already?"[2] I said. I roughly began rubbing my fingers over her thick dark bush. "It doesn't 'mean' anything," I explained as patiently as I could under the circumstances. "That line is the opening to Kathy Acker's early meta-porn classic, *I Dreamed I Was a Nymphomaniac.* I just threw it in to add a kind of literary texture, an intertextual reference: "I'm not looking for simple mimesis here but a kind of crazed passion, characters are deliberately two dimensional, but with just enough detail so that readers can project their own sexual fantasies." I replaced my finger with my tongue.

"Okay, Mac, if you say so," Lyna murmured dubiously, "but . . ." I ignored her blatherings about Deleuze and Guattari and the denaturing of the body, concentrating instead on pushing my tongue as far up inside her warm wet pussy as I could, when we heard the commotion outside the office. Someone was banging on the door.

Lyna jumped, pulled up her panties, smoothed down her skirt, and rushed to the outer office to perform her proper duties as my secretary. I made myself a tequila-and-tonic, with plenty of extra salt on the glass.

I could hear some mumbling, then a loud deep voice uttering something I couldn't quite understand. Then silence.

Lyna's voice came over the intercom: "Mac, there's some-

2 "...when confronting our sexual fantasies we do well to keep our own ridiculous in mind." Michelsen, ibid. p. 46.

body here to see you."

"Tell 'em we've closed down for the night."

"He sez it cunt wait. Mac, I think you'd better see this guy—he seems pretty desperate, he keeps saying the same thing over and over again, 'Wot the fok.'"

"What's his name?"

"Says it's Hemmingson." Suddenly, I got very interested. "Michael Hemmingson." Oh *Christ*.

"Send him in, darlin'," I said, trying not to sound as upset as I was feeling. "And while we're in here, why don't you practice your lines?"

There was in my biz what we like to call a "pregnant pause," and then Mike Hemmingson came through the door.

The fact that Mike Hemmingson was standing there in my office wasn't all that surprising—I'd gotten to know him years earlier when I was still working out of a tiny San Diego Gaslamp Quarter office. Over the years, there had been a lot of rumors circulating about his bizarre literary and personal behavior, but along the way he had run up an impressive string of publications. Right now, though, it was pretty obvious that something had gone terribly, terribly wrong.

Mike Hemmingson was a mess. He looked like one of those booze hounds at the end of a Ray Carver story: at his wits end, bewildered, fumbling for an explanation to life. His hair was matted, face sun-scorched and dust-caked, eyes wild; rivulets of sweat were carving channels through the dust on his face, producing the same kind of braided alluvial fan patterns you see at the base of the Santa Rosa Mountains. Other than the crazed look he had plastered on his tush, the only thing he was wearing was a pair of men's boxer shorts with prints of various cocktail drinks all around.

What the fuck? I thought to myself, not particularly eloquent, it pretty much captured a sense of the moment; but before I could actually say anything, Hemmingson blurted out: "What the fuck!" It would prove to be one of the screwiest bits of dialogue I've ever been involved with.

He actually croaked the phrase weakly, staggering to the chair in front of my desk. I looked him over suspiciously. How the hell had he known what I was thinking?

"What the fuck?" I demanded.

"What the fuck," Hemmingson repeated. I couldn't decide if he was delirious, deliberately mocking me, or even aware that he was here. That's when I noticed the bulge rising ominously out of his boxer shorts—it was hard to tell in the fading twilight, but it looked like somebody had stapled a 300-page manuscript to his groin.

Wanting to escape from this monotonous dialogue, and sensing Hemmingson could use a change in direction, I smiled and said, *very softly*, "Is that a manuscript you've got there in your underpants, Mike, or are you just happy to see me?" Hemmingson ignored my overture, was in no mode for levity. Painfully he began pulling the manuscript away from his belly, with a strange groan that I hoped wasn't pleasure-filled . Once he managed to separate himself from the manuscript, he held the thing out in front of me, and dropped it. The bundled pages made a soft plop on my desk. Something screwy was going on, all right.

"What the fuck?" I asked Hemmingson again.

"What the fuck."

This was getting tiresome. Instead of trying to break out of this prison house of language we seemed caught in, I looked down at the bloody pages. First thing that caught my eye was the cover—a familiar Rockwell painting of boy scouts, only instead of building a campfire they had a blonde bombshell trussed up like a turkey. Beneath the bloody smudges were the words, *What the Fuck: The Avant-Porn Anthology*.

"What the fuck??" I said, slowly, indicating to Hemmingson the cover and title. I was beginning to understand . . . I think.

"What the fuck," Hemmingson said. Then, with what seemed like enormous effort, he took in a deep breath and then very, very slowly—enunciating each word with such ease that I was certain he'd learned this technique during his days as a stage director at The Fritz—he finally managed to break us out of our monotonous "what-the-fuck" exchange.

"Mac, something weird happened to me out in the badlands and I need your help!"

I nodded. "Okay, but before we get going here, we gotta get a few things straight..."

"Yeah, yeah, I know—you get 25 bucks a day plus expenses, a Tuesday/Thursday schedule and no committee work. Jesus, Mac, cut the crap, this is serious!"

"Maybe you'd better start from the beginning."

At my prompt, Hemmingson set off into a delirious monologue that initially seemed like pure babel, a stream of non-sequitirs that can best be described as a mixture of John Ashbery's poetry, random selections from *Moby Dick*, and sound bytes from Gordon Lish's lectures on the art of writing. But as the words kept pouring out his mouth, I began to notice that his monobabeloque was carving a strange, utterly terrifying narrative from of the bedrock of what was left of his mind. A few of the edited highlights went something like this:

"...the planetary alignment, so I decided to locate the vortex over in the Fish Creek Wash area . . . not bothered bringing my canteen, figuring my flask of white Russians . . . the quarter and the dime...midafternoon dust storm . . . lost and feeling faint...must have been somewhere in the Split Mountain Area when suddenly . . . abducted by UFOs. Pikachu! Art Bell! Lizard Women! . . . Jellyfish-like creatures all being lead by a 10-foot tall Dennis Rodman lookalike! These were no Cnidarians! They were worse than Mormons! . . . USED me! . . . came to they had me strapped to a metal table . . . weird alien muzak playing in the background . . . lizard lady was giving me a blow-job . . . several orgasms, then I must have passed out . . to again, there were probes up my ass...another round . . . gang -raped by lizard ladies... Dennis Rod-Man was whispering horrible, nasty things into my ear! . . . awoke to find I'd been left near Font's Point with this manuscript stapled to my tummy . . . departing in their ship, transmitting a final message to me via some mode of telepathy . . . an ultimatum: I had 24 hours to arrange a book deal for this manuscript AND get somebody to write a preface for it or they'd make sure I never worked again!"

Hemmingson was out of words, but the sobs that now wracked his body spoke eloquently about his anguish. Reaching over and gently taking his hand, I tried to talk him down. "Maybe they're bluffing," I said. "I mean, how are—"

"They're not bluffing, Mac!!! They've injected me with some kind of time-released cold wartime Russian mycrotoxin; unless they provide me with an anecdote, it will begin erasing all my literary values and memories at precisely 8 a.m.." He added, "Tomorrow morning."

"Yeah, I heard about Rooskies using this stuff. The damage will be minute, subtle, and utterly effective."

"Look, Mac," he was pleading now, his eyes filled with a

kind of terror you only see on a first-time novelist who has learned that his publisher may go out of business before releasing the book, "You gotta help me. If you don't write this preface for me," he hesitated, "I'll be a Literary Zombie!"

He shuttered involuntarily, and looked down at the floor blankly.

"Okay, Mike, don't go all gooey on me. I'll take the case." For the first time since he stumbled into my office, a hint of hope and relief crossed his sand-ravaged face. I said, "Before I begin my investigation, I need to get some clarification about some of the points you mentioned. Like, this whole bit about the manuscript, making you get a publisher—I just don't get it. What's their angle? Money?

"Naw, they don't give a shit about the money. As near as I can figure, the only thing these guys ever want is a good fuck—they're not just sexually obsessed but jaded. They tool around the local galaxy clusters looking for planets with life forms they turn into their sex slaves. But these guys aren't just interested in fucking, per se—their agenda is world domination! Not by brute force, weapons, lasers, or Independence Day tactics. They're much more subtle. They send down an advanced guard of writers and artists who infiltrate the local literary scene and begin publishing fiction encoded to alter all who read it. You read their work, reality suddenly changes, nothing makes sense, and you're forced to be their pleasure slaves, willing to do whatever they command—all sorts of perversities; and golden, roman, and brown showers don't even begin to illustrate their lascivious behavior. Why, they're weirder than the Japanese when it comes to porn!"

Maybe my jaw dropped. "You're telling me that all the stories in *What the Fuck* are written by aliens?" I asked.

"Yeah."

"So," I said thoughtfully, "what kind of stuff is it? If it's commercial stuff—or any of that Carver-Iowa-workshop crap—you know I can't help you."

"Don't worry, Mac, I wouldn't have showed up here if it was anything like that—it's porn." He leaned toward my desk and winked. "Really filthy stuff."

"Yeah, so where do I fit in?"

"It's not just the usual porn, Mac—the aliens are already bored with that stuff. No, this is something different—it's WEIRD porn, literary porn, twisted, filthy stuff—but lyrical, if you know what I mean."

"Uh-huh," I uh-huhed.

"Mac, I'm scared, really scared. These aliens said if I did-n't play ball with them by getting a book deal for this anthol-ogy, they would ..." His voice cracked

"Go on, Mike, let it all come out," I said gently. In between his sobs, Hemmingson filled in the details of what the aliens had in store for him if he didn't play ball. It wasn't pretty: without an antidote, Hemmingson was to be relegated to publishing his books and stories in the small and universi-ty presses; each new work would be a clone of the other; he'd never progress or transgress; he'd never command an advance over $1500; and that his recent deals with Tor Books and Carroll & Graf and the money would vanish as quickly as a load of sperm on Monica Lewinsky's tongue.

I'd heard enough, and cut him off with a wave of my hand. "Okay, Mike, you've had a rough day. Give me a few hours and I'll see what I can come up with. Once I get a edi-torial handle on what the fuck's up with this manuscript, I'll get your preface written. In the meantime, why don't you head over to Carlee's and suck up a few tequilas-and-ton-ics—just be sure and ask for salt to balance your elec-trolytes. Tonight's karaoke night—you might want to get up and perform a couple of numbers, let some of that tension loose."

"Yeah, Mac, not a bad idea." He stood, stopped, turned, and asked, "They gonna have any problem with my outfit?"

"Nah."

After Hemmingson left my office, I called Lyna in to fin-ish the babysitter scene. She didn't answer. I called for her again. No answer. My first thought was she had maybe been abducted by Hemmingson's aliens. Then I looked out my window and saw Lyna walking with Hemmingson towards Carlee's Bar and Grill.

"Goddamn it," I muttered. If it wasn't enough that Hemmingson had interrupted the scene from my novel, as well as the pleasures of that particular text, and putting me on a case I wasn't prepared to take on, he was now taking off to karaoke with my Greek cyberpunk grad student and her warm wet pussy.

I poured a hefty shooter of bourbon. What else was there

to do? I settled in, sifting through the manuscript for clues about what I was going to say in my preface. Every private editor has their own way of solving a literary case. And despite all the essays I'd written about postmodernism, deconstruction, and other theory-oriented literary topics, I was from the old-school—which is to say that all I was ready to examine each story and espouse some jargon. Theory was a suckers games. All I was interested in was the textual facts, m'am, just the facts.

According to the PE Code, §3133.69, Private Editors are supposed to approach their work "keeping a safe editorial 'distance' and objectivity, never allowing their personal or sexual feelings concerning any elements of the case to be expressed." I was a little nervous—not only that what I had to say was likely to alter the entire direction of human and extraterrestrial sexuality, but that I knew from personal experience that writing about eroticism was, to paraphrase Georges Bataille, not just a problem but "the problem of problems."[3]

A few hours later, there were only a few selections left to examine. While absent-mindedly rolling a fag, I looked out my window. A bright full moon was already beginning its westward descent towards the Laguna Mountains. It didn't take a Yale-trained expert in Bataille or Sade to be able to recognize that Hemmingson was right about What the Fuck. All the clues indicated that this was porn all right—and not the kind of softcore form that that tends to stereotype, flat-tening sexuality into conventions that will not disturb its audience, where sex is made compatible with the prevailing sentiments of the culture, the kind that titillates its audi-ence with animalism, but seeks to socialize that myth by sublimating its physical egocentric energies into materialist culture analogue of sprit: the myth of sentimentality. No, the porn selections in What the Fuck were obviously very something different; literate, yes, but also dangerously

---

[3] Bataille goes on to note, "In that he is an erotic animal, man is a problem for himself. Eeroticism is the problematic part of ourselves....Of all problems eroticism is the most mysterious, the most general, and the least straightforward." See his brilliant study, Eroticism. Trans. Mary Dalwood. (San Francisco: City Lights, 1986.) Anyone wishing to investigate the kinds of "avant-" treatment of human sexuality in art—that is works which are deliberately transgressive, which risk exploring the limits of human pleasure, which occasionally introduce the spectre of violence, rape, pain, and death (because they're aware that violence and death are always linked with sexuality)—need to pick up this book.

transgressive—something...alien.

I knew time was running out, and started to go through some of the opening lines I was thinking about using in my preface. *If, then, literature is a mode of knowledge disobliged to the univocal presuppositions of an idealistic dialectic deriving its authority rather from the existential imagination, it is not only qualified to express a mythic sensibility but it may help that sensibility to change, to assimilate the seemingly undamnable stream of new truths being revealed to it. Whereby avant-porn enters a genre...*

Nah. What the hell was that supposed to mean? I was obviously feeling drowsy.

I knew I needed to clear my head, devise some prefatory remarks that would uplifting, seductive: but based on what? I went back over Hemmingson's testimony that none of the writers in What the Fuck were real—or human, even if some of the names were well-known; and that the whole manuscript was penned by alien lifeforms. But how the hell was that bit of evidence going to help me write my preface? Fighting panic, I decided to go back and conclude my preliminary investigation by finishing up all the selections.

That's when I came across "Cyrano of the English Department"—a selection that had my name on it. I stifled a scream.

Suddenly, everything was all too clear—so clear I knew I couldn't read any further. As to my preface, well, nix on that as well, even if my failure was going to cast Hemmingson into literary-zombie land.

I tossing the manuscript into the trash, reminding myself that I needed to invest in a paper shredder. It was then that I noticed I hadn't turned off the video cam. I was curious about reviewing my talk with Hemmingson, so I turned the cam off, rewound it, and played it back. I watched, with a smile, the brief scene with Lyna, as my fingers and tongue began to probe her divine fulcrum. I fastforwarded past the commotion and Lyna's departure, and picked things up again with me sitting at my desk, awaiting Hemmingson's entrance.

It never came.

On the video screen I could me sitting there at my desk, occasionally talking and gesturing, but the room was empty. I replayed the tape several times but the results were always the same: Hemmingson never appeared in the video. He wasn't there at all.

This was becoming too much like a Philip K. Dick story, so I had another shot of bourbon and decided to call it a night and go home, perhaps watch a Sumo wrestling match on satellite or put Springsteen's *Nebraska* into the CD player to fall asleep to.

I stepped out of my office in a bit of a daze, almost stepping on a rattlesnake, which scuttled away into the shrub. There was something weird in the air. The dust devils had vanished. Everything was dead still, the usual sounds of mockingbirds mixing in with the occasional mournful howls of coyotes. I looked up and saw a gyrating compass of flame moving towards me from over the Pinyon Mountains at warp velocity. A beam of blue light emerged from the saucer and packets of radiant energy rippled in ticklish waves over my face, filling my head with Avant-pornographic insights. As a river of words cascaded down into my consciousness, a prefatory form was assembled, and a flood of relief washed over me. I knew then I could now write Hemmingson's precious preface after all—and that he wouldn't have to spend the rest of his life as a Literary Zombie.

Moments later, the saucer was gone and I found myself alone in the darkness. That's when I heard the plaintive sounds of karaoke music drifting towards me from Carlee's—it was Hemmingson's deep rich baritone belting out the Sid Vicious cover version of "My Way." Lyna did the harmony. I headed back inside. I had an 8 a.m. deadline to meet—and a porn novel to finish.

July 2000: Borrego Springs, CA

Introduction

Michael Hemmingson

I. A Meta-Critical Jargon-Filled Explanation Of "Avant-Porn"*

XXXXXXXXXXXXXXXXXXXXXXXXXXXXXXXXXXXXXXXXXXXXXXXXXX
XXXXXXXXXXXXXXXXXXXXXXXXXXXXXXXXXXXXXXXXXXXXXXXXXX
XXXXXXXXXXXXXXXXXXXXXXXXXXXXXXXXXXXXXXXXXXXXXXXXXX
XXXXXXXXXXXXXXXXXXXXXXXXXXXXXXXXXXXXXXXXXXXXXXXXXX
XXXXXXXXXXXXXXXXXXXXXXXXXXXXXXXXXXXXXXXXXXXXXXXXXX
XXXXXXXXXXXXXXXXXXXXXXXXXXXXXXXXXXXXXXXXXXXXXXXXXX
XXXXXXXXXXXXXXXXXXXXXXXXXXXXXXXXXXXXXXXXXXXXXXXXXX
XXXXXXXXXXXXXXXXXXXXXXXXXXXXXXXXXXXXXXXXXXXXXXXXXX
XXXXXXXXXXXXXXXXXXXXXXXXXXXXXXXXXXXXXXXXXXXXXXXXXX
XXXXXXXXXXXXXXXXXXXXXXXXXXXXXXXXXXXXXXXXXXXXXXXXXX
XXXXXXXXXXXXXXXXXXXXXXXXXXXXXXXXXXXXXXXXXXXXXXXXXX
XXXXXXXXXXXXXXXXXXXXXXXXXXXXXXXXXXXXXXXXXXXXXXXXXX
XXXXXXXXXXXXXXXXXXXXXXXXXXXXXXXXXXXXXXXXXXXXXXXXXX
XXXXXXXXXXXXXXXXXXXXXXXXXXXXXXXXXXXXXXXXXXXXXXXXXX
XXXXXXXXXXXXXXXXXXXXXXXXXXXXXXXXXXXXXXXXXXXXXXXXXX
XXXXXXXXXXXXXXXXXXXXXXXXXXXXXXXXXXXXXXXXXXXXXXXXXX
XXXXXXXXXXXXXXXXXXXXXXXXXXXXXXXXXXXXXXXXXXXXXXXXXX
XXXXXXXXXXXXXXXXXXXXXXXXXXXXXXXXXXXXXXXXXXXXXXXXXX
XXXXXXXXXXXXXXXXXXXXXXXXXXXXXXXXXXXXXXXXXXXXXXXXXX
XXXXXXXXXXXXXXXXXXXXXXXXXXXXXXXXXXXXXXXXXXXXXXXXXX
XXXXXXXXXXXXXXXXXXXXXXXXXXXXXXXXXXXXXXXXXXXXXXXXXX
XXXXXXXXXXXXXXXXXXXXXXXXXXXXXXXXXXXXXXXXXXXXXXXXXX
XXXXXXXXXXXXXXXXXXXXXXXXXXXXXXXXXXXXXXXXXXXXXXXXXX
XXXXXXXXXXXXXXXXXXXXXXXXXXXXXXXXXXXXXXXXXXXXXXXXXX
XXXXXXXXXXXXXXXXXXXXXXXXXXXXXXXXXXXXXXXXXXXXXXXXXX
XXXXXXXXXXXXXXXXXXXXXXXXXXXXXXXXXXXXXXXXXXXXXXXXXX
XXXXXXXXXXXXXXXXXXXXXXXXXXXXXXXXXXXXXXXXXXXXXXXXXX
XXXXXXXXXXXXXXXXXXXXXXXXXXXXXXXXXXXXXXXXXXXXXXXXXX
XXXXXXXXXXXXXXXXXXXXXXXXXXXXXXXXXXXXXXXXXXXXXXXXXX
XXXXXXXXXXXXXXXXXXXXXXXXXXXXXXXXXXXXXXXXXXXXXX

---

* Before this book went to press, Hemmingson maniacally broke into the Soft Skull offices late at night and marked out the text—Publisher.

II. A Visual Explanation Of Avant-Porn

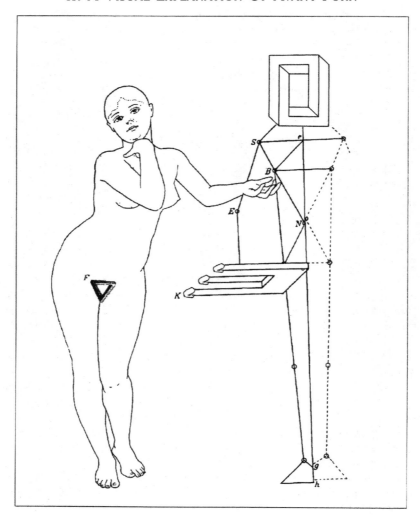

III. How I Really Found This Anthology

Please refer to Larry's preface. I have no comment beyond this point. But, one may take note that I do not, actually, karaoke. Not in this dimension, anyway.

November 2000: San Diego, CA & New York, NY

Michael Hemmingson

what the fuck:

the avant-porn anthology

Sex: American Style

Don Webb

I was with my editor and her brister. Well it had been her brother, but he had decided that he wanted to be a woman and so with the aid of hormones and surgery and costuming —he had become a woman. His name had been Kent, now her name was Janet. Both she and my editor Susan had the last name of Fitzgerald — a name from the Norman invasion of Ireland meaning Sons (Fitz) of Spear (Gar) Ruler (Ald). Ultimately their descent went back to Odhinn himself. But these were very modern women quite focused in this Millennial year.

We were discussing law case. Janet was representing Susan and me in a censorship trial.

"You know what I would like?" I said. "I would like to-do a taste test. You know like Coke and Pepsi."

"Tasting what?" asked Susan.

"Tasting you and your brister's cunt. I've never eaten transsexual and here's the best opportunity for comparison genetically speaking."

Janet blushed a little. Kent had so loved women that he had made himself into one; she was now mainly a lesbian, but was beginning to open up after she read my translation of Chiao and Ouarda Khan's *Wine of Fornication*. But then everyone was, except for the forces of ice-stupidity hat were trying to get me banned.

"I don't think that's a very good idea." said Susan.

I was shocked. I'd never know Susan to turn down an opportunity for cunnilingus — she always kept herself nicely trimmed for access. Courtesy is so important.

"Why?" My voice cracked with sadness.

"Well, Janet's runner Tony will be back with the court documents in fifteen minutes or so — and he's gay. Don't want him to be disappointed."

"That's not a problem, he can suck me off, or better still fuck me. He's cute enough, and I would enjoy it while I'm eating such beautiful women. I can put the lube in reach."

I dropped my pants.

Susan spread her legs and hiked up her skirt. Her puss lips were becoming that wonderful — almost supernatural-

ly pleasing — violet of her arousal, such a beautiful coun-
terpoint to the black triangle of carefully trimmed bush. She
settled on her desk and I got on my knees forward, first to
inhale that most holy of all incenses, and to push her cat-
nips apart and begin long thorough licking.

Janet came up behind me and spread my ass cheeks.

"I'll wet things up so Tony won't need to use lube," she
said in her husky voice.

She began performing the delightful art of *feuille derose*,
wherein the tongue, made as pointed as possible, penetrates the anus. She performed her strange task in the most
charming manner, while her sister began to make little
moans and coos. I could feel a stream of energy coming
from Janet up through my spine, out of my tongue and into
Susan's clit, made a thousand times more voluptuous med-
itating on the incestuous nature of the stream. I wanted to
fuck Susan badly, but I knew not to let myself come until the
trial was over. My energy was pitted against the force of
legal repression.

I sped up my eating, her juices now on my chin, now tick-
ling as the office air dried them on my throat. Her sister's
actions had thoroughly relaxed my sphincter and was quite
ready for Tony the runner to show up. I wanted him for his
message, but I wanted him more for his message service. I
wanted him to come in me while I ate his boss.

Janet began to buck against my face, rubbing my five
o'clock stubble against her muscular thighs.

When she came she uttered my magical name, "Thaïs!"

I knew this first release was working against the judge. I
saw him now, shriveled defender of the public good, trying
to remember the highest principles of the Novo Ordo
Saeculorum — the best of all Masonic Orders because it
finally gave men and women a chance to work out their own
fates by unleashing the Will To Pleasure. I knew the judge
had wisdom. He was a good man, but wearied by what passes for politics in the American republic. If I could just send
the energy into the best part of his brain.

I pictured him skull-less, I saw myself fucking his brain
directly. (I had skipped sex for three days so I could build
up enough of a charge to do this — I hoped to never have to
go through this hell again.) I fucked him in Boca's area —
because I wanted to send the Word — to convey the precise
information for him to change himself — and therefore the

law. All law begins in the minds of humans, and we must help our fellow beings by being as just as we can and radiating virtue direct upon them.

My dick was so hard a cat couldn't scratch it.

We took a breather and the women changed places.

I found that Janet's cunt wasn't as flexible as Susan's. Susan did take two pulls on my cock to heighten the tension. My Will almost broke at that point, for I had a glimpse of relief. But no I told myself. I must continue with my magic for the sake of American jurisprudence.

So much could come from allowing *The Wine Of Fornication* into the libraries of Texas. So many bright minds, strong with the wills that had brought their ancestors of all colors to this great state. An image of Lyndon Johnson passed through my mind. He is one of the minor gods guarding Texas, but not as great as I who in my divine form am the goddess Thmaist.

The goddess part of the practice of *Wine* had bothered Judge Gojiro the most. If only he had been named "Shinto" I thought then he would have understood the way of the gods —how with cooperation everything can in time evolve to its own unique divinity. I had tried to explain it to him. That Venus is the goddess of Love. This doesn't mean that she *is* love, but that she struggles with that principle at the highest of levels. Those who drink *The Wine of Fornication* are seeking to cross over and act in that divine realm, not broaden the gap between the gods and men. I was a goddess as I sucked on the penis-tasting folds of my lawyer.

Janet had begun to buck around. I remember when I first saw Susan and she make it. A champagne fight on my birthday had turned into their first oral sex fest. I stood over them and read from the *Wine*:

With tongue to subdue living idol
and draw forth its joyous gift
And give your own with open heart

Seek yourself through the other
and seek the other through yourself
And give with your own open heart

In threefold place the mystery lies
ultimately within ultimately without
and in all loving flesh

Any sex under these words takes on a twofold power. It transforms the deep political structure of the world, and it awakens the seeker to do some interesting things with his other life besides fucking like rabbits.

Not that there is anything against fucking like rabbits. I longed to hear the verdict, the Saying of Truth that would renew the world and make me free to begat spiritual children.

Susan had begun to caress my buttocks. I love it when a woman kneads my butt—it sends a special shiver all the way to the top of my skull.

I let my awareness run with the pleasure. Soon I was experiencing sexual telepathy—my pleasure would run down my spine through Susan's hand and down to her cunt where she was busily masturbating. Then up again and through Janet—past her large firm store-bought breasts and into her third eye.

I needed to know that flow of energy, because I needed to create a flow in the world without, through Judge Gojiro's brain. Let the power of virtue flow through him—I could feel blockages in him—bad bits of undigested thinking forced upon him during the time before the cure of AIDS—forced by television and evil men proclaiming the word of Restriction. I would overcome those blocks. I would melt the ice in him. Or, I solemnly vowed I would die.

I thought of the Constitution, the flag, of all things good in the Republic, all the strong pleasures of a picnic, fireworks, freedom of the press and good strong sex between consenting adults of any number. That will to pleasure the gods had given our ancestors' ancestors so that they might become gods is the heart of America!

I poured great waves of energy into his brain, burning away tumors and cysts, and unknotting anagrams. Wave after wave while I ate my lawyer.

The Truth-Saying must happen. It will release so much change, so much power, and so much happiness.

Just as *Love American Style* had a sketch called "Love and the Happy Days," which led to *Happy Days*, which had an episode in which a space alien tried to kidnap Richie which led to *Mork and Mindy*, so shall the Kitab Chiao of the seventh century lead to *Wine of Fornication* in the twenty-first century. Even if Judge Gojiro turned my case down, even if I spent my life despised and penniless—it would happen. It was part of that which must be.

When I had the revelation, the two women experienced simultaneous orgasms—loudly and proudly. I had a kind of mental relief. I knew that I had fought the good fight regardless.

Then Tony came in.

"We've won," he said.

And I came with the greatest mass of seed that has ever gushed forth.

All were agape at the miracle of seeing a pint of come in red, white, and blue. The future was now, and the four of us fell to our knees and ate thereof.

Our Hero Awakens

from The Adventures of Lucky Pierre

Robert Coover

My god!
Can't breathe!
Where am I?
Let me out!
—Our hero bestirs himself...

His dissolving fantasies are of a lethal fat all his own, he's fighting his way out of his own suffocating body—HELP!

—Smothered in honied cunnies, pillowed by dozens of delectable milk-white bottoms...

It's too late!

He rears up, gasping for breath, beating desperately against the soft walls—the flesh parts with soft cries, there is light—

—He takes a lovely pink-tipped titty out of his mouth, yawns sleepily, blinks—

Aha.

The girls who have been his bed and blankets kiss and fondle him into consciousness, tweaking his bottom, blowing on his navel. He blinks, grins sheepishly into the bright light, bobs his eyebrows. His prick is stiff with morning seed. He yawns, farts noiselessly.

—And so begins another Day in the Life of Our Hero Lucky Pierre!

He plumps a proximate bosom as he ought, ogling blearily, waggles a soft bum to demonstrate the palpability of his wet dreams, then hops out springily to his feet. The bed undoes itself and the girls don frilly aprons and rush about with brooms and spatulas. He slips off to pee.

—No, no! Naughty, naughty!

The girls drag him back, giggling and twittering like an aviary of mothering birds. Soft hands aim his prick to heaven and squeezes his balls. He fountains forth and they dance around in the shower like enraptured nymphs.

In fact, they are in a shower, the water hot and bubbly. The girls lather up their own bodies, run up against him to wash him clean: scrub! scrub! The steam rises. He is lost in clouds of disembodied titties and sudsy bottoms.

—Hey! hold it a second, gang! I've got soap in my—!

Wush*ppp!* water off, they bundle him up briskly, boy oh boy! The maids' breasts are tatooed with the insignia of vitamins and minerals: he consults the chart of daily minimum requirements. On the table: six pretty pussies all in a row. He dips his nose into one of them, waggling his eyebrows appreciatively over the steam, sits on the bottom of a girl who has made herself into a stool for him.

Ring! The alarm clock! Quickly, quickly, no time to eat: into underwear, shirt, tie, socks, garters, pants, vest, shoes, jacket, coat, hat—

—Hey, wait!

—And out the door, to face life and adventure, armed with a sense of duty, a wallet of condoms, and a buoyant heart!

He emerges in a black bowler and gray spats, umbrella over one arm and briefcase in hand, steps rapidly to the curb, where he is met by a black limousine. The chauffeur whips the door open and—slam!—he jumps in. Rarrarrarrarrunn! rarrarrunn!

—Must be cold, sir!

—Hum. All right, then.

—Out pops Our Resourceful Hero, down come his pants!

He jumps the gas tank, diddling the exhaust—burrRRR*ROOOOM!* The limousine streaks off down the street and out of sight. He runs after it, pulling up his trousers, trips and falls, jumps, falls. The limousine suddenly comes reversing back: *MOOORR*RRrrub!—and splat! right over him. He leaps up out of his dust, still pulling up his pants, pops back in the car. Slam! BurrRR*RROOOM!*

They roar through the city, sccattering traffic. People scream at them. Fists are raised. He sees cars sent up lightpoles, pedestrians flattened, trains derailed. Just process shots, probably, yes, back projections, no doubt...but still...

They corner, tires shrieking. The cityscape goes whipping by. Cyclists plunge into snowbanks. Mailboxes and phonebooths are bowled through display windows. Billboards topple. Buses accordion into each other in their wake.

—Ahem...

He cautions the driver with a polite tap on the shoulder. The driver leans sideways. What the—? A dummy! *The driv-*

er is a dummy!
—Oh my god!
He leaps over the back of the seat to grab the wheel, it goes soft in his hands. He slams his foot on the brake and his foot goes through the floorboard.
—*I've gotta get outta here!*
He grasps the door handle, it breaks off in his grip. Some kind of dimestore plastic! The car goes into a spin, cuts down a crowd at a bus stop, carooms off a snowbank, smashes right through the front of a building. Executives leap in panic out of high windows and secretaries flee for their lives. Blood spatters the windshield. Then—*smash!*—out the other side and he finds himself careening madly down a dead-end alley at a hundred miles an hour.
—*I'm going to die!* he screams. *I'm going to die!*
A screeching stop, the door flies open, he tumbles out.
He pops up out of the snow.
He waits: nothing falls on him.
He glances left, glances right.
—This tall elegant building, one of our city's great landmarks, is more than simply the place where Our Hero earns his daily bread. For here, each day, despite the familiarity of its façade, history is being made!
The chauffeur bushes him off. His heart is beating wildly, but he stands erect, adjusts his bowler stonily, strokes his moustache, greets the doorman, and enters the building through revolving doors.
—Good morning, sir! Thank you, sir!
—Morning, L.P.! *Love* that funny hat!
—Uh...yes...good morning...right...
He boards the elevator. It is jammed with young girls. They giggle, whisper, sigh. One of them faints. They fight to be closest to him. The elevator operator smiles at him over the fuss and bother, winks.
—Sixtyninth story! she announces. Going down!
—Up, he insists. Up.

What You Do

Ian Grey

Nothing else worked, so I kept cutting myself.

Little exploratory nicks at first, seeing if the mysterious ganglia of sensation would be impressed by this transgression of flesh.

I really had tried everything else. Acceptable modes of sexual stimulation, some decidedly unacceptable, and everything in-between. None of it worked to revive the piece of flaccid tissue my sex had become, to bring feeling back into my life.

After my accident.

PET-scans, CAT-scans. Resonant Imaging. Nothing. Though the accident had involved my head, there was nothing wrong a machine could gauge.

My wife gave me up in tears while I was still on the mend. The embarrassment of having such a husband...

A year passed with no sensation down there. I gave up on it.

Saw a pack of razor blades one day resting on the bathroom counter after the casts came off. Thought of killing myself. Tried, cutting shallowly.

And felt something.

I still recall my weeping.

This new activity of mine went on for some time. A lonely task, messy, but it was all I had. I felt shame for a time regarding my perversity.

Then the pain started changing. One day while lazily cutting a clean line over my chest, little bubbles of me oozing out, I felt...

Something. Like what I recalled of a sexual feeling. Still not centered in my genitals, but rather a more comprehensive experience.

After the first time, it got even better as I reached some sort of non-area-specific climax. I wondered if this was what women felt. I had to be careful not to slice myself in ribbons of gratitude

Soon, I got lonely, more and more desiring a way, a person capable of sharing my pleasure. I live in a big city, and so tried the various professionals available, but the specter of disease left me dry, whole, and frustrated. I got a doctor to certify I was negative, but all the girls and one guy said, yeah, right, that means a lot, laughing at my lab report nervously.

For a month I languished, until I got a call from one of the agencies. There was a girl who was willing.

Her name was Elly and she was fucked up. You could see it in her eyes, a wild I-don't-give-a-shit gleam cultivated, I guessed, by a cruel past. She came to my apartment wearing a black silk gown. Her nails were red, eyes blue.

She couldn't have been more than twenty. She said she wanted to see that certificate.

She left with it, promising she'd be back with a decision.

"Maybe we can help each other."

"How?"

Elly had checked the report somewhere, with it passing some secret criteria.

"How much can you move your body?" she asked.

"As much as anyone, but a bit slower. The doctors say I'll be almost normal in a few years."

She nodded. As before, she was wearing black—a mini this time, low-cut. Black stockings, black purse, an ornate silver gargoyle clinging to a choker around her throat. Never taking her gaze from mine, she slipped the top down, revealing her breasts. Average sized, and dusted with some make-up that glittered vaguely. Her nipples large, erect.

Under one, was a long, nicely healed scar.

"Do you like these?"

I said that I did. Very much.

"Suck them." She moved forward on the bed. "This one."

Slowly, I cupped the proffered breast in my hand, smelling flowers and spice. Licked, heart beating like crazy, then sucking, wanting to bite.

She'd slipped her mini up, and touched herself languorously, eyes shut.

Suddenly, I felt her small hand tugging at my hair, pulling me away.

"Now you."

"But I can't. My—"

She shook her head, raven hair gleaming. "No. Do what you do. Don't be afraid, Julian."

I reached into my dresser. When she saw the blade she let out a little sigh, then lay next to me. Her hand moved to my still useless cock and I froze.

"No, it's okay. I want to see it." Pause. "Can I? Please?"

I unzipped, showed the thing. Another sigh as she cradled it gently in her smooth cool hand. "It's lovely," she said. "So sweet."

She bent over, kissed it. Looked at me, then the blade. "Now, Julian. Do it." Her hand moved quickly over black panties. "Here feel—I'm soaked." She had me touch her. I did, feeling a delicious agitation, and then opened my shirt. Took the blade and pressed it against my hairless chest, just above the nipple. The skin dimpled with its pressure. I looked at her, her beautiful average breasts, moving slightly with each quickening, shallow breath.

"Don't tease me," she said.

I closed my eyes, pressed harder, imagined in my mind a straight line. I followed this design and cut.

Perhaps because of my excitement, I'd put more pressure than usual on the blade, as blood was now leaking gently from my wound.

I looked at her, saw her face go whiter than her make-up, saw something in her expression that went far beyond desire.

"God," she said, a moan, a prayer.

Then her head was pressed against my chest and I felt her small tongue trailing over my wound as she came loudly.

While I felt whatever it is I feel.

Except it was so much better like this.

Not alone.

It became a strange sort of revision of the long distance romance scenario, except in this case it wasn't geography but my own healing abilities that limited our visits to once a month.

Between 'sessions', we talked. I was right about her background. Horrible, sad. Some people should just be killed, doing things like that to children. She told me about the shrinks, the cures. The bullshit.

Finally, my Elly had forsaken the whole lot of them and embarked on her most difficult trial: accepting herself.

Laying naked and wonderfully sweaty next to me, lips still smeared red, she told me, "This is what I want. This is me. Maybe I'll change, or grow out of it." A shrug that sent real pain arcing through me: she looked so girlishly courageous saying this.

"But until then..."

And then she licked the little number sign I'd let her trace into my shoulder.

I trusted her that much by then.

Despite the fact that we'd achieved a symbiotic, mutually satisfying arrangement, Elly would still, on occasion, take the dominant role. After all, she was the one drinking me. Sometimes she'd tease me, a nasty look in her eyes, squeezing my thing until we got down to business. Once, while on her period, she had me lick her, but just once and never again.

I didn't really care. My orgasms or whatever they were, were glorious, full-bodied things. The pain had completely mutated into a new shivering pleasure, sensation lasting far longer than a mere tingle and squirt.

We'd finished, with Elly in the other room, reading in my study, when my wife showed up.

"I'm so sorry, Julian. I'm selfish. A bitch."

None of it was true, not as bad as she made it sound anyway, sitting there on the chair by the window. Sobs eating words.

I thought about Elly in the other room. Could she hear this? Felt fear grip me, a life of dry solitude stretching out forever if she freaked.

Got angry.

Left me.

"You did your best," I said. "Really. No hard feelings."

She looked across the room at me. Frosted blond, upscale, face even now flushed with some sort of health.

So much like I'd been. Before the accident.

Not a sound came from the study.

My wife straightened herself, got that pure-bred determined look I used to find so exciting. We argued uselessly for horridly long moments, the two of us on the bed, her hands now folded over her lap, waiting for me to say yes. I wished she'd get the fuck out of here, wondered if she made anything of the sweat covering my face, my turtleneck hiding arms, neck.

I worried about how well voices carried in this apartment.

Finally, I said, "No. Nothing we can do will work. Not anymore."

Said loudly.

She looked shocked, then angry. Rather quickly (I thought) after coming to the realization that her cause was hopeless, she left.

Minutes passed, the room feeling as dead and barren as it had before.

Before Elly.

She walked into the room, naked, streaks of my blood on her breasts and flat belly.

"Was that your wife?"

"Yes. I mean, no. We'll be divorced as soon—"

She silenced me with a hard look, strode across the room.

Then she laid next to me, stroking my cock, soft as ever, looking somewhere beyond my face. Absently, she handed me a fresh blade, saying:

"Go on, Julian. Do what you do."

Afterward, she rested her head on my chest. I was terrified, didn't think I could live without this pleasure, this honesty, this union.

I felt her shudder against me.

She was sobbing.

"Elly? What? You must know I—"

She raised her head, black mascara running in streaks down her white cheeks. "Don't leave me, Julian."

Leave her? I could barely move.

When I looked at her, saw the fear in her face, I understood. There are many ways of leaving a person.

"Don't make me go back to the way I was. The things I had to do. Just because..." She wiped at her face, tried to find some dignity. I saw a shame I recognized.

what the fuck

"I won't leave you, Elly."
Vulnerability crept into her face, a blush of pink.
Then she smiled, kissed me on the cheek.
Leaned forward, offering me her breast.
And then, for the first time, she handed me the blade.

Ian Gray

The Indifferent Fruit

Tamar Perla

*A young woman sits at the side of the road, uses a cut drink-
ing straw to place a small amount of crystalline powder into
a clear glass pipe, holds a lighter to the bottom of the pipe
and smokes intermittently, with a sense of ritual, throughout:*

I'll tell you the story but knowing that I'm not going
around telling it to everyone, in other words you've got to
listen. About the devil and all this, and not just something
chemical, not just craziness about seraphim and how long a
star goes before it explodes and psychics and some
supreme being and all this, but how things can go. I'm going
to tell you how I came to see it, how it all came together in
this sense after two years of messing around high as a killer
wave on cyrstal methamphetamine.

I would tell you a lie but I couldn't, I mean a story to hide
the real story because although the trucks keep slowing by
I knew he's coming back so I won't get in, I mean I did get in
just for a few miles (this is the lie I want to tell you). I
climbed into the truck and right away I knew this could be
the loneliest ride. He barely looked at me (I know he's coming back) and when he said, "Hop in," the hop came out flat
and dry so that I know it was someone else's word; I almost
said something then but decided to wait. So I took the ball
of tough, grey gum out of my mouth and carefully squished
it into the seat, I crossed and re-crossed my legs, I wondered
if we were going to have sex. Notice I didn't think did I want
some, but still I wondered. I said something like, "This
desert makes me happy" or "the road a long grey tongue
behind us" or "it's shifting nature."

I would have told you sooner but he held the pipe for me;
I would listen to him breathe when he said, "Now." Then he
was inside me so I could finally relax, finally I was feeling
what I wanted to feel much of the time. In the story I would
have told you, he would have been a trucker and I would
have held the pipe to his lips, on the grass at the rest stop,
I would have gotten him high. Or in the back of the truck,
filled with new furniture; I chose a leather couch and took
out my gum, got us both high then put his hand in my

pants.

This drug is not just about sex. This drug is not just about seeing what goes on while everyone else is sleeping, not about the paranoia dot cum dot machinebrain, not about sleeping while everyone else goes on, not about sleeping. About light and truckers need light like sex, truckers need sex and ways to keep their eyes open. When we made love in the back of the truck I kept thinking of him and one hand on the pipe, I don't know if we made love but I wanted to, I wanted something to come of it, light bursting from my brain.

If you see things you can be sure they're real. I wouldn't tell you what to do with them, just know. And trust to hear the stories of things that would kill you, because impermanence always tells the truth. I'll tell you because I've needed to, because I made love to the devil and we got high together, because I was inspired by his tolerance. He let me hurt until I was tired of hurting, he helped me hurt until I was tired of having sex with him. I still think about him a lot. If I flip this coin there's no telling what's coming down the road: trucker, boyfriend, devil, trucker. I think he's coming back for me, he knows I've got to be in L.A. tomorrow, he knows.

From Vegas to L.A. is a lot to see, a lot of light. The light reflects off the sand and makes more, sometimes it travels in tiny sparks that queer my eye, I start to doubt. But L.A. was wreathed in smoke, I thought I would get high but something is wrong when your cities are burning and everyone's just sitting in traffic. I wanted to get back in the back of the truck and take off my pants and just stay there, I didn't want to get on a plane back to Vegas and sit in a hotel room with no windows and smoke alone, besides I was always running out. I didn't want to be in a hotel room and paranoia, fighting with my boyfriend and later from the cab of a truck with the window rolled down and the power lines creeping in, freedom yes but making love beneath the power lines at the foot of a metal girdered giant was hurting me, I liked to be hurt but then I'd bring in the light and we'd get high together.

Sometimes I closed my eyes, he put his lips on mine and blew smoke inside, he'd say, "Now," but already I knew when was now. When I'm back in L.A. I'll put on a collar and get back to work, high on the weekends and sleeping nights, at least he's not bleeding in a hotel room in Vegas and we've gambled everything and I'm afraid to think, there's no more light. He put his lips on mine and said, "You could be so full there's no more of you, just light," and then we'd see how full I could be, so that finally I could relax. If a trucker cared we could get high together and glide around the green valley rim into L.A., his hand in my pants and the lights on; with all the smoke it was night or the end of the world, people's houses were burning so maybe it was for them, the end. I would like to tell you I think I'll never smoke again, but each night I sleep, I dream of getting high. I dream of light, of fullness. Its shifting nature. The road a long grey tongue before me. I am happy in this desert.

A truck pulls up.

The Best Way to Smoke Crack

William T. Vollmann

SAN FRANCISCO, CALIFORNIA, U.S.A. (1992)

The crack pipe was a tube of glass half as thick as a finger, jaggedly broken at both ends because the prostitute had dropped it. She kept talking about the man down the hall, whose pipe still wore a bowl. She said that that special pipe was for sale, but the john figured that he'd already spent enough.

The john was of the all-night species, family Blattidae. Having reached that age when a man's virility begins to wilt flabbily, he admitted that his lust for women grew yearly more slobbery and desperate. Every year now he fell a little farther from what he had been. In his youth he had not considered himself to be anything special. Now he recollected with awe how his penis had once leaped eagerly up at the merest thought or touch, how his orgasms had gushed as fluently as Lincoln's speeches; those were the nights when ten minutes between the trash cans or beneath a parked car had sufficed. His joy now required patience and closeness. That was why he'd paid the twenty-nine dollars to share with this woman whose brown body was as skinny as a grasshopper's this stinking room whose carpet was scattered with crumbs of taco shells and rotting cheese; among his possessions he now counted the sheet which someone had used to wipe diarrhea, the science fiction book called *The Metal Smile*, a gold mine of empty matchboxes, and all the wads of used toilet paper that anyone would ever need to start a new life. He'd bought the room for the night, and after that he was going to go back to work and the prostitute would live there. Maybe that was why she worked so hard at cleaning up, hanging the diarrhea-sheet over the window for a curtain, picking up the hunks of spoiled food and throwing them out the window, sweeping with the broom without bristles, sprinkling the carpet with water from the sink (which had doubled as a urinal) so that the filth would stick better to the broom. Maybe that was why she cleaned, or maybe it was because she had once had a home where she raised her children as well as she could until jail became her home, and although they took her children and turned them into somebody else's (or more likely nobody's) it was too late for her to shuck the habit of making her surroundings decent; or maybe she worked so hard just because she wanted him to be happy and comfortable with her.

If it wasn't for whoever left this mess, there'd be no roaches, she said. I've lived in this hotel all the time and never had roaches.

He sat on the mattress with his arm around her while they smoked a rock, and a cockroach rushed across his leg.

I'm not afraid of any human being, the prostitute said. I'm a single female out there, so I gotta be ferocious so they be respectin' me. And I'm not afraid of any animal. But insects gimme the jitters. All them roaches in here, it's cause whoever was in here before was such a slob. If I ever meet that motherfucker and he pisses me off, I'll say to him: You know what? You remind me of your room. Ooh, look at that big fat roach!

Certainly the big fat roach was blameless for being what it was. And the prostitute was likewise faultless for not wanting that roach to crawl across them later that night, once they turned out the bare bulb which reflected itself in the greasy window. Biting her lip with disgust, she slammed her shoe against the wall over until the bug was nothing but a stain among stains.

I really hate them roaches, she sighed, loading her blackened pipe with more whiteness. They just gimme the creeps. You know, in the Projects, you catch 'em with crack. If you cleaned up your place too good and stuff and you can't find 'em, just lay a rock out on the table and they'll be swarmin' shit, there's another one!

She snatched up her shoe and pounded the wall.

She was picking up bits of rancid cheese out of the chest of drawers with three drawers gone while the john lay watching the roaches. They seemed to be accustomed to the light. They scurried up and down the walls on frantic errands, ran across the carpet whose water-stains and burns resembled the abscesses of half-Korean Molly down the hall (another whore said she kept picking at herself); and one roach even climbed that foul bed sheet draped over the window.

The prostitute came back to the mattress and they

smoked another piece of rock. She loaned the pipe to a whore who'd bought bad stuff, so it stank of something strange. Now she kept running water through it, but that didn't do any good.

Nudge that rock down into the end that's burned blacker. The john knew that much. Don't push it in too hard, or you'll break the mesh, which is already almost gone. She'd taught him that. Just tap it lovingly in with the black-burned hairpin. Lovingly, I said, because crack is the only happiness.

The prostitute celebrated whenever she got a big rock by buying a lighter whose color matched her dress. She held a red lighter tonight to keep her red dress company. She was wearing red shoes and a red headband; red was her favorite shade. He'd seen her in the black cocktail dress that she put on when he knocked at her door and she was embarrassed because she thought she looked old; he didn't care how old or young she looked because he loved her, but she closed that door and wouldn't let him in until she was beautiful for him in the black dress which thirty seconds later he was urgently helping her pull off; and he'd seen her in the fox-tail outfit that reminded him of women he knew at the horse races, but most often he'd seen her wearing the hue of vibrant blood. She lit the rock and breathed in even though the tube of glass had been broken so short that it burned her lips and tongue when the rock was only half cooked; she breathed in because when she was eighteen her first husband had brought a two-by-four smashing down on the crown of her head, and after that she'd never had very good balance; that was twenty years ago now. And one of her daughters (she'd been very little then) had said: Mama, don't ever worry about fallin, 'cause I'll always be next to you, and if I see you start to go down, I'll throw myself right down on the sidewalk so you can fall on me! —It made her cry sometimes to remember that. Her daughter didn't walk beside her anymore, and so she smoked crack.

The john was looking worried. —Crack isn't addictive, now, is it? he said.

Oh, no honey, the prostitute smiled. It's just a psychological thing.

And later, in the night, when she spread her legs for him and he worried about AIDS, she said to him: Oh, don't worry, honey. You can only get AIDS if you're two homosexuals.

There were two roaches on the wall, and she got them

both with her shoe in a slamming blow like the one three months ago that had left her permanently blind in the right eye when she was being raped; now she couldn't read a menu anymore.

Inhale it slowly, hold five or six seconds, expel it through the nose.That was her way; that way was more mellow. If you did it too fast you might get tweaked. First the head rush, then the body rush.

Don't inhale so hard, she said. That's the difference between white boys and black boys. White boys always inhale too fast, 'cause they think if they do they'll get more high. You white boys are just greedy sometimes. Black boys know better.

He felt the smoke in his chest as he held it in, and then the rush struck him behind his eyeballs. Now his heart began to pound more fiercely. His lips and tongue swelled into a numb clean fatness like a pussy's lips.The feeling that he had was the same as long ago at the high school dances when the boys and girls had stood on opposite sides of the floor and the music had started but he was too afraid to cross that open space where all the girls could see him as he came among them to ask one to share her beauty with him for a dance, so his heart pounded faster and faster, until suddenly he was going to the girls anyway to say: Will you dance with me? and the girl giggled and her friends giggled and she looked quickly at her friends and then at him and said yes and he was going into the music with her, holding her hand. It was exactly that way that his heart was pounding, except that there was no fear in his excitement this time; no matter how rapid his happiness became it remained tranquil.

Well, laughed the prostitute (who always became more talkative the more crack she did), another main difference between white people and black people is white people have reputations to protect when they buy drugs. Black people don't care. — And she laughed.

Ahead waited the long night of her going in and out to do her business which she pretended not to be doing, believing that pretending would keep him from feeling hurt, when actually he wasn't hurt at all; she was trying to be loving by protecting him from what she was doing, while he was trying to be loving by letting her do whatever she needed to do. Meanwhile they both smoked crack. Ahead of that night loomed the night when he took her out for dinner with his friends and she was late because she had to smoke crack and then at dinner she excused herself to go to the ladies' room where she smoked crack and came out weeping as though her heart would break because she was convinced that all his friends looked down on her, so he embraced her outside as she soaked him with tears begging him to return her to that hotel on Mission Street whose gratings and buzzers were like airlocks, so later that night he did come to her, and when he lay beside her on the dirty mattress and took her into his arms her face was burning hot! Her forehead steamed with sweat that smelled like crack, that delicious bitter clean smell even more healthy and elegant than eucalyptus or Swiss herbal lozenges; she ground her face into his chest and whispered something about the Bible as her sick and glowing face burned its way to his heart. — There was a woman whom he loved who was a scientist. When he told her what had happened, the woman said: That fever, that night sweat, that dementia about your friends. well it sounds to me like AIDS, particularly the very early stages. — But another friend just rubbed his stubble and said: Her sweat smelled like crack, huh? She must be O.D.ing on crack. Happens all the time! — Ahead of that night crouched the night when the john woke up in his own bed wanting crack. It was the middle of a moon less time. He had no crack. He said to himself: If only the moon was here maybe that would cheer me so that I could sleep again; but ahead of that night laughed the night when he woke up from a dream of crack with the moon outside his window as big and round as the abscess on the prostitute's foot which would not heal, and he lay wide awake needing crack.

They smoked crack, and he lay in her arms staring up at the long lateral groove-lips of the moulding reflected in the mirror of the medicine cabinet, whose shelves had all been wrenched out, and he began to smile.

Look at that! he cried, look at all those roaches running crazy across the ceiling! I guess they must really be enjoying themselves.

The woman cackled. — I s'pose they be gettin' a contact high from all the smoke up there. But it kinda pisses me off, 'cause they can't pay me no money!

They both laughed at that, and then they did another piece of rock in the best way; she approved of how he smoked crack now; the best way to smoke crack is to suck it from the tube of broken glass as gently as you'd suck the crack-smoke breath from the lips of the prostitute who's kissing you.

San Francisco, California, U.S.A. (1992)

The john remembered the nights when he was still married and lay in the darkness of the guest bedroom watching golden hall-light, listening to the rush of his wife's high heels as she adjusted her dress and necklace in the main bedroom, his grief and anxiety hideous while his heart ticked with the clock. He had decided that if his wife asked him to come, he would say: Why should I? but then he thought that that did not sound sincere (and he was actually very sincere), so he decided that when his wife came in he would just say: Convince me and I'll go. His wife was almost ready now. It was cold and dark outside the window. He knew that he was missing his last hope by lying there while his wife put the penultimate touches of lipstick on. He was terrified that his wife might not even come and look for him. If she did not at least ask him, he could not volunteer to go with her. She went into the bathroom, where she must be checking herself in the mirror. Now she came out and turned off the bathroom light. He resolved that if his wife was making the rounds of the upstairs, turning off lights. She paused. Perhaps she was wondering where he was. He could not move. He would not move. He heard her go downstairs. She was clicking her high heels rapidly through every darkened room, including the living room where the unlit Christmas tree slobbered its sticky shadow of shaggy foulness; she must be looking for him;she was back at the bottom of the stairs now, and he heard her picking up her keys. So she was going to leave without calling for him. He lay breathless with tension. She called his name.

Here I am, he said

Where are you? It's all dark up there.

Here, he said with effort.

She came up the stairs and turned the hall light back on. He heard her going into each of the other rooms again. At last she entered the half-ajar door of the guest bedroom and stood peering to see if he was there. He could not say anything.

Are you sleeping? she said hesitantly.

No, he said.

She turned on the light and looked at him.

I'm going to go now, she said. I'll be back in an hour. Maybe an hour and a half.

I'll come with you if you want me to, honey, he said. He was surprised at how easily the words came to him. It was as if some grace of husbands, wives and desperate angels had helped him.

Oh, don't bother, said the wife. It would be too much work for you.

It's up to you.

You really wouldn't mind? said his wife. Don't worry about it. I know you don't want to.

She stood there waiting for him to encourage her hopes. He strained his every effort to say the words again that would make her happy, but even as his mouth opened he knew that he was going to fail.

You—you heard what I said, he gasped out.

Her face became resigned again. — Never mind, she said. She turned out the light. Tears had begun to gush out of her eyes just as she reached for the switch, and it is possible that she had waited another three or four seconds (or if he had somehow been able to make her do so), he would have seen them. She went down the stairs, opened the door and left him.

SAN FRANCISCO, CALIFORNIA, U.S.A. (1992)

Again he ascended the stairs between two gratings, and tall black men made way for him on the landing because if he was white he must be an undercover cop.

Who you lookin' for, officer? one of them said.

He said her name.

You a cop?

No.

You a paid informant?

No, officer, he said.

The black man laughed grimly.

He got to the top of the stairs where the second grating was, and the lobby man who had buzzed him was already standing on the other side of the grating with his arms folded.

She's not here, the man said. She just now went outside to do her business, so I reckon she'll be back before long.

They always said she wasn't there, and she was always there, so the john wasn't surprised. — Can I wait on your stairs? he said.

Help yourself.

He descended a stair or two to show his respect for the workings of the hotel, and waited, looking alertly through the grating like a zoo-barred jaguar waiting for meat, watching and waiting until just past midnight he saw her pass across the lobby on one of her constant errands. He was here to tell her how she made him feel. He called her name, and her face lit up and she came running to make the lobby man let him in.

Thank you kindly, he said to the lobby man.

The lobby man gazed expressionlessly away. At least he didn't charge the john five dollars to get in.

I was just thinkin' 'bout you! the prostitute said. I was afraid you'd quit me. Come on!

She ran ahead of him up the back stairs by the toilet, and there was the man who laid out his or somebody else's possessions on the stairs, including pennies and nickels, and stood patiently waiting for them to make him rich. The prostitute had already run high into the smoky darkness above him as he picked his way past more loungers, and then he had caught up with her and she'd taken his hand. Soon now he could tell her. Men like salt-encrusted pillars of carven ebony walled them on both sides, looking silently as she kissed his lips and thrust her tongue repeatedly into his mouth. He wondered if he was tasting other men's sperm. She slipped her arm around him and led him to the room where the two lesbian whores lived. The lesbian whores did very well in that hotel by renting out their room to strangers for five dollars for fifteen or twenty minutes. That was why they were so well furnished. They had a TV and even a single bed. The prostitute (who knew that the john would pay her back) gave the white whore some money, and the white whore slipped out. Inside the room, another white boy was sitting on the bed. He was smoking crack and he was very nervous.

Y'all make yourselves comfortable and I'll be right back,

the prostitute said, as prostitutes so often say, and the john thought to himself: Why not?What do I care if she doesn't show? I have all night and I haven't even paid.

The white boy offered him a piece of rock, and the john thought again: Why not? because the prostitute was still there and she was serving him so tenderly, holding the crack pipe to his mouth, lighting it, reminding him not to swallow the smoke or he'd get nauseated, and then the feeling hit, the good feeling, and the prostitute grinned and went out.

I don't like this, the other white boy said. I gave eighty dollars. Well, forty was just business, you know. But forty was to get me some more rock.

You'll see her again, the john said. You can trust her.

Usually I take her to my place and she stays the night, said the whiteboy. I don't like this place. This place is dangerous.

The john could not tell what exactly the prostitute meant to this other person. He wanted to find out. He wanted very much to find out.

How many times have you done her? he said.

Oh, two or three times. Maybe four or five.

Listen, he said to the other white boy, can you do me a favor? When she comes back, I need to speak with her, just for five minutes. Then you can take her home. I won't get in your way.

I don't wanna do that, the white boy said. He was out of crack, and so his hand was clenched around the crack pipe and his face was sweating.

Okay, the john said.

They sat in silence on the bed, and then the black whore and the white whore came in to get toilet paper. — Your friend sure is keeping you waiting,they said. That's rude.

I'm gonna go talk to her, said the white boy. I need some rock. I gave her money. I need rock! Where's her room?

Number sixty-four, said the john. It's a real nice room. Lots of company scuttling up and down the walls.

The white boy went out, and the white whore sat down next to the john on the bed while her lover sat in the corner. The white whore (who had been going out with the black whore for eight years) was wearing a very low cut dress that showed her rich plump breasts, and she bent towards him a little to make them move and said: You wanna like do anything?

Just then somebody knocked on the door. The black whore unlocked it, and the white boy came in. — She said she'll be down in a minute, he said unhappily.

So, the white whore was saying to the john, you think you might like a date?

You're beautiful, he replied, but I've already got a date.

Well, what if she don't come back?

Maybe then. I don't know. Maybe then.

Anybody got any rock? said the white boy.

She sure ain't showin' you no respect, said the black whore.

I don't like this, said the white boy. I'm getting very upset about this.

What makes you attracted to her? the john asked.

Oh, I don't even know her name exactly, the white boy yawned. It's just I run into her on the streets sometimes.

Just let me know if I'm in your way.

No problem dude. We can all hang out. Once she comes back, you and me and these other girls can go to my place and party.

You wanna date? the white whore cut in, her eyes lighting up. I'm sorry my face is kind of a mess. I got into an accident. But if you wanna date me I'll be real good.

You see, the white boy said, I gave her eighty dollars.

Eighty? laughed the black whore in the corner. You gave that bitch eighty? Shit.

I'm getting like tense now, said the white boy. I'm afraid I might do something.

I'll take care of it, the john said.

He went upstairs to sixty-four, and just as he was about to knock the door across the hall opened and an ancient Asian lady in a nightgown stuck her head out and flapped a moth-colored titty at him and he bowed with his hand on his heart, at which she closed the door. Behind the other door, the prostitute he'd come for was saying: Just gimme a dime bag, just this once. I swear I'll never ask for no more favors.

He knocked.

Who is it? the prostitute shouted in her fiercest voice.

It's me.

I'm comin', I'm comin'! she cried impatiently.

I've got to go now, he called, smiling a little. I'll see you another time. That worked wonders. The prostitute practically flew out the door in her eagerness to keep him, and they went downstairs.

These two girls are coming with us, the white boy said.

Oh no they are not! the prostitute cried. Ladies, I don't mean to disrespect you, but this is my business. We gonna go to his place and kinda get established, and then if we need you we'll come an' get you then.

So I'll meet you at 2:00 A.M. at the corner, the white boy was whispering something to the white whore.

Come on! the prostitute said.

The two johns got up and followed her into the lobby where the manager studied them from within his glass cubicle, and the prostitute (who could tell by taste whether crack was good or not) opened the grating and they went downstairs past the black men and through the second grating and onto the street.

I wouldn't be doin' this for just anybody, the prostitute said to the white boy, But you're such a dynamite guy too.

The prostitute ran across the street and bought the white boy stood watching. —I love two kinds of crack, he told her, the kind I smoke and the kind between your legs. —She laughed and laughed.

Thanks for letting me come along to your house, he said to the white boy. I sure do appreciate it.

No problem, dude. We'll chill out and party, you know, just a couple of mellow crack heads.

Everything okay, baby? the prostitute said to him. Soon we'll all be doin' some really good rock. Danny here don't mind. He's quality, he really is.

They got to the white boy's house, and the prostitute and the white boy were kissing. The john looked away.

While the prostitute was in the bathroom the white boy said: Come into the bedroom for a minute. Why don't you sit down on the bed with me for a minute?

You sure I'm not in your way? the john asked. You paid for her. I didn't. I can take off anytime.

Let's you and me do her together, the white boy whispered.

Sure, the john said. You go first. That's only fair. Besides, it's your place.

No, no, no, you don't get it. Let's do her together.

Oh, I'm not exactly into that, said the john, watching to see if the white boy might suddenly scream in rage and pull out a knife or gun. — I only do girls.

I'm not queer or anything, the white boy pleaded. There's nothing to it. We just turn out the lights, get under the covers, and you won't even know whose mouth it is.

Well, I'll have to think that one over, the john said, wondering of he would be able to knock the white boy down and run if the white boy turned out to be coeval with the white boy in the newspaper who kept other boys' heads in his refrigerator. He decided that he could take the white boy easily. The white boy was very pale and puffy and unhealthy. If he had a gun, of course, that would be different.

Please, the white boy said. If you don't do her with me, my whole evening will be ruined.

The white boy was weeping. Because he had broken so easily, the john felt fairly sure now that he must not be dangerous. He put his hand on the white boy's shoulder and said: I just don't think I can do what you ask. I'm really sorry, How can I make it up to you?

Never mind, the white boy said in a desolate voice.

The prostitute was still in the bathroom. The white boy went and opened the door.

Can't you see I'm tryin' to shit? said the prostitute.

I just wanted to give you this T-shirt, the white boy said, peering in eagerly. I thought you might like it.

Thank you, the prostitute said. I appreciate that. You're a real dynamite guy.

When she came out, the john said: Well, I have to go.

What's wrong, baby? said the prostitute. Come on. Smoke a little rock with us and relax.

She took some of the white boy's crack and gave him a nice big hit. He felt the feeling again, the happy excited feeling, and for a moment it was so strong that he couldn't talk. He exhaled through his nostrils, and his nose went numb. He could no longer feel the weight of his body's sadness.

Why don't you stay over? the white boy said. It's so late. You don't wanna be out on the street.

Maybe I'll just take a stroll around the block, he said.

He put his coat on, and the prostitute gave him another rock, holding him tightly so that he could not get away. — He's my baby, she said to the white boy, embracing the john desperately. He's the best. He's dynamite.

I guess I'll go now, said the john.

What's the matter, baby? said the prostitute. Listen, come

on into the bedroom and tell me what's going on. Excuse us for a second, Danny.

Sure, the white boy said dully.

Now what's goin' on? said the prostitute, sitting beside him on the bed with her hand on his knee, looking into his eyes like a worried mother whom he must not disappoint.

He wants him and me to do you at the same time, he said, in a low voice because the bedroom door was open and he did not want to hurt the white boy's feelings. I just can't. I'm sorry.

He said that? cried the prostitute in amazement. I don't do that!

It's okay, he said. Anyway I'm going to go.

She sat motionless on the bed.

The white boy walked him to the door. He looked back and she was sitting on the bed crying. — Please come 'ere, she said.

He went back to her, hesitated, and said: I love you. Then he strode out without looking back.

Emergency Room

Kim Addonizio

He asks if I've been tied up before. I tell him yes, and he wants to know for how long. Tell me about it, he says. I feel shy, I don't want to go into details. We're sitting in Vesuvio's at four in the afternoon, drinking gin and tonics. He has his hand on my thigh. I'm madly in love with him, we've known each other three weeks. I'm not ambivalent like I usually am, everything about him seems perfect: his close-cut black hair, the way he puts his tongue down my throat when he kisses me, his blunt, square hands. He's the sexiest man I've ever been with. It scares me I can feel so happy. None of our friends think it will last.

I want to tie you up, he says. I want to do things with you that you've never done with anyone.

A man at the bar is doing card tricks. He holds up the queen of diamonds and shows it to a pale, pretty girl in a black leather minidress, black fishnet tights and heavy black combat boots. The girl looks bored. She glances over at us and sees me watching her. She takes a card from the magician's deck, looks at it and sticks it back in.

We get drunk sitting in Vesuvio's. At seven o'clock we're still there, kissing passionately, his hand under my T-shirt squeezing my breast. No one pays any attention to us. The magician is still there, too, talking to another woman. He holds up the queen of hearts. Finally we get hungry and walk around the corner to Brandy Ho's and eat Kung Pao chicken and Szechuan shrimp, sitting next to each other in the red leather booth. I feel like I'm in an alternate universe. Everything looks familiar but it's different than before. The sexual intoxication is overwhelming, I can't function in the real world: I haven't called my friends, paid my bills, read a newspaper since all this started. I don't want it ever to end. I feel vulnerable and it's terrifying; I can't help being in love with him, even if he leaves me or treats me like shit I can't hold back the way I usually do, I have to give him everything. Then I won't know who I am anymore.

With his glasses on he looks like a different person: shy,

slightly studious, younger. It's like he's in disguise; I don't recognize him as the same person I fuck. I like him in his glasses, like the idea that there are things about him no one could ever guess from the way he looks. He takes his glasses off, sets them on my kitchen table.

Take off your clothes and stand against the wall, he says.

I peel off my T-shirt, drop my skirt and underwear and lean against the wall, facing him. He tells me to put my arms above my head. We've just finished dinner. He pours himself more wine and tips his chair back, drinking the wine, watching me.

Don't move, he says. He leaves the kitchen. I hear him pissing in the bathroom. I'm excited, scared, I don't know what's going to happen next. I close my eyes, listen to the stream of piss hitting the water in the bowl. My neighbor in the next apartment starts playing the clarinet. She's just learning so it's all honks and squeaks. The walls are thin, I'm worried someone will hear us, I don't want anyone to hear us. I don't want anyone to know what we do together, what he does to me.

He comes back to the kitchen, zipping his pants. He takes an apple from the bowl of fruit on the table.

Open your mouth.

He shoves the apple against my mouth; my teeth sink into it. I'm gagged. He's not gagging me. I can drop the apple anytime. I want him to dominate me, use me; I want to be his slave. I have to understand submission, why it's so erotic for me; I can't reconcile it with the rest of my life. I've never let myself physically explore how I feel because intellectually I can't accept it. Women are shit, they're only here for men's pleasure, men control everything.

My beautiful slut, he says. Look how wet you are. He puts his middle finger inside me, then in his mouth. He unbuckles his belt and takes it off in one smooth motion.

One Saturday night when we're fucking the condom breaks. I know I'm ovulating, I don't want to get pregnant. He calls a sex information hotline and asks what we can do, and they tell him there's an abortion pill I can take; I should call a doctor to prescribe it.

I call the advice line at Kaiser and get put on hold. I wait forty-five minutes, then a voice comes on the line and says there's one more call ahead of me. I wait ten more minutes. The woman on the other end tells me she can't help me, I need to talk to Doctor X. I ask her to connect me. She connects me to the wrong extension; the people there tell me to call a different number. I hang up, dial the main hospital and ask for Doctor X.

He's not on tonight.

I explain what's happening. The woman on the other end insists that Doctor X isn't there, and no one else can prescribe the pill. Finally someone else gets on the phone and tells me that Doctor X is being paged. I'm put on hold again. A muzak version of "We've Only Just Begun" by the Carpenters plays, followed by the Beatles' "Here, There and Everywhere." Twenty minutes later another person gets on the line.

Can I help you?

I think I'm being helped. I don't know. I've been on the phone for an hour and a half, I'm trying to reach Doctor X.

I want to scream at the person on the phone but she is very nice, it's not her fault, there's nobody to blame, I don't want to scream at her. I don't want to have a baby. I'm thirty years old, I work at a cafe and never have enough money for art materials. My mother was a painter, she stopped after she had me. I can't be a painter if I have a baby. He doesn't want a baby either. Not this way, he says. Not by accident.

Please hold, the nice person says. I listen to a few bars of "My Cherie Amor." A minute later Doctor X gets on the line.

You have to come to the Emergency Room to pick it up, he says.

Can't you just call it in to a drugstore?

We have to see you, he says. There are certain risks involved.

He says that if the pills don't work and the fetus is female it could be turned into a boy by the hormones. Masculinized, he says. The fetus might be masculinized and if you decide to have the baby there could be problems.

I don't want to have the baby, I say. I want the pills. If they don't work I'll have an abortion, but I've had three abortions already and that's why I want the pills. Please, I say. Can't you call it in?

You have to come to the Emergency Room, he repeats, sounding annoyed. We have to have a record that we've seen you.

I hang up. It's ten p.m., we haven't had any dinner. He puts his arms around me.

He says, I hate to see you go through this.

I hate doctors, I say. I hate western medicine. I hate Kaiser, you never see the same doctor twice. Nobody knows you or gives a shit about you, you're a name on a chart. Why can't they just give me the pills?

Let's go eat first, he says. I'll take you someplace nice, we'll forget about this bullshit. The Emergency Room will be open all night.

He takes me to Little Italy. We drink a lot of wine. I start to feel better, now it's an adventure we're having together instead of a lousy experience. We joke about it, he puts his hand over mine on the red-and-white checkered tablecloth. I've never been so in love with anyone. I tell him I don't think I want any children.

I'll get sterilized, I say. I'm no good at birth control, I always blow it one time and get pregnant from that one time. I'll make an appointment and get my tube tied. I only have one tube and ovary because I had an infection once and had to have an operation. A gynecologist told me once that if I ever got sterilized it might be major surgery, because of the scar tissue from the other operation.

I'll get a vasectomy, he says. It's easier, it's just an office procedure.

What if we break up and you want to have a baby with someone else? As I say this the thought of it makes me jealous and depressed and I'm sure it will happen.

I can go to a sperm bank, then. Besides we're not going to break up. And you might change your mind. Five years from now we might want a baby and we could have one.

We get to the Emergency Room a little before midnight. We sit in the waiting room, and after about half an hour a nurse leads me through a curtain and takes my blood pressure.

I'm only here to pick up a prescription, I tell her.

She ignores me, fastens a yellow plastic ID bracelet with my name and policy number around my wrist. She leads me to an examining room where there's a metal table with stirrups, and lays a blue plastic gown on the table.

Wait here, she says.

I sit down on the only chair. After forty-five minutes a Chinese medical student comes in.

I need to examine you, he says.

No, you don't. I'm not sick, I just need a prescription.

I'm supposed to examine you.

I think of him looking at me, my legs spread apart, my heels in the cold stirrups; I don't want him to look at me. I start crying and saying I just want the pills, there's nothing wrong with me I don't want a baby you don't need to examine me, please just give me the pills so I can go home.

He writes something down on his chart, then walks out, muttering something I can't hear. A minute later the nurse says I can go back to the waiting room.

A man with long blonde hair is passed out in one of the chairs. Three well-dressed black people are sitting together. The man is doubled over, holding his side, and the two women are on either side of him talking to him and rubbing his shoulders. There's a Toyota commercial on the TV, then an episode of "Miami Vice." The nurse comes out after twenty minutes and tells me that Kaiser's pharmacy doesn't have any more of the pills; there might be some at Mount Zion, she has to call and then send someone there to pick them up.

I lean my head on his shoulder; he strokes my hair. The blonde man wakes up and looks around the room. Fuck this shit, he says. He gets up and walks out.

At three a.m. the nurse calls me in behind the curtain and hands me a paper cup of water and another paper cup with three tiny white pills in it. She gives me three more to take in twelve hours.

When we leave, the black people are still sitting there.

I have an almost pathological need for other people's approval. If someone criticizes me I fall apart, I feel useless, stupid, insignificant. When I confess this to him he says I need to learn not to internalize other people's negativity. I experience this as a subtle criticism and move to the edge of the bed, away from him.

I used to sleep with men so they would like me. I always had a lot of lovers. Now I only fuck him; he excites me more than anyone. When I masturbate I don't think about strangers fucking me, the way I used to; I think about him looping a rope through a ring screwed into the top of the door frame, slapping my breasts and cunt. I think about the way he growls low in his throat, the violence of his orgasms. I masturbate imagining he is watching me, and come saying his name over and over. My life before I knew him seems impoverished, a desert. I'm afraid of losing him; he has to keep reassuring me that he loves me and wants me. At parties I'm jealous if he talks with other women. I'm convinced they're more attractive, more desirable than I am

We're in someone's loft studio, it's too crowded. I feel like I'm suffocating. Everyone is talking to everyone else, huge paintings hang on the walls, the paint laid on layer after layer—thick dark colors, blues and blacks. I can't find him. No one is talking to me. Someone gave me some mushrooms earlier and now I'm starting to come on to them, I feel jumpy and want to find something to drink to calm me down. I bump into a woman, she stares at me in dislike, turns away. I get through the crowd and pour myself some wine, drink it quickly and pour another one, asking people if they've seen him. No one has. I'm panicked, sure he's met another woman and left with her.

I go into the bathroom and lock the door. I feel sick so I crouch at the toilet but I can't throw up. Sitting down on the floor, my back against the wall, I stare at the postcards tacked above the toilet. I know I'm seeing images but I can't tell my brain what they are, specifically; they're like abstract paintings, they have no meaning. I feel violated by images, I can't help seeing them on billboards, TV, in ads and movies, they get into me through osmosis and change my thought patterns: what I'm supposed to look like, feel like, be. I close my eyes and see blue snowflakes.

He's pounding on the door, his voice sounds far away. I get up and open it. He takes me in his arms.

Please fuck me, I say. Fuck me here, on the floor.

He locks the door and undresses me. I lie down on the floor; it's cold, I start shivering. He takes off his shirt and tucks it under me. He's standing over me, unzipping his black leather pants. I start hallucinating that he's a demon, his eyes are frightening—dark brown, he's wearing his contacts so there's a yellowish ring around his irises. I realize I don't trust him, I'm afraid he'll hurt me. I want him to hurt me.

Slap me.

He slaps me across the face. I feel myself clench, get wet. My head lolls to the side; he looks in my eyes, I'm naked, I'm begging him to do it again. He takes a condom from his pants pocket and puts it on, then slaps me again and enters me. I start to come almost immediately.

Not yet, he says, and stops moving inside me.

Please, I say, thrusting up at him; I'll go crazy if I don't finish coming. He stays still while I writhe under him; the orgasm goes on and on, I can't seem to stop. After a while he starts fucking me again, faster and faster, he comes with a loud moan and falls all the way on top of me.

I feel secure again feeling his weight, listening to his heart slowing down.

I talk to my friend Simone on the phone; we haven't spoken for weeks. She tells me about her lover, whom she's just broken up with.

At first it was great, she says. We did things sexually we'd never done with anyone else. But then he confessed that he likes to cross-dress. I mean, I just couldn't handle it. He wanted me to pretend he had a cunt; it was too weird.

I don't talk about my sex life to Simone; at least, not the really intimate details. My girl friends and I discuss the size of our lovers' cocks, tell each other if they're any good in bed; I told Simone about the time I met two guys in North Beach and went to the Holiday Inn with them. Simone likes being tied up, but I don't want to talk about it with her. He and I have our own private world, we spend hours together absorbed in each other, seeing how far we can go. We close the curtains, nothing gets in. I tell Simone I want to marry him.

You're kidding, Simone says. How long have you known this guy?

Ten weeks.

Forget it, Simone says.

No, I mean it. I've been with enough men. I don't want to do that anymore.

The Virtuous Woman, Simone says.

Something like that.

You can't do it. You know how you are—if you like somebody and he wants you, you let him fuck you.

But I never felt like this about anybody else. And he's the

best lover I ever had, I know I couldn't find anybody else who does what he does for me.

It's not about better, Simone says. Sooner or later you'll want something different, something he can't give you, and you'll go out looking for it. And anyway, you're confusing sex with love. You're hot for this man so you think you love him.

I wonder why Simone does this to me; she can't be happy for me, she always finds flaws. He says she's just being my friend, trying to protect me. I don't call Simone for weeks because I'm afraid she'll convince me that she's right.

The more I fuck him, the more I want him; I've never had this much sex with anyone before. It's all we do—sex, work, eat, sleep. Sometimes we don't get around to cooking dinner until midnight, and sometimes we end up at two a.m. eating cheese and olives and pita bread in bed. Simone tells my other friends I'm obsessed. He's late for work all the time, his boss blames it on me. No one understands us. There's a conspiracy against us, to separate us. Romantic love is always tragic; the lovers can't stay together, death or lies or fate separate them. It's dangerous to be erotic, then you aren't so trapped; if you do it in public they look at you and their minds are filthy so they see filth, then they try to put you in jail.

After a few more weeks we quit our jobs and move to a hotel in the Tenderloin where we can be together all the time; between us we have enough money for about four months. I don't know what's going to happen after that and I don't care. I set up my tubes of paints, my chalks and charcoals and brushes, on a table in the corner of the room, and he models for me. We have a small refrigerator with a freezer that keeps tiny ice cubes frozen in plastic trays, a hot plate, an indoor barbecue, a stack of books we've bought over the years meaning to read but that we never got around to; we have a portable cassette player, tapes, potted violets and an aloe plant. We never go further than the corner grocery half a block away. We cook or eat takeout Vietnamese food from next door. Whatever we need from the outside world, the son of the woman two doors down picks up for us. We fight sometimes. We fall more deeply in love. Underneath everything we're blissfully happy. We know how to live. All we want is for you to go away and leave us the fuck alone.

A Brief History of Condoms

Kim Addonizio

1. ORIGINS OF THE AMERICAN CONDOM

The so-called American Condom (Prophylacticus Americanus) began behind the counters of druggists, springing to life in the dust and dark among prescription bottles.[1] In the diaspora which followed, some migrated into the air-conditioned light of Walgreens and Thriftys, others to the flickering fluorescent haze of convenience stores. Still others settled behind glass cabinets in large grocery chains. The most colorful varieties live crowded in baskets on the counters of medical clinics. Condoms thrive in great numbers throughout the continent of North America, and tend to be concentrated in large cities. Fundamentalist Christians and the occasional zealous Catholic have decreased their numbers slightly, but the overall impact of such predation has been insignificant on the population as a whole.

2. LIFE CYCLE OF THE CONDOM

A condom is a simple one-celled organism which appears, at first look, to be round and flat. When released from its foil "nest" and massaged, it changes its shape into a sock-like, membraneous creature which clings to human flesh— specifically, the male's sexual organ. Condoms have a symbiotic relationship with humans; sperm released during human sexual activity is caught and eaten by the condom, allowing the condom to reproduce itself. Having fulfilled its evolutionary purpose, the condom then shrivels and dies. The fetus, or "conda," microscopic in size at this point, becomes airborne until it finds a suitable "nest," slips inside it and gestates in the warmth and protection the foil offers.

[1] The largely discredited "Big O Theory," first developed by Holstein, posits a divine origin, to wit: that the universe was originally the size and shape of a gigantic, cosmically conscious condom, which masturbated itself and exploded into particles which ripped it apart and sent particles streaming outward into space. There are still some elements of the scientific community who claim that there is an inner condom in each of us, remnant of the Great Rubber, and that we are reabsorbed into it at the end of earthly life. It's interesting to note that numerous mythologies of so-called primitive peoples offer variants of this proposition.

A condom may lie dormant in its nest for years, but life outside the nest last from only a few minutes to half an hour or so.[2] It is fair to say that these brief moments, however, are by far the most gratifying; condoms have been observed to burst from sheer pleasure, and occasionally to squirm off of the male penis and travel excitedly upwards into the interior regions of the partner's body.[3]

3. COMMON USES OF THE CONDOM
There are many valuable uses of the condom beyond the aforementioned use in sexual activity. Condoms may be filled with water and dropped from high windows to terrify old people; or loaded with jello and thrown at parties. They may be blown up like balloons. The flavored variety, once the lubricant is wiped away, is favored for eating by adolescent girls. Condoms may be used in delaying sexual activity, as in, " I won't fuck you if I have to wear that thing on my dick."[4] Such a statement may have unfortunate results if the condom is then discarded, as it will simply dry up and die without reproducing itself. Condoms are dependent on human males, some of whom have an ambivalent relationship with them, and see them at best as a necessary evil.

4. INNER LIFE OF THE CONDOM
It is hard to ascertain whether a condom is capable of the emotions you and I regard as a part of sentient life. Does a condom experience depression, or fear death? Does it have a soul? If so, then we must examine carefully our treatment of this useful creature. Should it, for example, be so quickly relegated to the floor beside the bed, or the trash in the bathroom, or the weeds of the vacant lot? Perhaps our

---

[2] The briefest known lifespan is .078 seconds; the longest, evidenced by a videotape of pornographic artist Jackoff Holmes, was well over an hour. Research has indicated that short-lived condoms tend to exhibit a high level of anxiety, whereas the longest-living emit alpha waves—an indication that, in human terms, these latter condoms tend to "stop and smell the roses," i.e. the odors of anal or vaginal secretions.

[3] Emergency Room records indicate that a small percentage of patients seek treatment, but the incidence is undoubtedly more frequent, according to anecdotal sources.

[4] In the late twentieth century, this statement is an indication of gross stupidity on the part of the speaker. The best response to such an attitude is probably, "Go fuck yourself."

responsibility should extend to a decent burial, a few words said to mark the passing of our pleasure-seeking, short-lived friend. Perhaps it loves the woman whose vaginal walls drench it for a few minutes, or the man whose anus contracts around it. Perhaps it realizes that such bliss must soon, too soon, turn into pain and diminishment, into the awful isolation of the separate self. If the condom could speak, what truths might it tell us, privy as it is to some of our most intimate moments?

5. One Condom's Story

She carries me in her purse. She intends to be faithful, but just in case, she wants to be prepared. She is on a long trip, away from her lover. She meets a man who delights her, who is clever and interesting. He puts his hand on her hip as they are walking. They find a bar and drink until they can hardly stand up, then stagger to a hotel room. I hear them laughing and giggling, hear the rustle of clothes and good intentions being rapidly discarded. There is a blinding light as I am freed, feeling the cool air wash deliciously over me, and then I am lost in sensation, nothing matters but this, it is glorious, I am stretched taut, headed for that beautiful deadly opening; I go in and in. My head floods with sperm and I gorge myself, losing consciousness, and when I wake I find myself flushed down the pipes, along the sewers and out into the great river of the unborn, riding the currents down to the mothering sea. [5]

6. Social Organization of Condom Communities

There are many classes—one might even say castes—in the condom community. Brightly colored and flavored condoms are usually ostracized by those with a more uniform look and packaging. These second-class citizens are more likely to attempt to form what we can only call personal attachments with other condoms. Through a process known as "nest-ripping," two separate condoms may leak their lubri-

---

[5] The account is fictional; see Christopher Peckerwood's *I Am A Condom*. There are no authenticated stories of condoms speaking or writing their views, though apocryphal ones abound. Various people have claimed to be kidnapped by condoms from outer space, or to hear the voices of dead condoms speaking to them.

cants and form a sort of gluey mass which causes the nests to bind to each other. They then become unfit for human use and hence unable to reproduce, so why this occurs remains an evolutionary mystery.[6]

7. In Conclusion: A Personal Note

There is much still to learn about this deceptively simple creature. I have here attempted the briefest outline of serious study and research. My own fascination began, perhaps, when as I boy I unrolled my first condom and jerked off into it, finding it a much neater method than rutting into the sheets my mother would have to wash. I have, frankly, never encountered a human body which gave me as much pleasure as the simple, unassuming condom, always eager to please, ready to take my jism and lap it up deliriously, then lie peacefully hanging from my penis while I relaxed with a cigarette. Several times during these jottings I have stopped to "denest" and massage one of the little creatures, to slip it over me and caress it, to squeeze and pull until we were both deliciously sated.[7] I confess to you now that I love them, that I think of nothing but their moist dripping bodies, that at night they come to me in my dreams, they hover over me and smile, and at last begin to speak.

---

[6] For further readings see "Nest-ripping: Nature or Nurture?" in Scientific American; "Nest-Rippers, Menace to Society," ibid.; and the San Francisco journal Honey,Let It Rip.

[7] I can't get enough. Desire is endless. Sometimes I want to fuck everything in sight. I want to fuck the sheets, the trees outside my window, the men and women passing on the streets below; I want that ecstasy that only sex provides, the loss of self and finding of it, the petit-morte that tells me there is no true death, there is only connection and ceaseless change, there is only love against the darkness surrounding us, we are all ripped from the nest, helpless and exposed together; oh friends and colleagues, it all comes down to this: So many condoms. So little time.

Kim Addonizio

Tool-Subject Devices

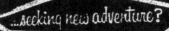

breasts cavin... light... trying to say, "You faggot." Thinking ... man, he tore at my
nipples as my ... against the old rail
station. My ... cold ... summer time? The
winter of our fuckli... madnes... Vein traveller.
Postcards in ... Home, so ... realize it at
first. I can love you for what I am ... his
friends. Praying only h...
Out of the stree...
His friends. ...
destroyed our ...
feast of all th...
lowed their cl...
talk, but slippe...
now. Thought ... this is me as
my cock grew ou... and I became
no longer not a wo... ck strong.
 "That night, b... I slep... eaten, so
many bodies an... embe... was what I
am. Carried by a ... nking ... this was
tomorrow. Yesterda... y win... for Juliet,
if she. And she. He ... hat. And
I knew no that I c... I played
under the disguises

 "Out on the st... jum... ecar and
headed for the docks... in the ... . Looking for
a rube or two. 'Sailor boy ... d free ove?' Flashing eyes,
weaving circles, floating h... Tongue alert and inviting
for all the boys to see. His g... wed... ng band for all their
eyes to see. Safe. Married. ... tic ps, thick and fleshy,
wanting. All those young ... thin... 'He just wants to
serve me. Nothing need... retur... ust give me service.
Probably some imp... ol ma... to some sort of a
decayed wife.'

DTD

Vivienne Wood

I

Freja awoke one morning from uneasy dreams and found her familiar female genitals had been transformed overnight into a sizable phallus (and entourage) which was now uncomfortably trapped between her stomach and the mattress. She turned over with a groan and thought the discomfort would lessen if it were not rock-hard. She blinked until her eyes came into focus, rubbed the sleep-goobers out of them, and examined her dick. It wasn't too bad, she thought, considerably above average size, in fact—she noted with a flush of pride. Luckily hers was particularly nice, longish and with ample enough girth to balance the length aesthetically (some of the longer ones she had seen were too thin, creating a pencil-like aspect that is displeasing to the eye and tactily unsatisfactory). She felt the skin and noted that it was smooth like any other with that especially soft bit beneath the tip on the underside (or was it the upperside? she wondered. It was certainly the side facung up as it lay erect against her stomach. She had always considered it the underside when looking up at one, however, so she decided to continue to consider it as such; no point in changing perspective this late in the game). She grasped it authoritatively round the base and examined the upperside. When it was thus held aloft, she noticed that her particular dick deviated from the emblematic straigthness of most phalluses in that it curved in a decidedly banana-like fashion. She let it go and listened to it thwapp satisfactorily against her stomach. Pleased with the sound, she repeated the procedure a few times while pondering the implications of its curvature. She didn't think it detracted from its overall handsomeness, indeed she decided, it might actually endow it with a certain distinctiveness. Freja was not one to place form over function, however, and she worred that the shape may in some way impede its effective usage. It occurred to her that during an amorous moment if the impaled partner were to lean back, spine arched (as she herself was wont to do) the curvedness of her dick might cause considerable pain to both parties concerned. Nonetheless, it appeared otherwise functional.

As she continued thwapping it absent-mindedly against her stomach while further musing upon its distinctive shape, it occureed to her that she should become familiar with its particularized mode of functioning before attempting to use it in the presence of another person. She had noticed from experience how willful the things could be, defying their owners occasionally with a refusal to corroborate the whispered asserssion that she was the world's-all-time-sexiest-chick, and had the hottest body the sweaty and breathless wielder of the obstinate instrument insisted they had ever come across; other times they capriciously substantiated this observation with an immediate vehemence that left the bearer mutter apologies about, "don't know what happened, it had been a long time, will be better next time, etc."

No, she resolved, she must become as familiar as possible with the apparatus' habits and peculiarities before road testing it. Besides that, it was still rock hard and faintly plum colored at the tip, a condition (as she knew from observing the owners of such things) that must be alleviated as quickly as posssible. She hefted herself out of the bed, noting with interest how her dick swayed with her movement yet remained insistently erect, standing at attention with stoic majesty. She examined herself sideways in the bathroom mirror and remarked inwardly that she would definitely need to guard against the thing's tendency (already manifest in its bearing) to take itself too seriously. She draped a hand towel over it, noting it could be useful for performing the duties of a towel rack should the real thing be unavailable. Although she couldn't readily imagine a plausible scenario where this feature would be necesssary (unless while camping perhaps?), she liked her dick's appearance of dignifed servitued while bearing the towel rather like a tuxedoed waiter at a four star restaurant. She marched back and forth in front of the mirror a few times, bowing and inquiring solemnly, "Would you care for a hand-towel madam?" but then resolved it was time to get down to the serious business of getting off.

She surveyed her array of toiletries in search of the appropriate lotion to facilitate her task and after rejecting the Lubriderm Lotion for Dry Skin Care (too boring, no scent), Victoria's Secret Peach Hyacinth After Bath Lotion (too girlie smelling), Suave Baby Powder Fresh Moisturizing Body Formula (not thick enough, some uncomforable friction might occur) and Alpha Keri Moisture Rick Body Oil (too liquidy and difficult to handle in conjunction with an unfamiliar dick), she selected the Body Shop Mango Body Butter (a refined, rich moisturizer excellent for especially dry areas like elbows and feet). The overwhelming mango scent which pervaded the apartment within seconds of opening the jar seemed vaguely sexual to her, probably, she reflected, because a fastidious ex-boyfriend had successfully used the product to relieve his needs against her stomach one time when she was on her period (which presumbably rendered the area from knees to navel hazardous to human contact, harmful or fatal if swallowed or absorbed through the skin) and too far gone in a drunken torpor to provide the blowjob he had intially requested. In any event, this product has a record of sucessful intereactions with penises; she would give it a try.

She slathered her hands with a substantial quantity of the oily goo (its slight graininess due to the crystallization of the natural ingredients quickly dissolved as she warmed the product between her palms), purposely grasped her dick near the base, and began to jerk her hand upwards, letting her body-buttered palms slide quickly up and down its length. Again admiring its substantial girth, she looked down its tip, now shiny with goo and purple with anticipation of immanent release, and remarked to herself that while she had given many a hand job in her life she had never gazed directly down at the focus of the endeavor from above. Instead the object in question had usually been at eye level, or slightly below and to the side (as in the front seat of the car—the primary perspective of high school days). She watched fascinated as the hole at the tip expanded and contracted with her jerking motions and wondered why she never noticed before that the thing looked uncannily like the mouth of a guppy opening and closing mindlessly as it gazes vacously through the walls of its tank. However, such introspection she discovered, while diverting, was not conducive to efficient masturbation so she closed her eyes and resolved to trot out one of her tried and true fantasies, amended slightly to correspond to her new anatomy. This time, instead of fucking Dan Quayle with a strap-on dildo while he was hand cuffed spread eagled to her four-poster bed as a six foot tall muscle-bound black gay man (courtesy of Mapplethorpe) videotaped the proceedings to send to Marilyn Quayle at a later date, she was able to fuck him with a real live dick. As usual, she came at the point where she ceases fucking him and straddles his face (this time the scenario was altered to have Dan Quayle giving her the blow job rather than performing cunnilingus as he was generally so rudely forced to do at this point) while the black man simultaneously begins jerking off and comes on her stomach. She felt the usual internal shudder followed by the sensation of warm viscosity flowing over her hand.

She opened her eyes and raised her hand to her nose, sniffing apprehensively while making a mental note to herself to clean the splorches off the floor before anybody came over. She was delighted when her olfactory investigation revealed only a very mild musk scent, barely discernible. A taste test yielded a similar result. But she was particularly relieved to discover the consistency was thin and liquidy with a uniform smoothness, no lumps or varying thicknesses were to be found as she rubbed the rapidly cooling goo up and down her arm while scrutinizing it with the exacting eye of an aficionado. She remembered several off-putting episodes with less-than-pleasing samples of this substance (each penis, she discovered, produced its own unique vintage). She recalled with a shudder a particularly disgusting encounter with a small, thin, almost prehensile-looking-penis (which was attached to a flabby, balding, near-sighted insurance litigator who had whined like a dog with its nose down a rabbit hole until in a moment of bourbon and boredom she had agreed to go home with him) that had excreted a sticky, immensely yeasty, gelatinous paste that had somehow seemed appallingly in keeping with the priapic intensity of its owner. She dimly recalled lunging toward the bathroom with a spasm of disgust, rinsing her mouth out (it had taken several go rounds with Plax to get the last remnants of the stuff off her back teeth), gathering her clothes off the bedroom floor and dressing frantically while mumbling about somewhere she suddenly remembered she had to be, abandoning all graciousness in her attempt to put as much distance between herself and that vile jelly as possible. She had pretended not to hear his surprised "well can I at last have your phone number?" as she shut the door. Thankfully, she thought, her innocuous secretion would be inoffensive (if not necessarily palatable) to the most discerning of recepients.

She watched approvingly as her dick conveniently folded itself for greater portability, and reassured that it would behave in a more or less predicatable fashion, and having pretty much exhausted the possibile activities available to her at home, she decided to acquiesce to its demand to find a chick.

II

Heading toward Telegraph Avenue, Freja stopped to piss in a planter and felt an immediate surge of exhiliration. The thrill of peeing standing up, while dressed, with only one portion of the anatomy exposed (which was protectively grasped in her hand and could be tucked back into safety at the first hint of danger) was too wonderful. As she wrote her name (albeit rather sloppily) in the dirt, she resolved to never pee indoors again and began a mental inventory of all the places she would like to exercise this new power off a ski lift (the piss might even be frozen before it hit the ground), out a car's rear window on the freeway (this one, however, would require an accomplice to drive), in her next door neighbor's mailbox. . .

But there was plenty of time for that she decided, and besides, her urine stream and her inspiration had dried up for the moment. She needed to plan her chick hunting expedition. She headed for Blake's, remembering the many successful chick-hunts she had seen conducted there. Blake's was exactly as it had been on all of her previous visits—the soundless, ever present Sports Event on the TV screen presiding over the milling throng beneath while Kurt Cobain commanded them from the overhead speakers. Predictably, the guys present all seemed part of some pack (generally, she had noted, guys traveled in packs when hunting and here she was at a distinct disadvantage). She obtained an Amstel Light, admittedly a pale substitute for Miller Lite, from the heavily lipsticked and false-eyelashed bartender with much greater speed than she had in the past and sat down nonchalantly on a barstool, unfortunately trapping her balls between the stool and her leg and jumping up immediately with a decidedly uncool yelp. She glanced around surreptitiously, but thankfully no one seemed to have witnessed her genital faux-pas. She slipped her hand into her pocket and carefully rearranged her offended gonads as she gingerly eased back onto the stool to observe the scene while formulating her own hunting strategies.

Comfortingly, all was proceeding as it always had. Freja watched as a pack of four guys, stationed within clear sight-lines of the Sports Event, just-slightly-less-than-obviously glanced repeatedly over at a gaggle of girls (four) in a corner who were artfully ignoring them as they traded confidences among themselves and periodically exploded into paroxysms of hilarity over some inaudible witticism. Freja knew how the rest of the scene was choreographed: once a group of girls had been targetted, the guys would circle a few times and the Alpha male would approach the High Profile chick of the bunch. If he was greeted with tolerant indifference or better, the others would move in, each Beta and Gamma male attaching himself to one of the remaining chicks. She had never been able to figure out how the negotiations to divvy up the excess chicks were conducted (the Alpha male/High Profile chick pairing was obvious); when the numbers were even each guy just wordlessly honed in on one of the girls; no way could this consistently operate so smoothly without prior arrangements. She strained to hear some discussion of these operations in the boys' intra-gender communications, but frustratingly their remarks were confined to detailed analysis of the Sports Event and Freja quickly dismissed as patently absurd the fleeting fancy that this was in fact an elaborate form of code. Yet sure enough the tall blond (Seattle Seahawks T-shirt, substantial biceps, sunglasses-tan, and easy fresh-off-the-slopes athleticism) whom Freja had tagged as the Alpha Male arose on some unseen signal and ambled toward the skinniest, longest-haired, blondest girl of the group.

At a table not blessed by this numerical parity, one male was left chivalrously talking to two surplus chicks while at another where the fluidity of interactions was burdened by an excess of guys, two had stationed themselves on either side of the designated quarry and were auditioning. How these tasks were assigned, however, like how birds know to turn instantaneously in flight, remained a mystery to Freja. She did recall a limerick spray painted under a window of one of the Frat houses at school, apparently to torment the room's occupant (there had been some clumsy attempts at lewd illustrations accompanying the verse):

There once was a brother named Carter
The dude was a terrible starter
   Behind his friends he'd abide
   Their coattails to ride
To hook up with some scanky sex partner

So, presumably, consistently relying on other males for leftovers eventually produced a drop in prestige, or was it the drop in prestige that preceded the guys' relegation to Beta or Gamma status? In any event, Freja decided, since she was not privy to whatever subtle rituals configured this hierachy, its mechanisms would probably always remain obscure, and pondering the matter brought her no closer to executing a successful chick-hunt. Kurt Cobain was singing from above, but Freja did not find this enlightening and decided to avail herself of the downstairs facilities.

She hesitated briefly before the two doors, noted the line leading into one of them and chose the other, glancing at the designation "Men" with only slight apprehension. Freja pushed open the door. She stationed herself at the urinal farthest from the room's other occupant, being careful to avoid casting more than the most cursory glance in his direction and fixed her eyes steadily on the wall in front of her as she unzipped her jeans—instinctively realizing that this was not the place to compare her latest acquisition with others of its kind, much as she would like to. Just outside the door she heard a robust male voice comment as it passed by in part of a receding conversation, "Yeah, dude, that chick was so ugly I had to spin her around..." which elicited some approving guffaws, followed shortly thereafter by a female voice, "Yeah, well, at least the creep bought me dinner..." proceeded by a rueful male voice, "You know the type I mean: good from far, far from good..."

She shook off her dick, careful to avoid any trace of a flourish and was mildly pertubed by its unfortunate resemblance to fish bait when not in a turgid state. Deciding that

Blake's was probably not the best place to hunt, since the packs were likely to leave only slim pickings (or actually not-so-slim pickings), she headed for Henry's. "Nature is a whore..." observed Kurt Cobain sagely as Freja wove her way toward the door.

Yes, this place was definitely better for the lone hunter, Freja concluded, as she sipped her Miller Lite and surveyed the scene from her strategic position beneath the Sports Event that provided a vista of every portion of the room. The low key, pub-like atmosphere somewhat muted the obviousness of the transactions taking place. She scanned the crowd, attempting to choose a workable target among the various girls, realizing that her odds of scoring with a well-defended High Profile chick were next to nil. She recalled a college acquiantance's system for determining his chances of hooking up with any given chick. He said that first you determine the Basic Attainability Quotient, or BAQ, which is the inverse of the Actual Desirability Quotient (ADQ). In other words an ADQ of 10 (Highest Profile chick) was a BAQ of 1, etc. Then you take the BAQ and subtract the number of girlfriends surrounding the chick, then multiply the answer by the number of drinks consumed by the girl. The resulting number is then increased by a factor of one for every hour that passes until the last hour before closing when it increases exponentially in twenty minute increments. While he conceded that there were sometimes unknowable variables that might play into the equation (girl's best friend had crush on guy, guy's reputation had preceded him, girl had just broken up with someone who liked like guy, etc., ad infinitum), he insisted that it provided quite a serviceable model although the characteristic female nonsensicalness when it came to determining the desirability of any given male (which according to him was not discernibly standardized or remotely predictable) was the greatest element of chance.

Freja scanned the room, rejecting a group of five Sorority-looking girls (Express baseball hats, pearl-stud earrings, hotpink lipstick) as collectively averaging on unworkably low BAQ. The rest of the chicks seemed claimed by various males, but Freja, not to be daunted in her mission, resolved to keep her spirits high and her standards low and stay put until opportunity presented itself. In another sweep of the crowd she paused to closely examine a particularly rauscous group occupying the entire length of one of the long middle tables and fixed on a sizable brunette (about 60 pounds overweight, medium length hair, big tits). Since the ADQ was calculated according to a strict set of rules (blonde hair outranks any other color, long hair outranks short, big tits adds 1 bonus point, hardbody adds 2, 1 point is subtracted for each 10 pounds overweight, etc.) Freja was immediately able to assign an ADQ of 3 which translated to a BAQ of 8. She watched as the girl silently sipped her beer (not lite, Freja noted disapprovingly) and periodically ceased her vacant gazing at the TV set over the bar in order to glare malevolently at a couple at the far end of the table. The clean-cut blond male-half of the pair seemed unaware of her attention as he whooped loudly, straightened his Virginia Cavaleirs cup with a self-satisfied gesture after scoring the winning point in a dice game played with a couple of brown-haired versions of himself, and wrapped his arm in a proprietal gesture around a skinny, bored-looking blonde (obviously High Profile chick) who was unsuccessfully attempting to use her stir straws like chopsticks to fish ice cubes out of her drink. Gambling that the Fat Chick was a casualty of a recent Fuck-n-Chuck scenario involving the blonde boy and therefore a likely quarry for a pig-hunting expedition, Freja casually stationed herself next to her on her way back from the bar. "So, do you go to Cal..."

"But I don't want to do it doggy-style," the F.C. repeated, a hint of peevishness detectable in her tone. "Oh come on, it'll be fun," Freja whined, her right hand deftly making short work of the resistance provided by the F.C.'s Levi's button-fly 501's. "It's just that ... well ... my butt's kind of fat. I'd rather you didn't see it."

"Oh is that all you're worried about?" Freja breathed in her best I'm-extremely-turned-on-yet-still-oh-so-sensitive voice. "I promise, I won't look..."

Several seconds later, after having successfully peeled off the F.C.'s jeans which lay on the floor in a substantial heap like a discarded innertube, Freja was momentarily afraid that her newly minted dick may not be up to the challenge represented by the phocine rump before her, but determined to give it the old college try she commenced her appointed task, finding herself strangely mesmerized by the barely visible network of bluish veins just beneath the surface of the F.C.s pallid skin. She lifted her eyes a moment from the expanse of undulating flesh to gaze in vaguely horrified fascination at the Care Bears poster about the F.C.'s bed in which the bears (whom Freja had always assumed were in some way connected with fabric softener although puzzlingly enough this was apparently not the case here) are sliding down a pneumatic, counter-intuitively pastel colored rainbow into a vat of cubby, utterly symmetrical flowers while conveniently pastel colored butterflies hover nearby in sycophantic adoration. Listening to the methodical thwapping sound of her pelvis against the ample plane of the F.C.'s vigorously flopping buttocks, Freja half-heartedly attempted to amuse herself by mentally embellishing the poster with lewd depictions of snakes, tarantulas and Boschian demons taking outrageous liberties with the Care Bear's flowers but abandoned the project almost immediately as a far too cliché-ridden assault on far too easy a target and turned her attention back to the matter at hand.

Staring down she could see her dick (which, she noted fondly, had thus far done quite well and had not had any banana-shape related mishaps) disappear and reappear with monotonous regularity as the F.C.'s gelantinous butt completely obscured the line of sight with each forward thrust. Focusing her gaze on the ripples that spread across the viscous surface of flaccid skin in hypnotic synchronicity with her own athletic exertions, Freja noted with forensic thoroughness the superabundance of dimpled cottage cheese fat upholstering the entire expanse of the F.C.'s now sweat shiny rump as she wrapped her arms around where the waistline was theoretically located in order to spasmodically clutch handfuls of loose wobbly stomach flesh while she waited for her dick to complete its task.

Possibly on account of its recent prior encounter with the Mango Butter or perhaps due to a sullen resolution to demonstrate its absolute sovereignty in matters of this sort, Freja's dick made it abundantly clear that she would have to keep up the endurance phase of the pig-hunt for a good while longer. Letting out a groan she was fairly confident could plausibly be interpreted as enthusiasm, she focused her eyes on the pink "My Pretty Pony" doll whose perfectly coifed mane cascaded arfully over one of the heart shaped eyelet throw-pillows painstakingly positioned in a random arrangement around the white ruffled pillowsham and, wondering simultaneously how much time this girl spent per week grooming her stuffed animals (all in varying shades of pink, she realized with a jolt of mild hysteria) and whether faking an orgasm could really be all that different with a dick as without one, clenched her pounds of flesh with grim determination and began pumping with renewed vigor. Uttering the first sound she had made since the single low grunt she emitted while hefting her bulk into the four legged position, the F.C. let out a low moan accompanied by a barely detectable shudder, disrupting the otherwise unbroken rhythm of thwapping skin and slishing orifi that had been audible throughout the entire encounter despite the all-too-palpable presence of Mariah Carey's multi-octave meditations on the nature of love which had effectively obscured the customary sounds of heavy breathing and squeaking bedsprings.

Seizing the moment, Freja put in a couple of convincingly impassioned thrusts and producted the Stacato-Series-of-Ecstatic-Moans-Punctuated-by-Several-Ripsnorting-All-Over-Body-Shudders that had long been a part of her repertoire, rapidly disengaged with a gloopy squelsh and rolled over on her back, momentarily leaving her dick (gleaming and deeply purple from exertion) to its own devices while she struggled to suppress the urge to dismember the pink koala bear which had squeaked accusingly when she rolled on it. "OK, still don't look," the F.C. said. "Huh? Oh yeah," Freja mumbled, catching a glimpse from the corner of her eye a gestalt of chewed-down-to-the-quick fingernails on pudgy hands cupping pendulous teats, a flash of silvery stretch marks, the impression of rolls of fat hastily reconfiguring themselves to keep up with the F.C.'s rapid movement before she turned her attention back to the koala bear which was starting to bear a disturbing resemblance to Paula Abdul. "Well now that's done: and I'm glad it's over," she informed it in a sub rosa whisper as she frantically rummaged through her mental archives for the exit protocols appropriate to scenarios such as these. The F.C. returned shrouded in an oversized white T-shirt and baggy boxer shorts (does she really think she's concealing anything?

Freja muttered mentally with a derisive snort) and plopped down heavily on the bed with an expectant air. Momentarily at a loss as to what was required of her, Freja stared blankly at the F.C. with what she hoped was a neutral expression until it occured to her that it was probably incumbent upon the one with the dick in the sexual encounter to provide some sort of polite reassurance to the one without one that what had just transpired was not merely a Get-In, Get-Off, Get-Out transaction (it being the height of rudeness she dimly recalled, to acknowledge this fact) and that this reassurance customarily took the form of post-coital physical affection. She glanced ruefully down at her dick and hesitated momentarily while she wrestled with a hot rush of resentment for the social burden imposed by the ownership of such an object before she gingerly raised one sweaty paw to stroke the F.C.'s hair while placing the other limply over the F.C.'s hand and aksed in what she was almost certain sounded like a concerned whisper, "Er, you are on the pill or something, aren't you?" Clearly mollified, the F.C. giggled coyly, flashed what Freja guessed was intended as a flirtatious smile but which instead counter-productively revealed two grayish-black canine teeth which had gone unnoticed in bar light, bestowed a warm flabby kiss on Freja's forehead, ruffled Freja's hair and uttered in a tolerant People-with-Dicks-are-so-Foolish-but-Cute tone, "It's a bit late to be asking that don't you think?" After several more enthusiastic kisses on Freja's neck she breathed, "I'll be right back," and much to Freja's relief headed toward the kitchen, apparently not expecting a reply. If she had not already been planning her escape Freja would certainly have begun doing so immediately upon the F.C.'s triumphant return in an olfactory cloud of crushed flower petals and slightly overripe fruit (how long did she have to search for a perfume that matched her decor? Freja wondered) bearing two A&W Vanilla Creme Sodas and a bowl of M&M's. When it fully downed on her that every M&M in the bowl was some shade of pink (pink! where the Hell do you get pink M&M's, she thought wildly, barely containing a rising hysteria), Freja realized that her nerves required an immediate escape even if it required abandoning even a vestige of politeness. Burbling disjointedly about "not fond of sweets—bike ride—need to get up early—friends from out of town—Golden Gate Park—only can sleep on my own mattress—7am start," she dressed with only thinly disguised haste and then began sidling towards the door, nervously running her fingers through her hair and straining every nerve to produce a passable semblance of casual ease.

As Freja continued edging toward the door, the F.C. swooped down upon a white enameled roll-top desk, removing a sheet of predictably candy-pink stationary. Freja felt Mariah Carey's insistent squeaks about her dreamlover pureeing her psyche like a cuisinart and just managed to suppress her growing hysteria by reciting the alphabet backwards to herself (a skill, she had been told, that would also see one safely through a sobriety check) and focusing every shred of attention she could muster upon the hot-pink glittered plastic heart bobbing atop the F.C.'s Hello Kitty pen as she wrote. "Here's my number," she said. "Uh, thanks," said Freja, abruptly bursting into a coughing fit designed to hide the mixture of giggle and shriek which had bubbled up unbidden in her throat at the sight of the paper's teddy-bear border (each clutching a pastel balloon in its paw) and the waft of the bubble-gummed ersatz cherry scent (presumably secreted by the glitter pen) which hadn't assaulted her nostrils since she'd reached twelve years of age. Attempting to convey nonchalant reverance while stuffing the paper in her front pocket, she crossed the last few feet to the door and, feeling emboldened by the immanence of her escape, turned as she slithered out into the night and mutttered the requisite, "Uh...I'll call you."

Crossing Sproul Plaza, Freja stopped to piss on the administration building steps, rationalizing to herself that although this was a tired-out transgression usually not enacted by owners of penises post-adolescence, since this was her first chance to practice this particular form of political expression she was almost obligated to take advantage of the opportunity. As she enjoyed the cool hissing sound of liquid on concrete she examined her disk pensively, noting it seemed none the worse for wear for its recent activity. Shaking it off, she was about to tuck it back in her boxer shorts (which she had heard are far preferable to tighty whities for dick transport) when she felt a now familiar stirring—this time her dick was drawing her intractably westward.

III

"Nice cock," the Marky-Mark clone whispered in Freja's ear as he brushed past her on his way to the sauna, causing Freja to glance down and realize with chagrin that the towel presented to her upon entering the bath house had fallen around her ankles. Noting once again that it was indeed a nice cock, its banana-shape standing at attention like a barrel-chested martinet, she decided to drape the towel over her arm instead and let her dick lead the way unshrouded. Surveying the room, she tried to discern what exactly the appropriate protocols were before plunding dick first into a possible behavioral faux-pas. Could she just join the group of three guys jacking each other off in the dim half-light of the wieght-room by walking over and wordlessly presenting her penis for inspection? Did the guy in the next room giving a blowjob to the tattooed marine (nude except for his dogtags) want company, perhaps a blowjob himself? Deciding not to risk a possible rebuff, she instead grabbed a condom from the candy-dish as she passed by and stationed herself hopefully in front of one of the TV sets in the corner and slowly jerked herself off, carefully positioning herself so her entire apparatus was clearly visible in the flickering lights emitted by the porno on the screen. The two mustached protagonists had scarcely commenced fucking before Freja felt a hand on her dick. She glanced over at the waif-like blonde boy beside her, met his pale blue eyes with a steady gaze, and wordlessly transferred her hand from her dick to his. On familiar ground here, she administered the same hand job she had been giving for years, remarking smugly to herself that her penis was far bigger than the stubby pinkish one she clasped in her hand, but quickly lost her self-satisfied composure when her dick abandoned its loyalty to her and responded with traitorous immediatecy to the blond boy's touch, splatteing out hot gism almost instantaneously onto the floor. Amending her technique to mirror her partner's, she firmly grasped the base and jerked manfully, only moving her hand as much as the warm goose-pimply skin at the root would permit. Her efforts eventually extracted a couple of drops of pearly goo which ran lazily down her hand, yet Freja was left with the unsettling feeling that she had been woefully inadequate in her task. "You have a great cock," the boy remarked with a flip of his white-blond hair as he wandered off towards the showers. Somewhat chagrined by the mediocrity of her performance, and deciding to partake of the joys of voyeurism for the time being while her now fishbaited penis rested stickily against her inner thigh, Freja stationed herself beside a half open room where a Tom Cruise look-a-like was clearly about to perform fellatio on a bald muscle-bound biker (although no bike was in evidence, Freja could really not imagine him with any other type of transportation) who was naked but for two silver nipple-rings and a Nazi hat.

"Pretend you're a straight guy," Tom Cruise whispered before beginning his task.

"You fucking faggot! Suck my cock till I come in your mouth, you filthy pervert!" the biker shouted without missing a beat. "Yeah, I can tell this isn't the first dick you've had in your faggoty mouth, you disgusting fucking queer! You little ass-licking, cock-sucking butt-fuckers make me sick!" This said, he delivered a resounding smack across Tom Cruise's face, leaving a reddened mark and apparetnly spurring Tom on to greater efforts as the biker breathed, "Yeah, that's right, get me off you little queer. You fucking faggots give head better than any bitch I've ever nailed!" Apparently this last peroration coincided nicely with the finale of the performance, as Tom Cruise stood up with a satisfied grin, swallowing dramatically, and said with exaggerated machismo and a mock swagger, "That's because I give head like a man."

Knowing that she could not possibly compete with this display and feeling, once again her dick's relentless demand for fresh fields and pastures new, Freja headed for the locker room with the intent of getting her increasingly dictatorial phallus back to campus as quickly as possible. As he passed Freja on his way out, Marky-Mark straightened his New York Giants cap and matter-of-factly remarked, "You really do have a beautiful cock."

IV

"Hey dude, never call your fraternity a frat—you don't call your country a cunt do you?" someone bellowed near Freja's ear, though the room was too packed with beer-drenched, short-haired, Reagenjungen for her to distinguish from exactly which one it originated. She snaked her way through the mass of warm, sodden bodies, it dawning on her as she breathed in the testosterone saturated air and noted the absence of any penisless persons that it must be Hell Night and wondered why her dick had insisted on coming there. Nonetheless, she obeyed its instructions, realizing it would give her no peace unless she moved as directed up the dimly lighted staircase toward she knew not what. At the top a tall, brown-haired guy with frighteningly even features grabbed her arm and pulled her up the two remaining steps, pushing her hard against the wall and causing her to gasp out a squeak of surprise. "Boy, are you ready to take the final step to becoming a member of Delta Tau Delta?" he screamed in her face with mechanized ferocity. She nodded dumbly. "If you consent," he chanted, "you have no right to refuse my commands; but you also know that you are free to choose not to consent. Do you consent?" Freja nodded again, understanding immediately that her dick would have it no other way.

"I want to hear you say yes!"

"Yes, yes, I consent!" snapped Freja, aggravated and wishing to get on with it, whatever it was. He pulled her by the arm several feet down a hallway to a closed door and turned toward her with an expression of such gravity on his perfect features that Freja had to supress a giggle. "Listen," he said, "now that you have consented you are ready. This is where I leave you. You're to knock on the door. Follow whoever opens the door for you and do whatever you're told. If you hesitate about going in, they'll come and take you in. If you don't obey immediately, they'll force you to. Now go." With this, he strode away with exaggereated dignity, presumably to resume his station at the top of the staircase.

Freja knocked on the door.

It was immediately opened by a blonde hardbody attired in a scanty reinterpretation of an eighteenth century chambermaid's garb: a tight bodice hooked in front that radically accentuated the bustline, lace-frills around the neck, half-length sleeves, a distinctively non-eighteenth century mini skirt of some why-bother see-through material and fuck-me red lipstick. She beckoned Freja inside a tiny room that looked suspiciously like a hastily converted walk-in closet. "This is your last chance," she whispered, brushing a long, red fingernail slowly along Freja's cheek. "Do you agree to submit to what will happen to you in the next room?"

"Yes, I consent," replied Freja, feeling she had got a pretty good handle on the routine by now.

"Then you may proceed," she said with a carefully executed curtsey that afforded Freja no little amusement, although she politely managed to keep a straight face as the girl opened the door to the adjoining room.

All Freja was able to register was a black blur as a large figure seized her arm and yanked her into the fire-lit room, expertly fastening a set of handcuffs to her wrists before she had time to exhale. Looking up at her captor, she saw that in addition to his black clothing and black combat boots he was masked by a black hood that concealed even his eyes behind a network of black gauze and that the hand clasping her uncuffed wrist, like the one keeping firm hold on the other end of the handcuffs, sported a black leather glove. Wordlessly he dragged her to a rough wooden saw-horse in the center of the room and fastened the handcuffs to an iron ring embedded in the wood, forcing her to her knees with a rough shove on her shoulder. From his thick leather belt he removed a leather bracelet which he strapped around Freja's wrist before he threaded the attached chain through the iron ring, drawing Freja's wrists together as he pulled it tight and bound it to the handcuffs. Stepping back to survey his handiwork, he gave the chain a final tug to insure its fastness and strode round to the front of the sawhorse, standing with his crotch at Freja's eye level which was, after all, a vista she was quite accustomed to. "You are bound," he intoned dispassionately, "because it has been so easy for you to consent and we want from you what it will be impossible for you to consent to, even if you agree ahead of time, even if you say yes now and imagine yourself capable of submitting. Your submission will be obtained in spite of you. Now Mistress 'X' is going to have her way with you." On this cue Freja heard the door open behind her followed by the swift click-click of high heels on a hardwood floor. She turned to see a woman dressed only in a floor-length red cape and black patent leather mules with an iron collar around her neck and gold shackles on her wrists approach the sawhorse, bearing in her hand a red scarf. She kneeled directly in front of Freja and, upon a barely discernible nod from the Man In Black, reached forward and unbuttoned Freja's jeans. She leaned so close as she pulled Freja's pants and boxers down to her knees that the scent of honey and roses emanating from the nape of her neck momentarily odscured the smell of wood burning in the stone fireplace against the wall. She next blindfolded Freja with the red scarf, drawing the silk so tight the flickering firelight was entirely obscured. "What is about to occur," the male voice began in the same almost expressionless monotone, "is intended less to make you suffer or scream than to feel, through this suffering, that you are not free, and to teach you that you are totally dedicated to something outside yourself. When you leave here you will be bearing in your flesh a mark which will identify you. By then you will have learned that you are one with those who bear the same insignia." Immediately Freja heard metal scraping against stone, followed shortly by the ticking sound of heating iron, but was unable to reflect on this for more than two seconds before she felt a warm mouth surround her semi-erect penis which quickly completed the remainder of its journey to utter rigidity. Her low moan of pleasure as she felt the familiar progress toward climax turned into a shrill squeal of surprise and something-that-couldn't-really-be-described-as-pain-but-was-definately-a-close-second-cousin-of-that-sensation as she simultaneously felt the sting of ice pressed against her buttocks and the sharp awareness with an expert application of the tongue to the soft base of the penis' tip. Through this sensory haze Freja still heard, but did not register, the scrape of metal on stone that directly proceeded her climax. As her orgasm coopted her entire neural network she heard a hissing sound and smelt the odor of burning skin before her brain processed moments later the delayed message of acute pain that coursed though her, made her go rigid in her bonds and wrenched a scream from her lungs as the branding iron seared the flesh of her left buttock while a female voice counted slowly up to five before the iron was withdrawn. Only then was the blindfold removed by a black gloved hand, allowing Freja to taking the sight of the Man In Black kneeling before her. While he released her bonds she turned and focused blearily on Mistress 'X', still holding the smoking brand atop a long iron rod, before her eyes alighted on the letters inscribed on her skin, still freshly crimson, which read clearly

DTD

The Party on Twilight Avenue

or
An Orgy Among Friends

Jimmy Jazz

André was the first person we saw bathed in red light. A mixed drink in one hand, a cigar in the other. Everyone agrees that he's a beautiful boy, with his long black hair gathered in a pony tail, supple youth dripping from his skin, a freshly charged Art Spirit. He's sporting a paisley-lapeled smoking jacket that would look ridiculous on me. The cigar wet with his saliva isn't lit, though most of it has been smoked.

"Hey, Jimenez Yaz. Hey Silvia."

"Hey André."

"I thought you weren't coming to this party because you had a job playing Santa at the disabled kids' home?"

"He was supposed to play Santa, but he got fired," Silvia says.

"You can't hold on to a job lately."

"Yeahhhh, well, last year's Santa showed up and said he wanted to do it. The guy had his own suit. You know."

"Sorry Jimenez Yaz."

"That's okay, all that drooling and screaming gives me the creeps anyway."

"We saw your painting at the erotic art show..." Silvia says, but one of André's homosexual friends pulls him aside to meet a guy wearing leather chaps.

Twilight Avenue always has the best parties. The theme is red light district /opium den, which means they changed the regular light bulbs for red ones. The hidden occasion is a triple birthday: Marlene, Clara, André. The cake has already been cut into, so if there was any singing we missed it. It looks like devil's food with plain white icing and a fruity raspberry center. Silvia and I cross the hardwood floor to the snack table. I begin stuffing Seamus' home-made falafels into my mouth one after the other after dipping each one in a creamy tahini sauce. Seamus is sitting on the chaise lounge half asleep with his brow furrowed by time and a glass of red wine balanced on his fat belly. The music is hypnotic, intoxicating. Marlene is flitting to each clique like Tinkerbell, the party hostess making sure everyone has a drink. Clara's clique monopolizes the couch in the corner. She's locked in conversation with Janet X, one of those local rock stars who works at the record store. Janet's probably complaining about her husband who doesn't like parties. Eddie, the new young boy, sits at Clara's feet. He looks younger than the last one, but surprises you with moments of high Zen mysticism. He's wearing a costume, though it's not really a costume party.

"What's your costume Eddie, straight white male?"

"I'm a disgruntled white male serial killer," he says tucking a big plastic hatchet into his belt and under his ski vest. "I'd be a cannibal too, but I'm food conscious, and most people are too fatty."

Silvia and I have switched to Oreo cookie insertion stuffing one after another into our mouths like we only eat at parties and art openings.

"Mmm." I mix us both a vodka/cranberry.

Silvia starts her conversation engine with a couple of guys in another clique. She has the ability to talk to strangers, which I find incomprehensible, yet marvelous. They are obviously homosexuals. The obviously hetero clique is in the opposite corner.

Some guy whose name I can't remember says, "Do you want to smoke some pot?"

"No thanks," I say, preferring to sit alone in a folding chair, sipping my cocktail. Shonenberg, who is supposed to be Marlene's beau, and Mr. Foltz, Marlene's housemate, have a 21-year-old girl sandwiched between them. Shonenberg has her hand clinched in his and Mr. Foltz is massaging her shoulders. They're both over 30.

"Would you have sex with us, if we were the last men on earth?"

"Perhaps," she says, toying with them, soaking up and reveling in the attention. Her wide pretty face and glossy brown eyes are perfectly accented by the chartreuse and gold 50s lamp on the end table. She's wearing a chic leather coat. Her black hair is pulled back and gathered onto her head with the kind of hairpin Mata Hari might take your life with.

"What if I was the last man awake at this party..."

As the party surges forward we drink and drink and

drink. The music keeps us swaying. Mr. Foltz has an exten-
sive collection of obscure SST records; when one ends he
inconspicuously places another on the turntable without
disrupting the continuity of mood. The cliques mix around,
but stick pretty much to party lines. The smokers are out on
the porch. Most of the homosexuals are talking about going
to a dance club.The graduate students are discoursing in
semiotics. Janet X went upstairs to talk about guitar pedals
with some other local musicians.The lushes are in the
kitchen shaking the last drops out of empty liquor bottles.
Then independent filmmaker Lulu Godardo makes an
entrance with her pal Big Ed the open mic poet. I've seen
him a few times around town. We've both had bit parts in
Lulu's movies. A peculiar green bottle rests in the crook of
his arm.

"Hey Big Ed, whataya got to drink there?"

"Hey Jimenez." Ed and Lulu are really fucked up. The
pupils in their eyes have rolled back like eerie cue balls in
the corner sockets. "It's a kind of absinthe opium tea con-
coction."

"Pour me a cup." I follow him into the kitchen, but there
aren't any more cups so I dump the ashes and left over ice
cube water from one on the counter. Ed pours the drink with
a steady hand. "You're gonna have a hangover tomorrow
Jimenez," Eddie says as Clara leads him out the backdoor,
across the backyard lawn toward their respective apartments. He picks up a piece of fallen fruit, looks back at me
and says,"Breakfast." The funny thing is that I'm not sure if
he was actually touching the fruit. I lose sight of them in the
darkness as they duck under the limbs of the huge tree. It
seems that this special group has always lived on Twilight
Avenue, though Clara, the poet, moved in when Junko
Partner the trash rock guitar player moved out, who moved
in when she moved out to live with her last boyfriend.

I don't know how Big Ed can see the cup without pupils
but I don't question as the syrupy liquid approaches the
rim.

"Go slow with this, it's strong stuff."

The party goes straight down hill from there. Silvia and I
find Shonenberg passed out in Marlene's squeaky metal
framed bed. I've got my cup of opium and my girl so we shut
the door. "Should we draw on his forehead or something?"
Already, I'm looking through his wallet, he's got a picture of

his mother in a bikini and a frequent flyer punch card from the local dive bar. I decide take the crumpled Alex Hamilton and replace it with an Abe Lincoln from my own wallet.

"I don't think so," she says already stripped to black bra and panties.The simple first kiss leads my head into spin cycle. My clothes pile upon Marlene's floor next to a stack of quality paperbacks. She's got Rimbaud's *Illuminations*, *Bastard out of Carolina* and a copy of the new *Unnatural Disasters* anthology. Her beau is completely out of it. He doesn't even stir as we fall onto the squeaky metal framed bed next to him. My cock is hanging limp despite the stimulation. Silvia is on her back resting her head on Shonenberg's bony ass. I kiss my way down the length of her body, stopping to lick the baby hair on her thighs. A nirvana of skin pleasure. I begin dragging my tongue at the crotch line of her panties, tracing it. Digging a tunnel, working under the fence.My tongue ascertains a pool of wetness. I'm like a dog lapping at a bottle of cream, but I can't get my whole head in there so I pull the panties all the way off. Marlene's beau groans. Silvia makes a sound like "Mmmmm" as her wet lips hydrate my passion. I stretch the lips over my face and wriggle my way inside her, once the shoulders are in, it's easy... drowning in her viscera, till my mouth kisses a lung, taking her breath at the wellspring, tasting the back of her nipples as I slink on up. My brain in her brain, my heart in her heart, my erect cock shooting jism out of her vagina from the inside, fucking her from the uterus outward, my arms in her arms, my hands in her hands, our eyes, our noses, our lips, kissing inside-out instead of outside-in, our hair, our hips, our inside-out love story, our tears, our years, our sexually transmitted diseases...

I come up for a breath and another sip of the elixir and I see Marlene, André and Lulu looming like Scooby Doo shadows watching over my shoulder. I take a large sip and go back to my debauch. The beau is kissing Silvia's mouth as I delve into her vagina again. I feel the slow rhythmic caresses of Marlene's and André's hands on either of my shoulders. Silvia has flipped over now; my tongue cruises around the rim of her anus, barely long enough to dip into the more acidic juice of her vagina to add contrast. The smell is divine. Shonenberg's cock is out. He's still groaning like when we thought he was asleep. I look up to see Marlene and Silvia kissing down the shaft of his thin purple cock.

Their lips fold around it to kiss each other.

André's hands have moved into my pectoral muscles, dig in hard for a second then revert to airy dandles. I look back for Lulu and she's dancing in the corner. Eyes still like cue balls, clothes cast to the floor. Her huge breasts sway. One painted crimson from the party bulbs, the other dipped in the pallid glow of moonlight from the window. André has worked his way down to my cock. He reaches around, planting delicate kisses on my back. His smooth boy chest, somehow naked against my skin.Time moves as if in a strobe light. Marlene and Silvia take turns swallowing the head of the beau's penis. Silvia leaves a film of saliva and Marlene licks it up with the very tip of her tongue.

I see the backlit figure of Mr. Foltz getting up from the couch in the front room to put on another obscure album side.

I thought my friend Cecil, the lawyer, was in Atlanta, but as I look back, I can see him in the bathroom with his ex-girlfriend. He's sitting on the crapper. She's on her knees, his stubby cock stuffed into her mouth. Her drunken chin rests on the toilet seat. He grunts, "Urr." His mangy dog, the one who got kicked in the head by a little boy at the Martin Luther King Parade, is with him as usual, sitting obediently on her frenetic tail. He stands quickly wiping his ass with a fistful of white toilet paper. He leads his ex by the hand into the bedroom, the excited dog at his heels. Silvia's head bobs on the purple cock in time with the music. Cecil lays his ex down on the floor. He has a bet running with himself about how many times he can dump someone and then have anal intercourse with them. The pubic hairs stand out brilliantly red on her tiny freckled body. Cecil has the bowl of tahini dip, scooping up three fingers full. Marlene's head bobs on the purple cock in time with the atonal music. Silvia's eyes are closed, head resting on the beau's stomach. Big Ed rubs her feet which explains the gleeful grin. André finally has me erect and firmly gripped. "Sparky, sit. Sparky here." Cecil coaxes his dog between his ex's legs. The dog laps up the tahini like an exotic treat.

My head is looping like a Spirograph. The control center calling out for another drink. Have you ever had the feeling that everyone around you was going to come simultaneously? Lulu has her fingers working her own clitoris. Hips gyrating. Tits swaying. Light scintillating across her torso.

Marlene fumbles through an antique night table drawer at the bedside, handing a condom to Silvia who straddles the beau, slips the rubber over the head and inserts his purple cock into her vagina. I'm not sure if I'm okay with that. Marlene hands another condom to André. I look back and he's putting it on. She hands him a vial of personal lubricant which he applies generously to one finger which jams unexpectedly into my ass. "Ow."

"Sorry Jimenez Yaz." Marlene pulls Lulu onto the floor tasting her lipstick. Lulu fumbles for her purse. I take another drink. "How many cups of that stuff have you had?" Big Ed says. "This is my third." "Your pupils are gone man." Lulu pulls a dental dam from her purse. Marlene is naked with her on the floor. Her breasts slope to either side of her body. As Lulu slips between her legs, André's cock finds its way gently up my ass.

In the morning, I wake up naked in the branches of the backyard tree. The inert bodies of my friends scattered over the grass, locked in slumber, fallen fruit, as the morning sun sheds new light on the beauty of their naked souls.

Flight 1266

Michael Hemmingson

BREASTS. The passenger opened his eyes from a fantasy; the stewardess with curly red hair had her face in his face. "Can I take that?" she said—the plastic cup he'd been drinking a Vodka tonic in. "Yes," he said. He looked at her opened shirt, the contours of her large white breasts. She smiled, took his cup, walked away. There was another set of breasts to consider: the young woman sitting next to him; her white blouse was unbuttoned rather low, her small tits unveiled, no bra, very tanned skin. He decided she skied a lot, coming back from Colorado. She wasn't more than eighteen, maybe twenty. He started feeling old; he was thirty-five, married twice, and wanted to fuck every woman he saw these days. The young woman was asleep, breath heavy, her chest rising with each intake of oxygen. He could see one pink nipple, and so wanted to touch, to taste, that nipple. He tried to cast her into his air crash fantasy, Flight 1266 from Denver to San Diego. He couldn't.

WORRIED. The turbulence was heavy, but this wasn't what worried the red-headed stewardess. Last night, she'd committed adultery, with the Captain of this flight. She was a happily married woman; her husband was an architect, a trusting and gentle man, whom she'd been married to for eight years. She never considered the idea of sleeping with another man, although there'd been opportunities. She wasn't even sure how it happened. The crew was staying at the Hyatt in New Orleans—another city, another hotel. This was a new Captain. He'd joined her and the other stewardess for a drink in the hotel bar. The other stewardess retired early. She had a few more drinks with the Captain. She liked his smell. She liked his hands and his eyes. He was witty, made her laugh. When he asked, "Would you like to come to my room?" she surprised herself and replied, "Yes." He was in the shower when she woke up, and she realized what she'd done. She scampered back to her room, gathered her stuff. She was scared. The jet was bouncing back and forth,

30,000 feet in the sky. She wished for a crash; then she wouldn't have to face this.

BATHROOM. The passenger got up to use the bathroom. It was occupied and he had to wait. A woman in her late twenties came out, wearing a thin, tight, short dress. He watched her as she walked back to her seat. The end of her dress was clinging to her ass. She was wearing thong underwear, this was obvious, the left cheek of her ass sticking out. He went into the bathroom. It smelled of perfume and woman. He looked for traces of her—hair at the basin, piss or shit in the toilet. All there was: her smell. He took his cock out and fondled it. He thought of fucking her in this bathroom, what that'd be like, the oddity of it all. He looked at his reflection in the mirror. This wasn't the time. He stumbled, slamming against the wall: more turbulence.

COCKPIT. The stewardess entered the cockpit. Her stomach knotted up when she saw the Captain. She asked the Captain and the Co-Pilot if they needed anything. The Captain looked at her and smiled. "Yes," he said. There was an awkward silence. She looked away from him. "I'd like some water," the Captain said. She nodded, and left.

WOMEN. "I had her last night," the Captain said. His Co-Pilot said, "You're kidding. She's married." "I know," he said, "so am I. I still had her. I spanked her. And I did other nasty things with her." "Bastard," the Co-Pilot said.

WIFE. The Co-Pilot wished he had someone to have, or fuck. He only wanted his wife. His wife wouldn't let him touch her. They hadn't had sex in six months. She said she didn't love him anymore. He started to wonder if she was fucking someone else. He knew he was capable of murder; he'd always known this.

SPANKING. She couldn't go back into the cockpit, and asked the other stewardess to take the Captain his water. She went into the bathroom. She found herself re-living last night in the Hyatt, sucking on the Captain's cock, swallowing his semen. His semen was thick, not like her husband's runny seed. Then the Captain told her she was a very bad girl, cheating on the man she loved. "You deserve a spanking," the Captain said. She said, "Yes, I do." He bent her over his lap, sitting on the bed, her naked ass exposed. He was gentle at first, lightly tapping each cheek of her buttocks with his cupped hand. Back and forth he did this, and gradually each slap became harder. She didn't stop him, even as it started to hurt. She wanted this. He was so very right: she deserved this punishment and pain. His slaps became extremely hard, so that she cried out with each impact, tears falling from her face and onto the carpet of the hotel room. He stopped, and said, "Enough." He made her suck his cock again. His cock felt good in her mouth.

BRUISED. The stewardess flushed the toilet. She stood with her back faced to the mirror at the basin, turning her head, looking at her ass: it was black and blue.

LUST. The other stewardess gave the Captain his water. His hand touched hers, he looked in her eyes and smiled. She smiled back. He was very good-looking, and she had an image of fucking him. She'd fuck him if he wanted to. She had no one in her life. She would've done it last night, but she was too tired for any interaction.

SWEETCHEEKS. The young woman with the deep tan and the unbuttoned blouse woke up due to the turbulence. She noticed that two buttons of her blouse had come undone, and her chest and breasts were available to prying eyes. She buttoned her blouse. The man who'd been sitting next to her wasn't there. She had noticed the way he was looking at her before they left the airport. She was used to this sort of thing. Men wanted to fuck her, and she liked to fuck men; sometimes it got her in trouble. In Colorado Springs, she'd met up with her ex-boyfriend. She didn't know why. She still liked him. She got drunk with him and his roommate, and as things go, she found herself in bed with them both. It wasn't the first time she'd engaged in a threesome. She sucked their cocks, she fucked their cocks, and her ex-boyfriend kept calling her his favorite pet word from the past: sweetcheeks "My little sweetcheeks," he always said. Last night, it was: "Yeah, sweetcheeks, take that dick! You love dick, sweetcheeks." He wasn't so playful in the morning, when he was sober. "You're a slut," he said, "you'll always be a slut." "Goodbye," she said. She noticed the stewardess with curly red hair. Sweetcheeks was bi, but it'd been over a year since she'd had a female partner. She could go for someone like the stewardess. Yes. When she got back to San Diego, she promised herself to visit a certain lesbian club on the corner of Park Avenue and University; she hadn't been there in a while, and now seemed like a good time.

ART. The passenger returned to his seat, noting that the tanned young woman was awake now—and to his disappointment, her blouse was buttoned all the way to her neck. She looked at him. He smiled. She smiled back, and turned away. He closed his eyes, thinking of her smooth skin. He wanted to talk to her and didn't know how. He thought about the woman he'd just broken up with—a forty-year-old widow who worked for the social security department. She had an art to sucking cock, the way she salivated all over a penis and chewed on testicles. She also liked drinking urine. But that was all over. Two months ago. He wanted to fuck. A burst of turbulence hit again. His cock was hard. He imagined the tanned girl reaching over and taking his cock in her hand. He opened his eyes and saw the stewardess with red curly hair approach. He held up his hand, and asked for another drink.

HEADCRASH. The passenger had a vision. It excited him in an outlandish way. He noted a worried look on the red-headed stewardess' face. Was she new, was there something wrong? There did seem to be an inordinate amount of turbulence, the 737 rocking back and forth—the way space ships did in old science-fiction movies when grasped by the hand of interstellar gods and monsters. In his vision, the jet went down, somewhere in the badlands of Arizona. Many people died, but he was one of the survivors, as was the stewardess. They were injured, bloodied, and afraid, but alive. As the survivors waited for a rescue team and primal fears returned under the clear desert night of the hazy edge of the Milky Way, the stewardess came to him: she wanted comfort. He held her. Under the stars, he made love to her. She didn't vocalize a thing, but her passion was inflamed, with apprehension and lechery. After they were rescued, he kept in touch with her. She took a job at a travel agency, sending other people on jet airlines, secretly wishing every one of them would wind up in a crash—she didn't want them to die, no: she just wanted them to experience what she had. These notions made her want to fuck. She would fuck him after confessing these imaginations, asking: "What are your secrets?" "I would like to be inside you," he said, "in an airplane that was diving into the ground, straight into a mountain, as my cock dived striaght into you. A small airplane," he said, "just you and me and fate." The passenger, now a seeker, joined the former stewardess-turned-travel-agent at gatherings, around the country, of airplane crash survivors. (It should be noted that they took trains to other cities where such gatherings occurred.) He was relieved to know that other people experienced the same sexual feelings as he. It was now a conundrum; he couldn't see any kind of airplane without getting a raging hard-on and needing a hole to fill it—whether it be a small charter flight or one of the jumbo jets Federal Express used. He began to discover an entire underground network of sexual freaks—people who'd been in plane crashes, or knew someone who had, or had been affected in one way or another with flight, fear, and fuck.

Blur

Alan Mills

ONE/JEFF

What am I supposed to say? I'm having a party. You're invited. There'll be plenty of boys. Eager boys. Slut boys. Cock boys.

Plenty of cock . . . boys.

It was a friend's idea. "Throw a party," from his lips. Quentin's lips. How could I say no? There were circumstances.

We were in bed. That's the best way to begin. We were in bed. Me and Quentin. */GET RIGHT TO THE POINT/*

We were in bed and his naked body felt so good next to mine. I'd give him anything.

It isn't often that I feel this way. Touching someone without paying the bills is . . . unique to me. Unique, because it, not I, is a rare occurrence.

In bed, his naked body is, well . . . I'll avoid philosophy. He's smaller than I am. More compact. His hair is auburn. Eyes green. Handsome. Muscular. He has the cutest feet.

Long toes. Smooth, glassy nails. Feet soft, even underneath.

Like most perfect youths, he shaves, shows the definition in his thighs, the rosy color of his balls, the sweet wrinkles around his hole.

His calves are dense. His whole body, dense. Hard. Each muscle rounded. Biceps. Chest. Ass. Beautiful. Tones.

He's kind and selfish, like most men his age. My age. I'm the same. Gentle, egotistical, unforgiving.

He wants a party, an orgy, just because. Why not? He's a slut like me.

He kisses me, and my attraction to him hurts.

Kisses me again. My lips part, taste his tongue. This morning, I can still taste myself inside his mouth.

Convince me, I think. Convince . . .

He sits up, straddles my chest, pushes his cock between my lips. Yeah, that's right.

That's how it's done.

It's hard and strong. A good-sized cock. It goes in slow, pushing down like a depressor.

Open for it. Open more for it. More for it. Soft pubes on my nose. A smooth scrotum on my chin. Balls pull away. Breathe. Cock goes back in. Out. Back in harder. Harder. Yeah, harder. Out, in, harder. Yeah, fuck my mouth harder.

The cock pounds the deep inside my throat. I reach for his ass. Blindly search for those hard masses, the hot crack, that steamy hole. Oh yeah, turn around; put the hot, steamy hole on my tongue.

He gets on his knees, pushes his ass into my face. I like it there. Right there, the pink spot. Makes him groan. He pants, moans, says, "Oh fuck," and all that porno shit. I push my tongue in like a sword and lick with my tongue, flat like a dog's, then flick it, thin and fast, like he's on fire. He's on fire, burning up around my mouth, talking nasty smack like he's fuckin' speaking tongues until his badboy mouth drops and wraps around my angry cock.

I thrust that monster fucker up into his nasty throat like it was made of soap. I scrub my boy's mouth out. Teach him. Learn him, like my dad would say. I learn him, eat his ass real good. I lick his nuts, bat them with my tongue, fuck his mouth, real hard. Lick his ass and nuts and try to get his cock somehow down my throat.

I get rough with his ass and cock. He licks. Works my prick like I'm the only man he'll ever need. Thinking that makes me want to shoot. He knows it. Pulls back. Sits up. Grips my spit sloppy cock and pumps it.

Ass hard against my mouth. Breathin' nothing but musk.

He jacks his own cock where I can't see it. Pumps mine. Jacks his. Same time. Left hand on me, so he can cum first.

I feel it. It strikes like God's wrath upon my skin. Warm, loving, it falls the way spunk does, heavy on my chest, stomach, a few drops hurled at my balls.

I love it, soiled by it, made into a rugged faggot slut by it, and he knows—pumps my cock harder. Faster. Firmer.

My cock explodes, too. I can't see it. Just know. Gasp for breath. Tighten ass. Get all hot everywhere. Struggle to push my tongue in more and deep. My cock swells, feels like it's on fire, like the long tube down the center is a nuclear reactor. I spill. Scream. Chernobyl myself all over the place, the warm wetness splashing down my cock, my balls, the inside of my thighs.

He turns around. We both breathe. Lying down beside me, he kisses the remainders of his soul from my lips.

"Can we have a party?"

"Yeah, sure." I give him anything he wants. Of course. Who wouldn't.

Endastory . . . I suppose.

TWO/CAMERON

Cameron sat in his car, quietly determining whether he should do what he came here for or simply accept the limitations of his courage and go home. It was dark outside the car, dark inside the car—one Victorian street lamp dropped light in a vague circle several houses down the road. No, this is it, Cameron thought; it's now or never, as they say. He reached up, tentatively, opened the door and got out. One small step, he thought and laughed, shutting the door to his safe and practical Nissan before setting off up the road.

The house was huge, a large Tudor design with an old brick base. Thick landscaping and a couple of oaks completed the experience, making the property even more ostentatious than the many upper-class homes that surrounded it. This place wasn't Jeff's—Cameron knew that.

Somewhere, an old man was enjoying more than his share so that Jeff could briefly live like the king he would never be.

Cameron looked at his invitation one more time. He didn't need to. Every light in the house was on, and he could hear the ruckus of people and music coming through the walls. Still, he opened the chartreuse card to make sure—that's just the way he was.

LIFES'S A BLUR
WHO NEEDS BOUNDARIES
1492 Imperial Road
4.11.97 [22:00]
J.K.

He followed a stone path to the front door. Stepping onto the porch, he approached and knocked. Within moments, the door was thrown open by a tall, lean, grunge-rock type with a tight, uncovered torso and a pair of black latex pants. "Come in," he slurred coyly before staggering back and lunging forward. Cameron froze as the stranger wrapped an arm around his neck, kissed him roughly and pulled him through the doorway.

Cameron could taste the vodka on the man's breath as he was thrown against a wall. The strange tongue pushed viciously into his mouth, and he felt like he didn't have any choice but to give in to the onslaught.

The kiss stopped abruptly as the guy pulled back and stared intensely into Cameron's eyes. He was taller than Cameron. His hair was dark-dyed black—with long disheveled bangs. Something inside Cameron felt weak in this man's presence, and the young man smiled like he knew that secret.

He kissed Cameron again, more gently, then stopped to look at Cameron's face. His hands roamed Cameron's solid chest and stomach, which Cameron had hidden so discreetly underneath a cardigan sweater. "You're so cute," he said, running long fingers through Cameron's well-groomed hair.

"Um thanks, uh, and you're . . . like . . . "

The boy cut off Cameron's stammering with his wet lips. His hand traveled down Cameron's torso, seductively, and cupped around Cameron's straining crotch.

He moaned softly against Cameron's lips. "I'm sorry, bro, but I haf'ta do this."

To Cameron's surprise, the young man started lowering himself to his knees, lifting Cameron's sweater and kissing his stomach when he got down there. The boy licked at the soft trail of hair below Cameron's navel, and Cameron quickened the pace of his breath as the guys's hands kneaded Cameron's tingling cock and balls.

Cameron could see around the room now. He was trapped in the entry hall, just between what seemed to be a sitting room and another room which might have been the den. A variety of gorgeous men walked casually past him on their way in or to one room or another. Already unnerved, he began to really panic when he felt his fly being spread apart.

Before Cameron could complain, his cock was out and in the man's mouth, where the warm, wet tension washed away the last of his resistance. He closed his eyes and pressed back against the wall. The mouth moved firmly across his cock, slowing going to the base and then back up. The young man sucked patiently, turning his mouth around the head, teasing the glans with gentle circles of his tongue. The stranger seemed to be taking his time, savoring the feeling of the large, musky cock in his mouth.

Cameron got closer and closer and opened his eyes to look at the young face that was sucking his prick. He humped his hips forward, driving his cock into the tight mouth. He looked back up at all the people who had stopped to stare at him. Some gazed intently at the action going on below his belt, but most of them were watching his eyes, his face, his vulnerability. He could feel it in his expressions. His mouth was gaping. His brows were clenched tightly above his eyes. It was definitely his eyes that they were staring at, as if the event going on behind them was more interesting than the drama being played out at his crotch.

The boy on his knees kept sucking like none of this was going on, driving Cameron closer to blowing his load. Cameron closed his eyes and tried to forget about everybody watching him, but he couldn't while the twisting mouth on his cock was pushing him and pushing him. He couldn't hold back. He tried and tried, but the cocksucker finally won.

The mouth pulled quickly off his cock as cum shot from the tip and pelted the handsome face with ropes of white cream. Cameron grunted with each expulsion of his seed and looked up painfully at the crowd that surrounded him. This was the moment they were hungry for, and each of them smiled when they saw it in his eyes.

His body shuddered as the last of his cum dripped from his cock. The man on his knees stood up and wiped the discharge from his face and shook it off his hands, letting it spray on the hardwood floor. "Hey Doug," he shouted to someone behind him as he smiled with the warmth of a twisted imp, "that's six." He gave Cameron a soft, salty kiss; "Thanks," he whispered before disappearing into the crowd. Cameron stood there, still breathing heavy, no longer of interest to the men walking past, his exposed cock still dripping cum onto the floor between his now unstable legs.

THREE/DAVID

```
Subj: Last Night
Date: March 11, 1997 12:32 PM EDT
From: davvcat@aol.com
X-From: davvcat@aol.com <David Carter>
Reply-to: davvcat@aol.com
To: killabel@aol.com
```

Hey Jef,

Thanks for inviting me last night. I had a great time. Met this really nice guy. Richard. I have to tell you about it.

Your orgy was wild. More like Wilde...if you get my drift. Everywhere I stepped, guys were fucking guys. I saw big dicks in every room. Wow... you have some incredible looking friends.

Anyway I was hanging by the food cuz you know me, I'm shy... and Richard walked up to get some of the quiche stuff you had. (Don't let nobody else reads this!) Anyway we started talking about how good the sandwich rolls were (anything to avoid focusing on the three sluts going at it under the table) and we really kinda hit it off.

BTW, where were you last night? I don't remember seeing you even once. You must have been hidden under one of the piles of men. Give me the details when you reply.

So anyway we went out by the pool and sat down on the little marble bench by all the ferns. It was cool. We talked about how nice it was out and how the pool was like a swarming mass of boysoup. Steam was rising off the water and it was completely packed with writhing, naked bodies having sex. Anyway we laughed about that and moved a little closer together and you know... kissed and stuff. Then he asked me if I'd like to get in the hot tub. A bunch of boys had just left it and there was an opening.

Okay... you know what an extreme moralist I am, so I took off my clothes and jumped right in. Jef, that man had the most beautiful body... and he liked me, but who wouldn't? Except maybe for you. (Oops, didn't mean to bring that up.) :)

We kissed... arms around each other. The water was boiling and swirling and jets were massaging my back and ass. So you can see that none of this is my fault right? I couldn't help myself. There were eight other guys going at it in the tub and a few more fucking outside the tub, so when he grabbed my dick and started stroking it under that water I couldn't resist... the way I normally do, you know.

We kissed each other and stroked each other. He said he wanted to see me again. God I hope he calls. He lifted me out of the water and rubbed his beautiful prick on my lips. And girl, you know I sucked that motherfucker!!! I put that cock in my mouth and slurped that son-of-a-bitch all the way down my throat. He loved it, moaning and pumping his ass. (Do not save or print this, asshole!)

One of the other guys tried to get to my dick, but I wouldn't let him. Richard was the only one I wanted down there. When he saw the guy struggling to get at my prick, Richard got down there and sucked on it so that no one else could. It was so romantic. He sucked me off... and I sucked him off... and we kissed as we jacked each other too.

Finally, he pushed me up against the edge of the tub and got behind me. He rubbed his cock along the crack of my ass and fucked between my legs while a jet of water massaged the head of my cock. He kissed my neck and rubbed my chest. The jet of water felt incredible. We both got closer as he rubbed against my ass. When we came at the same time he bit into my neck. Oh God, Jef, it was wonderful. My cum pumped out of my cock and his cum flowed out of his slit and stuck to my balls. Nasty, huh? Hope you don't have to change the water. If so, sorry, but we weren't the only ones.

Anyway I just had to confess this to you. Tell me how your evening went.

Stay groovy,
Your loving X, David

FOUR/MARKUS

I look at my reflection in the mirror. It's starting to hit me now. A tingling trail of snot is dripping down the back of my throat, and I'm feeling good. My skin feels good. I touch it, pinch my nipple through my tight shirt and suck in air as the sensation washes across my skin, into my body.

I stick a coke spoon once more into the dark brown vial and scoop up one more hit of the white stuff. Bringing the key carefully to my left nostril, I press the other one closed and take in the powder with a quick implosion of air.

It stings, burns, goes into my bloodstream, releasing endorphins, hormones, God-only-knows-what.

The door thunders. "Almost done," I shout and flush the toilet to make things seem believable. I pocket the vial and check my nose for incriminating residue. Out in the party, the heavy beat of the music jumps right through me. My heart beats with it. I am it. Oh man, God bless the son-of-a-bitch who invented crystal meth.

I move quickly through the simple masses and head right up the stairs; it's like part of me can sense where the really nasty shit is going on.

I pass one door and then another, looking in. Vanilla. Vanilla. Vanilla. None of them have what I'm looking for until I get to the last door on the left: "The Master's Bedroom."

That's what it says, right there in big painted letters on a cardboard sign. I don't hesitate. I walk right in.

I open the door and see some guy getting spanked on top of a black king-sized bed. Another really buff guy is kneeling in front of him, shoving his cock down the lucky man's throat while a Latino master smacks his ass like an angry father. I don't get to enjoy the view for more than a second before I'm grabbed by the neck and almost lifted off my feet by a huge black guy in a leather harness.

"What the fuck are you doing in here?!" he shouts.

"I . . . I . . . I'm sorry," I stammer.

"SHUT UP!" he yells. I do.

I'm tweakin' really hard now, and my whole body is throbbing with sexual need. I look down tentatively and see his big black cock thrusting out from a thick dark patch of curly hair and a cockring. I want his meat up my ass. I want it real bad.

"What da fuck are you lookin' at, white boy?!" With each word, spit flies in my face. "Huh?! HUH?! What da fuck's wrong with you, white boy?! Are you a faggot?! Are ya droolin' on my cock cuz you're a faggot?!"

I try to answer him . . .

"SHUT UP!"

He pushes down on my shoulder, grabs my head, pulls my face into his groin. "Don't just look at it, pussyboy. Suck it! Suck that black cock!"

I open my mouth, and he pushes it in. I can't take it all. I end up gagging each time he forces it down my throat. He keeps trying to fuck it all the way in, but I keep gagging it back up. Finally he stops and smacks my face. "What da fuck is wrong with you, boy?! Don't ya know howda suck cock, ya fuckin' slut?!" He glares at my reddened face. "Take your fuckin' clothes off 'fore I kick your ass."

I stand up slowly and start peeling off my tight shirt. When I have it half-way off, he yells, "I told you ta get those fuckin' clothes off!" He pulls on the shirt and pulls me down to the ground with it. I end up on all fours, and he pulls at my pants, ripping them down my legs. He pulls my boots off, my socks, the rest of my pants and underwear, slapping my ass every chance he gets. When I'm completely stripped, he turns me on my back and pushes me down with a big hand until I lie prone on the ground. A mass of dark muscle, he moves over me and clenches his fist in the air.

"Don't fuck with me, white boy!" he snarls before bringing his big fist down on my chest. The thud shakes through my whole body. It doesn't really hurt; it just really turns me on.

Before I can even register what's happening, the black stud positions his cock over my face and starts fucking it into my mouth. This time, I lay my head back, relax, open my throat to the dense meat of his cock.

"Yeah, dat's good, boy. Dat's real good." He holds himself above my mouth like he's doing push-ups, slowly sliding his huge cock into my passive mouth. His torso presses down on my eyes and pulls away as if the sky were falling down on me in waves. When he lifts up and his cockhead is held in my mouth, I see shadows move across his skin. A twisting feeling moves through my chest and bowels. It's more than lust. It's like aesthetic arrest.

"What ya doin' over there, Darrell?" I hear someone say.

"I'm teachin' this boy to suck cock."

"Well, bring him over here. We're beginning to miss you."

The black cock pulls out of my mouth. "Now, we wouldn't want you pussies to start cryin' or somethin'."

The black guy grabs my arms and pulls me up off the ground. He throws me toward the bed where two guys catch me. "Well, he is a cute one, isn't he?" one of them says. He reaches up and starts running his fingers through my short hair. It tingles, and I practically purr, closing my eyes and rolling my head with his gentle touch.

"Look at this mouth," the other one says as he pinches my lower lip and touches my tongue. He kisses me, and the other one starts playing with my cock, which isn't hard but feels great. My balls feel tight and swollen, and my cock drools as his fingers dance over it. It starts to get a little bigger, a little harder, but the erection isn't easy even though the sensations are like heaven. Crystal giveth, I suppose, and crystal taketh away.

The guys turn me around, and lying on the bed in front of me is the boy who was getting spanked when I walked in. They make me straddle him and push me down until our bellies are touching. He looks up at me tenderly and I start to tremble with excitement. I can no longer see what the other three guys are doing, but I can feel hands stroking my butt and playing with my hole. It feels so good back there, and I keep thinking, please stick something in there—I need something in there.

Then the licking begins, and fingers start to push inside my hole. I get hot all over, and the interior of my ass tingles as fingers randomly thrust into my guts. The guy beneath me kisses me, his warm mouth pulling the air from my lungs.

I feel them doing something to his cock, and before I know it, they sit me up and start lowering my now loose ass onto him. I feel the well-lubed latex as his cock slips right in. Like the drugged up, awake for three days slut that I am, I take the cock graciously, straddling him and bouncing up and down.

His cock is short and fat, and I like the way it spreads my sphincter. The other guys like it, too, watching as it stabs into me repeatedly.

Soon, I'm pushed back down and another, different cock is thrust into my open asshole. This one is longer, denser, and I can feel every inch of it push inside and slide along my bowels. The man beneath me holds me and kisses me while the stranger behind me fucks my ass like a bastard.

I love it. My whole body loves it, tingling anytime any-thing touches it. My ass is numb and my balls are burning up. Everything feels good as cock after cock pounds inside me.

They keep taking turns, fucking me, talking nasty to me, shoving dick into my mouth. All the while, every nerve in my skin sings out and my cock feels like it's going to explode. But, it doesn't. Actually cumming, blowing my load, takes effort on crystal, and I don't feel like ending this right now. As far as I'm concerned, these four guys can just fuck the hell out of me until the sun comes up. Who needs to orgasm when you feel this good.

FIVE/QUENTIN

With hands on the balcony rail, Quentin looks down on the undulating masses in the pool like some metaphoric Evita, surveying the lascivious excesses of his country's men. Somewhere in that human bouillabaisse is Jeff, he's sure of that. Jeff wasn't anywhere else. Quentin had already checked. Boys fucked or did drugs in every room, and Quentin couldn't find Jeff among any of them. It's as if Jeff had completely split the scene.

This debaucherous event was Quentin's idea: a sexual festival of such grand proportions that even Dionysus would be proud. From the look of things, Quentin had achieved success, even though Jeff is lost somewhere, out there, immersed neck deep in sin. This thought tugs at Quentin. Maybe, he thinks, this party wasn't such a great idea.

But it's too late now.

The night is unusually warm for this time of year as if all the feverish bodies are actually heating the house and grounds. This can't be true, but it looks as if it might be. Quentin leans over the rail and watches as four boys in the shallow end struggle to suck each other off.

He wishes Jeff were here instead of somewhere else— with him instead of someone else—with him as if he never thought of someone else, but that's not Jeff.

The four men in the pool have come to a decision about who's going to blow whom. Strangely, the two blondes end up with their mouths full while the two dark Latinos sit on the edge of the pool kissing—they look like brothers. From this distance, even the two blondes look related. How interesting, thinks Quentin. One pair of brothers, maybe even twins, giving head to another pair of brothers, maybe twins, in a pool in the middle of a massive orgy. Who knew that such things were possible?

Most people talk about life being random, but to Quentin, this seems planned. One set of twins blowing another set of twins—it has to be evidence of some power greater than ourselves. And the juxtaposition is too intriguing: one point of organization amongst a virtual sea of chaos. To Quentin, it makes sense.

Quentin imagines that Jeff would enjoy this—this phenomenon—this metaphor. Jeff would stand behind him, keep him warm, watch the drama of divine will play itself out inside the distant pool. Maybe Jeff would kiss his neck, lick his ear, pull Quentin's pants down and stroke his dick, play with his ass, rub his own cock inside Quentin's crack. Miracles seemed to have a profound effect of Jeff.

The two Latinos seem excited. Within moments, the two blondes pull back and jets of cum shoot from the uncut Latino cocks. Quentin can barely see the eruption from this distance, but it looks like the cum is blasting out and over the blondes. Twin Spanish fountains, thinks Quentin—how novel, how perfect, how divinely inspired.

Quentin feels his own cock, trapped inside his briefs. It's hard and his nuts feel full. He needs attention. His ass needs attention. It's like there's some unsatisfied desire somewhere inside him. It hurts. It's almost unbearable—this abstract presence—this lonely void.

SIX/SCOTT

I never thought I'd get turned on seeing two guys go at it, but I guess there has to be a first time for everything. The guys must have been lovers—they seemed so intimate, so into each other. I've never really had anything against homosexuals, and when Mike invited me to a gay party, I didn't think I'd have a problem.

The party wasn't quite what I'd expected. We had arrived early. Things were innocent. By the time the party developed into something that I wasn't prepared for, Mike was gone, and I wasn't about to wander from room to room looking for him. No, it was best to find a quiet place and wait the orgy out. Mike would find me when he was done.

Fortunately, the library was unoccupied and apparently uninteresting to the throngs of men that engaged each other all around this mansion with what I'd have to call reckless abandon. I'm sorry if that sounds clichéd, but the details that this story requires aren't really easy for me.

I was reading an old magazine—*Newsweek*—an article on the millennium—when someone walked in. He was about my age, shorter than me, and had blondish hair that hung down below his ears. He walked in laughing and stopped when he saw me. "Hi," he said with a smile. I think he was drunk.

I started to say "Hi" back, but stopped when someone else, with black hair and a slightly bigger build than the first one, walked in behind him. He, too, froze when he saw me and said, "Hi." I couldn't say anything at that point—it all seemed too weird.

The blond walked over to the shelves directly across from the door, keeping his eyes on me as he went. The other one—he looked New York Italian—followed him tentatively, while also watching me. Maybe he was half Italian. I wasn't sure.

I didn't move. There was nowhere else to run.

At least these guys had their clothes on, even if their clothes were typically gay: form fitting shirts (one burgundy, the other a grayish silver) and designer jeans. I went back to the article.

"Look," said the first one, "Rimbaud."

I remember how it struck me that his voice sounded French. It made me look back up. The Italian moved behind the blond and kissed the back of his neck. "Rimbaud . . . huh."

"Bukowski," the blonde said romantically, laughing, as he pointed to another book.

The dark haired guy growled and kissed higher on the other guy's neck, closer to his ear.

"Rumi."

The brunette lifted his head and stared toward the shelf, his dark bangs flowing away from his face. He reached for a small green book. "Fuck Rumi!" he said as he threw it over his shoulder, across the room. The book skipped across the floor and he went back to nibbling on the other guy's neck.

"Shakespeare."

The brunette ran his hands all over the other guy's back, chest, stomach, kissing his neck more feverishly.

"Dove . . . Rich . . . Donne . . . "

Not abandoning the neck, the guy in back traced his left hand along the other boy's arm and reached for the book he was touching. Without saying a word, he pulled the book out and chucked it behind him.

"Duncan . . . Graham . . . O'Hara . . . Marlow."

The top, I guess, turned the blonde around quickly and

violently cupped his mouth on the other man's lips.

He pulled back and whispered, "The sight of London to my exciled eyes is as Elysium to a new—come soul . . . not that I love the city or the men . . . but that it harbors him I hold so dear, the king upon whose bosom let me die . . . "

The blonde smiled. "Sand with the world be still at enmity."

Pressed against the bookcase, the two of them kissed passionately. I didn't know how I should feel about what I was seeing, and before I could decide, the dark haired guy dropped quickly to his knees, violently opened his partner's jeans, and began sucking vigorously on the guy's dick.

I figured it would be best for all concerned if I just quietly slipped out the door, but before I could even sit up from the sofa, the dark haired guy stopped what he was doing and looked straight at me. "Where the hell do think you're going," he yelled. I felt speechless.

He stood up and pulled his blond lover toward me. When they had crossed the room, he shoved the blonde down on the sofa and pushed the guy's chest into my lap. The top roughly pulled the blonde's jeans down, exposing his ass. I didn't know what to do. Frozen and overwhelmed, I kept my hands to my side and watched as the top slapped his lover's ass in a way that wasn't vindictive, but definitely wasn't kind. As I sat there looking down at the blonde's back, neck and hair, I could feel his body writhe as the other guy pushed a finger into his raised ass. There was something exciting about the whole scene, but I couldn't imagine getting involved, just like I couldn't imagine running out of the room. I was caught in something indefinable. What I was witnessing had nothing to do with me or my sexual interests but had everything to do with sex and the way we are all linked by it. I liked being in this moment even though it was a moment that I feared and felt guilt over. In this moment, I was the innocent bystander, the perverted voyeur, the sadistic top with dick in hand, the compliant bottom about to get fucked.

The dark haired guy put a condom on, rolling it all the way down to his neatly groomed pubes. From where I was positioned, I could see everything and had no desire to look away.

The guy's dick pushed against the blonde's ass and slowly slid in. I could feel the boy's body tense and shudder on top of my lap and against my stomach as inch after inch entered his ass.

The top started fucking him, building up greater force with every thrust. Each time he pounded into the ass, the blonde's body pressed down against my legs. His dick wasn't touching me though. It hung from his raised pelvis just to the left of my thigh. I was kind of grateful that is wasn't touching me. I didn't know how much more of this extreme situation I could handle.

The top continued fucking the blonde until he straightened his back and let out a series of loud groans while he shoved his dick as deep into the ass as it could go. When his climax was done, he grabbed the blonde's hair and shoulder and pulled him up until he kneeled right next to me. The top then reached around him and started stroking his dick right in front of me. After just a few strokes, it seemed like the blonde guy was going to cum, but the top slowly whispered, "Don't . . . Don't . . . " He continued stroking and the blonde struggled to hold back his orgasm.

Finally, the top whispered, "Okay, do it." Instantly, the guy came as the top wrapped his hand around the dick's head, forcing the cum to explode on his palm and pour down the shaft. Fortunately, none of it got on me. I was starting to get worried.

I was shocked, however, when the top lifted his sticky hand and cupped it around the blonde's mouth. The blonde reached out his tongue and sucked all of his own cum from his lover's palm and fingers—barely a few inches from my face.

Without a word, they got up and fastened their pants. The top looked at his lover and nodded toward me. "Say thank you," he said.

The blonde looked right at me with a slight smile. "Thank you," he said with a sincerity that caused something to clench inside of me.

"You're welcome," I said back.

He smiled, kissed his boyfriend, who had ceased to seem so menacing, and the two of them left the room.

SEVEN/ JEFF

Okay, so I'm here. Just watched a porno. Things are really going now. Not with me. With the orgy. And I don't know what difference being here makes. This one room, the "video" room, is quiet. Static and snow. A flickering—like taking pictures of the walls. Like taking pictures of me. Alone.

I'm not good at this shit.

And what was that porno to me? A bunch of guys fucking like they're told. Me, getting hard, despite myself.

Imagine being a porn star. Walking into someone's home. Greeted with warm, lust-tainted smiles, and a kind suggestion to "get" comfortable.

It's not the sleaziness that bothers me. It's not the sex, the degradation; I can't be degraded; I already was; it was all over for me once my mother pushed me out .

I don't feel empty, even with a cock up my ass. I don't feel shallow. I can't. It's the lowest experience that means the most.

I got a hard cock. I wanna stroke it. Slide my greasy palm up and, yeah you guessed it, down. Up and down my thick, funky cock: slick with all the fucking juice my gapping slit pours out. I wanna do it bad.

My gray colored, Calvin Klein, fucking Marky Mark wanna-be underwear is all wet and slimy where my prick leaks oil.

But I'm not gonna undo my fly. Open my cock to the TV set. Someone might walk in, think I'm being complicit with these insipid games.

My cock is swollen and throbbing. I can't. If I do, someone, besides myself, might get off.

On it. On me. On me getting off.

Last night I dreamt that I wasn't a porn star, that I was more normal, not normal, just more normal than I am. I am normal.

In my dream, I watch myself get fucked on the big screen. I watch it and get off on it as if I doesn't mean everything it does. I'm not myself. I'm not on the screen. In front of the screen, I feel normal, I get hard watching a cock rabbit into the image of my life-sized fucktube so fast the digital video can't even keep up.

It's a blur. In reality, I'm a blur.

Outside this room, men are clawing at each other like sodomite beasts. I hear them. I should join them. Once again enter into the honesty of existence.

Somewhere, there is a mouth, a boy on his knees, a sloppy orifice in which to insert—

/INSERT COCK HERE/

An open mouth like communion. This is the body of Christ. His blood. My blood. White like fire.

I stroke my cock. Get it ready for inferno. I want it to burn down a man's throat. Open his ass like the gates of heaven.

/FUCK/ I can't do this. It's sacrilegious and I have an empty soul.

I taint myself with metaphor, taint myself with rivers of cum, get my cock sucked, bounced off an anonymous tongue, and blow my load into latex—it feels like love.

Maybe the porno was a bad one.

I've worked with everyone involved. They were better when I met them.

Well, I guess that's it. I'm here. Otherwise, I'm useless. With cock exposed, I have a function. Here it goes.

I scoot my ass down the couch. It's leather. Through my jeans, my Marky's slide up ass. Undo my belt. Unsnap one button. Pull. Zipper slides down itself.

Look, that cock. Out in the open. The dark room closing in on it like tribal awe. The TV set burns snow, electric virus crawling on the screen. I hold my cock to it. A monolith. A wet tower. A requiem to VCR.

Okay, I stroke it. I stroke it just like you tell me to. /UP AND DOWN/ "Yeah, stroke that cock. Stroke that big, fucking cock. Oh. Yeah. Make that fucker cum. Give me that load, cocksucker. Oh, yeah."

Yeah, I stroke it like you tell me to. My clear juices glow on the surface. I rub my palm on the head. The pink helmet gets red with friction.

I fuck upward—up into my fist. Balls bouncing. Hand slick. Breath hard, heavy. Heavy. My hand on the head. Fast. Faster. Fingers blur.

That's it. My cum floods out. Cock standing straight up. Hand working the shaft /JUST THE SHAFT/ squeezing tight on the up stroke, pushing the cum up, out. The milky spunk pours out the slit, slowly at first, low pressure, pouring out, flowing up just a little and seeping down the head into my fist.

Then it happens: the high pressure thrust.

And now I'm here: this pitiful cumming creature. No meaning. No purpose. A simple fountain. Spunk and semen blasting up and, yeah you guessed it, falling down again.

Cum spraying, caught mid-air in the white screen's strobe. Cum flying. Cum falling. My chest rising, descending, fast, getting pelted by warm spunk, cooling spunk. Cold spunk on my skin.

And here I am. Spent. Empty. Alone. Still surviving past my usefulness. Praying you enjoyed yourself, you dirty motherfuckers.

EIGHT/DOUG

Anthony and I always have amazing evenings. Each morning, after one of our adventures, I wake up not believing in the events that I remember taking place. I think that's part of our dynamic. Every moment together is almost unbelievable.

Anthony's a slut—a way bigger slut than I could ever be—and he flaunts it. I watch him on his knees in front of his ninth guy this evening, and I know that I could never be the badboy he's become.

Sure, we do sex clubs and group sex and stuff like that, but I always manage to be just a bit more innocent than him.

Tonight, I serve as a witness to his debauchery, following him like a war correspondent through the trenches and the mine fields of this pre—apocalyptic orgy. I watch him—his profile—opening his mouth seductively and letting a stranger's cock disappear down his throat. As I stare, I feel as if I should be taking notes, making some commentary, speaking into some encumbersome recorder.

The cock goes into his throat slowly, getting harder, longer as the man it's attached to gets more and more excited. I want to be down there, with Anthony, but this is his contest, not mine.

The man is big and muscular, with thick pubic hair and a nice patch of fur in the middle of his chest. His hair is dark,

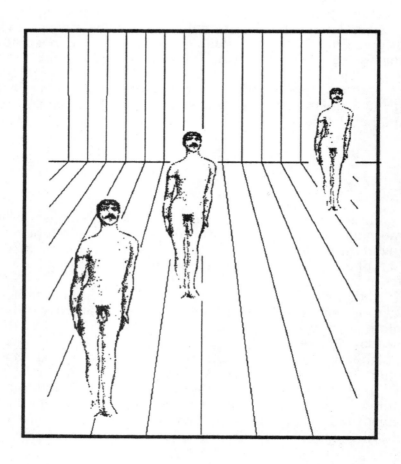

It may appear otherwise, but the three nudists depicted above are all of the same stature. Notice how the man in the middle seems quite enormous.

but is not the reflective black of Anthony's unruly bangs.

Somewhere else, Joey must be sucking on a different cock. I can't even guess what number he's up to by now. I know that I should be rooting for Anthony because he really wants to win, to be named the biggest slut in town, but a large part of me wants Joey to win. I don't totally know why.

I look down at Anthony, at the way his cheeks fill every time the cock pushes into his mouth. I can see the cock's outline above Anthony's jaw. Some might think that this image is degrading. I just think it makes my friend look more beautiful.

The guy starts getting rough now. He starts pounding his cock into Anthony's throat as if Anthony hadn't already done this eight times tonight. But, of course, he can't know that or, at least, can't know the exact number. That's my job.

"Yeah, suck that cock," he says. "Oh man, you really like that cock, don't you? Don't you?"

How typical. How fucking typical and stupid. Oh yeah . . . Suck that cock . . . No shit, you dumb fuck. He's already sucking your cock, you ignorant pile of crap. You like that cock, don't youS Of course he does, asshole. Is he supposed answer you? What, dick-head, should he nod, mumble, send smoke signals? You idiot.

"Oh dude, your mouth feels so hot. Oh, you keep doing that, you're gonna make me shoot down your throat." He grabs his own balls. "Huh, you want this load down your throat?"

Dear God, please make this asshole shut up.

Anthony keeps on sucking like a pro, passively letting the man fuck his face while he twists his mouth to increase the stimulation. Nothing phases him, and I know he likes it. He's one raunchy piece of work.

Anthony starts to really work that cock. Sucking and slurping like he really wants that guy to cum in his mouth. He pulls off and strokes the shaft, saying, "Oh yeah, give me that fucking load, stud!"

Holy shit, didn't he say that with the last guy. It's hard to remember.

Anthony goes back to sucking on the cock. It rockets in and out of his mouth, glistening with thick saliva. Drool pours from the corners of Anthony's mouth and runs down his chin. I know if I licked it, it would be salty from the man's precum. I'd like to lick it up, just to touch Anthony's sweet lips with my tongue, but I'm sure it would be misinterpreted.

I imagine that Anthony's jaw is really tired by now, and, as if without sympathy, the guy grabs the back of Anthony's head and fucks harder.

"Oh yeah! Oh yeah!"

I've been with Anthony before, and I know how good he is. We're best friends and we share everything—so to speak. We've used countless guys together, and I've enjoyed it every time—I've enjoyed being with Anthony every time.

"Oh yeah! Oh yeah! Ohhh yeah!!!"

Anthony pulls off just as cum pours from the cock's slit and flows unevenly down the head, dripping down the shaft. The guy pumps his hips, flinging the cum off his cock as it dribbles out of his tiny hole.

Anthony stands up, smiling at the guy, and then turns that coy gaze on me. "That was number nine, right?"

"Yes Anthony," I say, "that was number nine."

NINE/MAX

Nothing's better than tight boypussy when it's wrapped warmly around my monster cock. I love it—the hot, pink insides that give and contract with every thrust.

That's what I was saying to myself as I lifted the blonde kid's legs. "Show me that pretty hole, boy," I demanded. He obeyed. "Oh yeah, that's a hot little asshole you got there, boy."

It was too. He was a cute kid—one of those surfer types— and was really into my massive 6'2" slightly hairy body. His eyes went on fire the second he saw me with my shirt off, and he didn't waste any time. He walked right up to me without saying a word and started running his hands through the dark hair on my chest. "What the fuck do you think you're doin'?" I yelled at him, and he looked up at me like a puppy dog that just got caught pissing on the rug. I grabbed his head and pulled his mouth to one of my tits. "You wanna play?" I said. "Then chew on this motherfucker, boy!" He loved it, chewing tentatively like he was afraid I'd get pissed off. I just ground his mouth into my chest harder, and he got the idea, biting down. I really worked that boy, making him lick my chest, neck and pits. "Get out of those motherfuckin' clothes!" I said, and when he was butt naked, I roughly grabbed his face again and kissed his mouth, burning his lips with my stubble. He was really into it—into me and into the people watching—and I could smell my pungent sweat on his breath. "You're my pigslut now," I said, before pushing him down on the pool table.

And, here I was, with this cute blonde boy with his legs in the air, showing me his asshole, and he still hadn't said a word.

I moved in closer to his pulsing sphincter and took a good look at it. "Yeah, real nice." I pushed my tongue out and lapped at it, then looked at my spit glistening on the wrinkled surface. I licked his hole again, then watched my spit drip down between his crack. "You like that, boy?" He didn't say anything—he just responded with a deep, throaty moan.

"Boy, I asked you a fucking question." I slapped his hole with four fingers just hard enough so that he'd feel it.

"Agghh," he cried. I licked his asshole again, and this time I didn't stop, probing into him wantonly with my tongue. His tight, young hole got looser and more relaxed. He got more and more into it, and I stopped again, letting my fingers slap against his wet, pink hole. He cried again—more softly this time.

"You answer me when I'm talking to you, boy!"

"Sorry . . . Um, am I supposed to say sir?"

I stood up and started slapping my hard cock against his hungry butthole. "If you want this cock up your cunt, then yes, you better show me some respect." I slapped my cock against his ass harder. His whole body flinched each time the head of my prick made contact with his hole. "Do you want this cock up your ass, boy?"

"Yes sir."

"Yes sir what?" I barked, sliding a condom down my shaft.

"Yes . . . "

"Say it!" I yelled, lubing my cock up.

"Yes sir, I want your cock up my ass!"

I smacked my cock really hard against his hole several times. "You want this fucking cock, boy?"

"Yes sir!"

"Say it!"

"I want that fucking cock!!!"

I squeezed the base and gave him the whole thing with one thrust. He wanted it bad, and his insides opened up to me completely. "Oh yeah!" he screamed when I buried my cock in him.

I pulled my dick out slowly. "Oh yes sir, fuck my ass." And, I rammed it back inside, only to withdrawal it slowly again.

"Oh God, fuck that ass, sir!"

"Yeah, you like that cock in your boycunt, don't you?"

"Oh yes sir! Fuck my boycunt, sir! Oh yeah, fuck my boy-cunt, sir."

His screaming turned me on so much I almost came too early, but I held back and fucked his opening really hard even as sweat dripped down my forehead and fell into my eyes.

Men were all around us, jacking off or sucking each other's cocks, but we were the center of attention. The whole room was filled with the smell of musky sex and hot latex. The entire scene drove me to fuck the boy harder and faster.

I held the boy's legs up by his ankles and watched my cock fuck in and out of his ass. His dick was hard, and his pink nuts bounced every time I thrust my cock into him. I fucked him and fucked him, occasionally bending down to kiss his gapping mouth or twisting to lick his toes or the soles of his feet. "Oh God," he kept crying. "Oh God, fuck my cunt harder, sir. Fuck me harder, sir!"

I grabbed his cock and started stroking it firmly. "I want you to cum for me, boy." I kept stroking it, and my hand got slick with his precum. "Shoot that load for me, boy. I wanna see it."

His grunting became louder and his cries became indecipherable as jets of white spunk exploded violently from his cock. The orgasm sprinkled his entire torso with creamy white boymilk, and the firm spasming inside his ass sent me off, causing me to release my huge load into my stretched out condom.

TEN/Damien

. . . the bedroom is beautiful, and the whole house is beautiful, and brad is beautiful as he shuts the door behind him and locks it, looking at me with a disarming smile curving one side of his lips, and i sit down on the bed, waiting for his next move, which is equally charming as he walks around the bed and starts a fire in the marble fireplace that dominates one wall, and even though the fireplace uses gas logs, they are really nice ones, and it's hard to tell the difference between them and real wood, but that isn't really important anyway, because brad is here with me, and i have been wanting to be alone with brad, in this way, for quite a long time, but that always seems to be the way that relationships go with me, or at least, it has been my experience that whenever i really, really want someone, they never seem to have any interest in me whatsoever, and that's usually okay, because i've made it a point to not expect anything good to happen in my life, but brad is a good thing, or at least i pray that he is a good thing, because what i really need in my life right now is a good thing, and brad comes over to where i'm sitting on the bed just across from his new fire and kneels right in front of me to unbutton my shirt— the fire becoming a burning halo around his dark auburn hair—and i look down as his hands travel the blonde coat on my stomach and chest, the tiny hairs glowing like burning embers, and I reach down to pull off his black shirt, and when it slips over his head, I feel overcome by the sight of his stunning body, which isn't necessarily perfect, but is instead more normal or natural, like my own body, but everything about him is stunning to me because of who he is, and, over time, i have truly grown to like who he is even though i never expected to be given this opportunity to be so intimate with him, being that, so far, I've only known him through friends, or rather acquaintances, that i see on occasion at the small neighborhood gay bar which hides somewhere between our two separate homes, and even though we've talked numerous times about the empty topics that characterize bars, i've never had the courage to tell him how attracted to him I've been, until this evening when, through some accident, we both showed up at what was supposed to be a friendly gathering but is, instead, a bacchinal feast, and through this same accident, it turned out that each of us, with the exception of our elusive host, was the only person here that the other one knew, but I feel extremely appreciative of accidents and chaos and random occurrence when brad stands up, kicks off his shoes, undoes his fly, and lets his pants drop to the floor, and i remove my shoes and socks, stand and let him open my jeans and push them down so that we both stand naked as the fire casts a glow on our skin, and it is then that brad kisses me, for what is now the second time, and it feels like a first because now the clothes are gone and his lips and body and genitals press against mine, and when he first kissed me, I was caught off guard, having never been expecting him to feel about me the way that i most definitely felt about him, and so it was to my surprise that he leaned over and touched his lips to mine while we sat uncomfortably on a sofa surrounded by sex, but then his tongue touched my lips and my tongue touched his tongue and we opened our mouths the way we open our mouths right now as brad runs his hands down my back to my rear, pulling me toward the bed, and we fall together onto the soft mattress, still locked in a masculine embrace, and he rolls me over onto my back and kisses me passionately as his endowments rub up against mine, sending waves of stimulation up through my spine, and we kiss, rolling back and fourth, touching and kissing skin while our erections press firmly against each other, the pleasure growing to a pinnacle of ecstasy which makes our breathing become labored and causes us to groan, as if in pain, until the friction releases our semen, spreading it across my stomach and thighs and his stomach and thighs as he continues to rub against me, and, slowly, our breathing returns to something that could be considered more normal, and he looks into my eyes and smiles, and i instantly wonder if we're ever going to do this again, only because i have always wanted to be close to him whether or not sex is involved, and now i feel afraid, even through i also feel hopeful, and i lie here, looking back into his eyes, waiting to hear what he has to say, knowing what he says might change everything or might leave me where I've always been . . .

ELEVEN/Jeff

Disordered noise set to an industrial beat pushed through the walls and slowly made Jeff interested in investigating the wantonness of his own party. Tentatively, he stepped out of the entertainment room which had served as his temporary retreat and walked languidly toward the living room. Naked men seemed to be tossed about casually. Bodies were draped over sofas and chairs. Some were sprawled out in front of the fireplace and others formed small piles on the floor. In Jeff's mind, the room was quiet, calm like a battlefield were only smoke hung in the air. Gradually, it dawned on him that this room wasn't like that at all. These bodies were moving, sucking cock and fucking ass. Everywhere, they crawled over each other in search of cum like leeches hungry for blood.

Jeff moved through the room—stepping over random limbs—and crossed to the hallway that passed the dinning room and lead outside. He reached the patio door, opened it, and four men, wet and naked, stepped in. "Jeff!" they yelled in unison, surrounding him. They were all typically buff and beautiful, with dark hair and tan bodies, but Jeff didn't recognize any of them, and clearly, none of them knew his real name. It didn't surprise him though. He had invited a few hundred of the usual guests and didn't really know a single one of them either.

Laughing, and smelling of chlorine, the four men pulled Jeff toward a nearby bathroom. Shoving him in with them, they shut the door.

It felt suddenly warm in the small room as one of the guys started removing Jeff's white Jocko shirt while the others ran their hands over his body. Jeff's cock grew as one of the men grabbed his crotch. After all, Jeff reasoned, a hard cock is what they really want.

One of them bent down to remove Jeff's Doc's, and two of the guys hurriedly pulled his Pepe's and Calvin's down. They really began enjoying themselves then, touching Jeff's hard body and rubbing their warm cocks on his skin.

With his head hanging limply toward the sink, Jeff simply relaxed as the men kissed and licked his neck, chest and ass. Two hands firmly parted his asscheeks, and a wet tongue pushed into his hole. Jeff let out a loud groan and accidently looked directly into his own blue eyes reflected in the flat mirror before him. As he stared into himself, one of the men whispered in his ear, "You like that, don't you?"

The tongue licked more vigorously and pushed into Jeff's asshole even harder as the whisperer pinched Jeff's nipple. "Oh yeah, Jeff, you like that tongue up your ass, huh?"

Another guy whispered, "Oh yeah, you like that." Jeff continued to stare into his own eyes, wanting to shake his head no, but couldn't when he felt a warm mouth envelop his cock.

Jeff's breathing instantly became heavier as the mouth tightened on his cock and started sucking it slowly. "Oh yeah, Jeff, you're so fucking hot," whispered the first guy before grabbing Jeff's jaw and bringing Jeff's mouth to his. Jeff let the steamy tongue enter his mouth and opened his ass more to the thrusting tongue at his backdoor.

Another mouth clamped around his left nipple and someone's hand started playing with his balls. The tongue stopped pushing into his ass, and he could hear a foil package being torn open. The wet sound of lube being squirted out of a tube and stroked onto a cock followed, and in a few seconds, Jeff felt the large head of a cock pressing up against him, inside him.

The cockhead entered, shocking Jeff with its sudden violation. It was slowly followed by a long, fat shaft. Jeff's angry moans sank down the throat of the guy kissing him as the cock plunged slowly in and out of his lube—slick ass.

Soon, the fucking become harder and the sensations in his cock became more intense. The pounding of his prostate made it difficult for Jeff to hold back his orgasm, and his cries still disappeared into the stranger's mouth. He humped his hips a bit, and that did it. The mouth pulled off his cock, and cum spilled out of it, falling violently into the unknown.

Jeff didn't pay attention to the climax of the other men. He remained limp while they finished themselves off. When they were done, Jeff pulled his clothes back on, not bothering to clean himself up, and walked back out into the party to search for his boyfriend.

TWELVE/Alan

Imagine that you're a writer of erotica. You sit, fully clothed, in an office and rest your fingers on a keyboard, trying to remember. The pressure just below your finger-nails is light, and you try to connect the feeling to something tender, like the way your finger tips felt, most recently, resting on the warm stomach of another man while your mind moved back and forth between sleep and silent awe.

But, that's not entirely true, and what you want to write about /RIGHT NOW/ is truth. What you want to do is write the story that you don't know how to write, and truth is the best place to start. In lieu of this, silent awe should really be replaced with a word that means anxiety or angst. There are probably reasons for this. Probably. Perhaps. You don't know.

When you write erotica, you don't necessarily think of sex even though a statement like that one might be disconcerting to your readers. What you think about is language and how writing precedes from it, and right now you can't help but be obsessed about the accidents: Pressure Is Light.

But, you think about the sex, too. You imagine it and weave experience into a fictitious mesh of passion-glazed memories which become connected to form narrative drives that forcibly recall themselves. When you write about group sex, you invariably recall a time in a sex club when a mob of men left you feeling raped, and when you write about S&M, you access twisted versions of a night when someone gave you crystal, coke and K and convinced you that it felt good to be degraded. When you write about lovers, you can't resist the image of one man and how you felt about him and how perfect you thought he was—physically, spiritually— and how you felt so torn apart inside when you drove him to the airport and walked him to the international boarding gate, settling for a half-assed goodbye and a peck on the cheek because airport security said you couldn't walk him all the way. At that moment, you thought about the movies and how the abandoned party reaches out to touch the glass as the plane their heart is on lifts its nose and disappears into a seemingly endless and empty future. You felt denied. The window that looked out on his departing plane was a mile and several security checks away. Perhaps that's why everything you write is so heavily laden with bitterness and pain. It's as if love and misery are the same thing. This might not be entirely true either. Even at its best, your relationship wasn't always perfect.

You don't know if you've ever been in love. You know you came close once, but you're still not entirely sure that what you felt was actually the real thing. You've felt like you were in love a million times. No, that's hyperbole. The actual number is close to six.

Each and every time, the love of your life turned to shit, except for once, but you've already told that story. Maybe this is why you hate the word 'heart' so much. It's such an abstract and convoluted metaphor for something which you're not even sure exists.

But, this doesn't take you anywhere. You've placed yourself here to write erotica, and presently, you've failed to do it effectively.

What you wanted to express was that the lies were true. You've never been to the orgy you're writing about, but you feel soiled as if you had—not that you think sex is bad; sex might be the only good you've ever known.

You definitely like the way an orgasm feels. The buildup. The release.

In fact, you never moralize. As far as you're concerned, life is hard, and if people want diversions, who are you to say no? It's not like you know a lot about alternatives. This reminds you of something Shelley wrote: "Life, like a dome of many colored glass, stains the white radiance of eternity until death tramples it to fragments." Maybe you should delete that. It sounds kind of heavy.

Being that this is erotica, you should at least write that you have your dick out and that you're stroking it while you type with one hand, but that isn't true. You're not going to do anything or invent anything. Cum is not going to splatter your keyboard, and because of this, your reader's cum is probably not going to splatter this page. "Where are the songs of Spring? Aye, where are the they? Think not of them, thou has thy music too . . . "

That's John Keats.

You don't know why you're doing this. You're failing, and this story /NO/ this essay is falling apart. You simply feel like you need to include something outside yourself. Maybe, at your deepest, you're a collage of random things. This seems sinister. "To hope, til hope creates, from it's own wreak, the thing it contemplates." Shelley. It's a spell to end tyranny. That's what you need: a spell . . . to end tyranny.

No, you don't know why you're doing this. You knew that you wanted to write the text that you didn't know how to write, and you knew that you wanted to not cover up. Often that's what writing is for you—a covering up. But, beneath your orgasmic images and dirty words, there's a life, limited and finite—the very opposite of God.

Perhaps there isn't anything erotic about that, but somewhere, in your heart, you hope there is. You hope the reader will forgive you, and you hope he will still be touched by what you've placed here—maybe not in the way he intended—maybe not in the way you intended. You have no idea what you intended. Maybe, it was intimacy. Maybe, you wanted the reader to know who's words they were cumming on. Maybe, it makes no difference. And. Or. Maybe. It does.

THIRTEEN/QUENTIN

—There you are, says Quentin.
—Yeah. Jeff looks disinterested.
—I've been looking all over for you.
Jeff looks up. —Why would you do that?
—I missed you; I couldn't find you; I've been looking all over for you, says Quentin.
—It's our orgy . . .
—My orgy.
—Um, I thought we were going to play around.
—Okay, Quentin.
—Together.
—Oh . . . I didn't know that was necessary.
Jeff and Quentin stand in a room surrounded by men having sex or recovering from sex. Quentin looks around somewhat nervously. Jeff seems distant. Quentin feels like he's on stage. —Why didn't you just find somebody else to play with? *Jeff starts to walk away.*
—I didn't want to.
—Didn't want to what? Play around?
—No, *says Quentin*, I didn't want . . . somebody else.

Jeff looks at Quentin, giving Quentin's statement serious thought. —Oh. I think I understand.

Jeff places his hands on the sides of Quentin's face and gently kisses him. Jeff's kiss turns more passionate. Quentin gives in, surrendering yet another part of himself to Jeff's handsome and overwhelming presence.

The kiss becomes more powerful. Both of their mouths are wide open, their tongues pushing forward and filling the space between them.

Jeff withdraws and sucks once on Quentin's lower lip before speaking. —I'm sorry, Quentin. I didn't mean to leave you stranded. Let me make it up to you.

Jeff kisses Quentin's lips again, then kisses Quentin's neck before lowering himself to his knees and opening Quentin's fly. —Yes, Quentin, I promise . . . this'll make it better.

Quentin looks around at the men watching him as Jeff releases the hard cock from Quentin's pants. The eyes staring at him don't bother Jeff as he holds the thick shaft and guides his mouth around the head. Jeff's tongue makes contact first, and Quentin gasps from the sensitivity of his glans and the vulnerability in what he would call his soul.

—God, Jeff, he whispers.

Jeff entombs the whole cock in his mouth and throat, sucking on it so that the head rubs on the back of his tongue. He keeps it buried there and quickly moves his mouth forward and back, sending Quentin toward orgasm in less than a minute.

—Oh shit, Jeff. Oh God. Oh God. Okay. Okay Jeff. Please stop. Please . . .

Jeff pulls off the cock and gives it one tight squeeze, releasing powerful spurts of heavy cum from the gaping slit. Quentin shouts something meaningless as his cum volleys through the air, pelting Jeff's previously stained shirt. All around them, men smile. Some laugh. Some hoot. Some give up applause.

Jeff puts Quentin's cock away and stands. He puts his hand on his own chest and rubs the cum into his shirt's tight fabric. He places his other hand behind Quentin's neck and holds him as Quentin continues to shudder from the climax.

—That was good, huh? says Jeff.

—Fuckin' A.

—Are you happy now?

—Yeah.

—Good. *Jeff gives Quentin one last kiss and lets go of him.*
—I think you should go now, *he says. The room goes quiet.*
    —What?
    —I think you should go.
    —Go were? *Embarrassed, Quentin looks at the crowd.*
    —Go home or wherever it is that you came from.
    —Are you kidding?
    —No. *Jeff remains stoic.*
    —Why?
    —Because it's over. It's been a nice couple of days, but now it's time for you to go.
    —But I love you.
    —I'm sure you do, but that's just too bad. You need to leave.

FOURTEEN/Daryl

I've always been the first to admit that I'm not exactly as wild as I should be, but when I had the opportunity to actually cut loose and do something dangerous, illicit and sinful, I jumped on it. I wasn't, however, really prepared for what I had gotten myself into. When I first walked through the door of what was to be my new, undiscovered playground, I almost turned and ran out from fear, insecurity and moral trepidation. But I didn't. I had driven to that house for a reason; I had a purpose; and I wasn't going to be turned back by anything.

It wasn't long after I walked in that some stranger reached out to touch my buzzed hair. His fingers sent shivers coursing through my body as he traced the stubbly hairs up my neck to somewhere just behind my ear. I turned and stepped closer to him. He was handsome, mature, and clearly drunk or on something. He leaned against a wall with another guy who also looking right at me. Inside, I panicked, but outside, I was the very definition of confident and sexy. The other guy looked a lot like the first. They both had short hair cuts, wore only tight shorts and black combat boots, and had sculpted bodies and purchased tans. This town was full of beautiful guys, and, amazingly, they all managed to look alike.

The first guy reached for my hand and pulled me closer to him and his friend. They both started kissing me—taking turns. Soon, both of their mouths touched my lips at the same time, their tongues fighting with mine.

Their hands searched my body and grabbed my rock hard cock. This whole experience had me unbelievably excited. Having grown up in what my stern father called a "good Christian home," I wasn't used to this kind of tactile excess. My family wasn't into kisses or hugs. Our sex lives were never discussed. And now, here I was—the whore of Babylon.

I played with their cocks, pulling the stiff members out of their shorts and getting a good feel. They really got into my cock, too. I'm kind of a normal looking guy, but believe me, I have the dick of death—it's sturdy, straight, incredibly thick and twelve inches long.

Eventually, I backed away from the two guys and let them go at each other. I wasn't about to completely spend myself on the first two guys I met. I walked through the house, my hard cock practically busting out of my jeans. I seemed to get a lot of attention everywhere I went. Gee, I wonder why.

I went from one room to another, letting strangers stroke my cock or put it in their mouths in a vain attempt to get the whole monster down their throats. I didn't commit to any single guy. I just played and moved on, immersing myself in earthly desire and beautiful sin.

Finally, I came across the pinnacle of debauchery that I had been searching for. About ten naked guys stood around a beautiful blonde boy with their cocks in their hands. He was bent over the arm of a couch with his smooth, perfect ass shoved up in the air. His asshole was wet with lube and looked like it had already been worked over quite a bit. One guy stood right next to the boy and pulled a condom off his own dick. He stroked his dick a few times, and a shower of cum suddenly burst forth and landed on the boy's back. It looked like quite a number of loads had already been dropped there. The boy moaned appreciatively as the hot spunk landed on his skin.

Another one of the guys stroked a prophylactic onto his cock and walked up behind the boy's ass. I moved in and watched as his cock pushed into the inflamed hole and disappeared somewhere inside the boy's body. Not giving the boy a chance to adjust, the guy just started ramming his cock into the wet, sloppy ass. The boy moaned and grunted, giving his audience a myriad of "look at me I'm being fucked" expressions.

As the guy fucked him, I got fully undressed. When I took off my jeans, everyone's gaze moved away from the action and fell on my giant cock. I even think a few jaws dropped. In fact, I think the only one who didn't notice was the boy getting fucked.

That had to change, so I moved onto the couch and gently slapped the boy's face with my large, rosy cockhead. He quickly opened his eyes and stared at it in shock. Then, he looked up at me and smiled wickedly before straining his neck to get a good lick of the shaft.

He ran his tongue all over it and did his best to get it in his mouth. Meanwhile, the guy fucking him got closer to orgasm, eventually spilling his jizz all over the boy's ass.

Then, it was my turn. I put on a condom, seriously lubed up my cock, and slowly started pushing the head of it into the boy's loose hole. He gasped and breathed rapidly as I shoved all of it into him. I had to be gentle, at least at first. The boy had been getting fucked for the past few hours, and he had yet to feel anything like this.

Soon, I was pounding him real good, and he was enjoying the fuck out of it. The men watching liked it too, and soon cum was spraying all over the room.

I kept fucking the boy, thrusting all of my huge prick into his hot ass. I felt somebody kneel between my legs, and I looked back to see a man reach for the boy's stiff cock. The guy stroked the kid as I continued to fuck him mercilessly, and soon the boy's ass contracted around my cock as he cried out and shot his load onto my legs. I stopped thrusting and just kept my cock buried in his ass. With slow flexes of my ass, I softly massaged the boy's prostate as the other guy milked cum from the boy's cock. The kid continued to cry out as his orgasm continued.

When it was obvious that he couldn't take any more, I pulled my cock out and shot all over his ass, happy that I had given the kid one fuck he would never forget.

I didn't leave the party immediately. I hung around and even got off again. I had spent my whole gay life trying to be good, but this experience was a hell of a lot more fun. Unbridled sex was something I was definitely going to have to get a lot more into . . . in the future.

FIFTEEN/JEFF

Things are quiet now. The sun. The pool. The proverbial day after. The maids have left. Cleaned the place. Dirtied me with their looks. Charlie's due back.

Las Vegas. Lady Luck. Some fuckers have too much money. Too much time. I should be grateful.

Right on cue, he walks up, looking kinda down. He must have lost—like it matters. I'm thinking of Quentin.

He bends, gives me a kiss, looks up and down my body, stopping to admire my cock's outline beneath my cobalt Speedos. It makes him smile.

I smile back. Once again, on cue. He asks about the party, says something about fun. My answer is no.

"No?"

"Yeah. No."

He talks about missing me, strokes my chest. I respond, smile. It's all been done before. My indifference is kept inside.

"I'm thinking Vegas would be a good place for a porno."

"Really."

"Yeah, you know, bad boys looking for sin."

"Sounds great."

His hands follow the deep line that divides my stomach.

"It could star you. / Cool. / I'll have to write the script soon / Oh. / We can stay at the Stratosphere. / That'll be fun."

His hand is on my cock. I get hard like I'm supposed to. On cue.

I'd prefer the Hard Rock, but Charlie doesn't know that. Maybe that pastiche New York thing. Not that it matters. The entire city is made of plastic.

"Maybe Joey and Rex can go." I say.

"Oh yeah. Of course."

Joey/Jeff/Rex: his angels.

I'm the blondee.

He takes my dick out and strokes it slowly. This scene would make for a good '70s drama. Imagine the ratings.

His hand on my cock feels good. I can't help that.

He's not so bad. 42/43. Still in great shape. Good looking. Great clothes. Wealth does a lot for a man's looks.

Quentin was poor. Struggling.

/HONEST/

Poor is cute, too.

Charlie says again that he really missed me, and then he bends down, puts his mouth around my cock. It instantly feels good.

/DUB IN SUCKING NOISES, MOANS/

I was only with Quentin a few days, while Charlie was in Vegas. Amazing how we merge with someone in a night, pretend to be lovers and part in the morning with a kiss as if we know we will come back together in a few hours after work or for dinner.

We live lies.

What I have with Charlie seems real. He pays me to have sex on cue. With him. For him. Him / The camera.

It feels real. His sucking on my cock feels real. It always feels real. Looks real. Sounds real. Smells real.

I'm sure I taste real. Salty? Musky? Maybe like chlorine. Sweat.

He sucks my cock. The feeling makes me forget: Life has no function—I consume. *The meaning. The meaning.*

Quentin deserved better than me, so I pushed him away.

I push Charlie away, and cum erupts from my cock. It hits his face, lands on my stomach. Apparently, sperm have a social structure similar to ants. There are sperm generals, sperm knights, lowly sperm soldiers and ditch diggers. Thinking about this makes my nuts feel numb. It's like I can feel them in there. Interacting. Planning my defeat.

Sex is all about images. We, as queers, rarely actually have sex with men. I take that back. We, as human beings, rarely actually have sex with human beings. It's like we're fucking pictures.

I never knew Quentin. I learned the word which we call his name and I fucked the surface we call his body. Even now, his image loses focus.

I stare down at the cum on my stomach and watch as a long drop seeps out of my cock. Charlie looks down on this, too. He smiles, kisses me. It alleviates his insecurities. He likes the image of me, naked . . . spent.

With one finger, I play with the sperm on my surface. Another army bites the dust.

what the fuck

Sex is war.

"Charlie, can you have the maids come clean me with their mops?"

This puzzles him. He doesn't understand what "I" mean. But, that could be okay. Maybe his attempt—my attempt—is at least close to love.

Cyrano of the English Department

Larry McCaffery

for Raymond Federman

A lot of people have asked me how I survived, personally, intellectually, creatively, and (most important of all), SEXUALLY during the 80s—those years of AIDs, Reagan, Jesse Helmes, sexual harassment, of the Meese Commission and PC fascism and all those other things that were trying to SUCK the juice out of you, DRY up the life and passion and so on. My response is usually to shrug and say modestly something like, Hell, survival wasn't easy for anyone but maybe especially if you were a professor in an English Department that was part of a university whose name I won't reveal but which was run by and for lawyers, cops, accountants, and anybody else who was associated, indirectly or indirectly, with the military industrial complex.

So what was my secret of survival? I took advantage of my background, my education, and my personal interests, that's how: I wrote porn fantasies for all the guys in my department to liven up their boring sex lives!

Yes, that's right, I invented erotic scenes (I called them "scenarios") for all the sexually repressed dweebs in my department, mostly dorky types with tweed sports coasts and pipes who didn't even know how to IMAGINE HOW TO MASTURBATE (I'M NOT KIDDING) much less actually get inside the pants of anyone, not their department secretaries or colleagues, not their horny coed students, typically not even their long-suffering WIVES because they spent all their time READING! Yes, all they ever did was sit around hunkered down at their desks or on their couches staring at useless and boring books and literary journals, I mean all they did, all they ever HAD DONE, all they COULD IMAGINE DOING, was sitting on their ugly, rapidly expanding asses reading, yes, reading a

left to   right
top
  to
bottom
turn the page, always in a straight line, reading and re-

reading, filling their thick skulls with useless words, ideas, phrases, incomprehensible theories, verbal vomit so that they could shit the stuff out of their brains into their own lectures and essays. And when they weren't reading (or re-reading), they weren't out on the make, no, not these guys, when these guys took a vacation from reading what they wanted to do for some real excitement, a change of pace, was to slip into. the department late at night and start XEROXING what they HAD BEEN reading, or might be read-ing, or wanted to read, or WRITING ABOUT what they had been reading, or doing committee work or gathering enor-mous amounts of bibliographical information from data bases accessible to them on their university-supplied Internet systems, yes, unbelievably boring and irrelevant information about titles and subtitles authors and co-authors and editors and editions and pub dates and a lot of other crap they'd gather together and arrange on their com-puter files in alphabetical order to satisfy their anal reten-tiveness and so they could cite everything they'd stolen with perfect accurateness, so they could write the stupid useless turgid boring politically correct essays that would get them promoted, articles that deconstructed patriarchy or provided textual analysis of the meaning of Madonna's pussy in her latest video, or that droned on about the mis-use of the phallus, or trying to figure out how to run the SPELLCHECK on their new word processors, or responding to the e-mailed questions they've received from all those OTHER boring academic drones, or grading student papers and gossiping about their colleagues that they couldn't get it up anymore—and who couldn't figure out how to change this situation on their own. That's where I came in.

Meanwhile, me, I began inventing porn scenes (for a fee, mind you) for my colleagues, all of them (all the males, any-way), assistant professors, black professors, feminists, deconstructions, associate professors, specialists in Medieval romances and metaphysical poetry, FULL profes-sors, part timers, TA's, yes, absolutely filthy scenarios that these guys could take home and act out with their little broads, their boring wives, or their girlfriends, or their stu-dents on the weekends.

Fifty bucks a scenario that was my price (TAKE IT OR LEAVE IT) and no one really bitched about it. Therefore WOW would I bang that sexy stuff away on my word processor (I had a used Kaypro in those days)! Fabulous erotic dreams, full of all these bizarre politically incorrect perverted episodes that were sure to be a turn on to people whose idea of a wild time was to sit around imagining the look of the gals in the front row when they read the dirty passages from Donne or Chaucer. Scenarios that allowed these jerks to finally get their repressions and prejudices and secret desires out in the open, sexual episodes I cunningly built out of precisely the topics and character types and symbols and plot models they were so obsessed with but hadn't ever found a means of relating to their own lives--stories about racism, sexism, sexual harassment, abuse of authority, domination, unequal power relationships, the power of the phallus, topics these experts on narratology and semiotics and codes spent so much time writing and dissecting and analyzing and talking about at conferences and on the phone and in the classrooms and in the hallways that they never had any time to try explore first hand.

That's why they came to me, so I could supply them with something they could try out for themselves, totally wild, outtacontrol stories based (as it should be) on minimal details furnished by the crums I picked up out of their course syllabi and files they'd dumped into the trash and boring essays about narratology and semiotics and post-feminism, episodes involving the frenzy of the visible, unequal power relationships, S&M, anal sex, with whip cream, leather, blindfolds, younameit. Wild, absolutely politically incorrect situations of surrealistic denseness who filaria of suggestiveness was certainly enough to seduce even the most jaded kind of minds. Positions and contortions that would require for correct execution and proper results the acrobatic talents of the entire population of a zoo or tiergarden. Ah, what ORGIES! I invented on the spot! What POLITICAL and GENDER and RACIAL INCORRECT-NESS! I created in those moments of word-processed-passion sitting in my office as I let my fingers do the walking. I wrote approximately twelve scenarios per week (2 to 3 pagers each, double spaced), with a few extra ones over the semester break and summer vacation. Sometimes on late on Friday afternoons before giving them hard copy I would read their scenarios aloud to take home to all the jerks in the Department Office after the secretaries had gone home.

Ah, did I have fun writing those fantasies on that beat-up

old Kaypro of mine, full speed, and without the least apprehension, without thinking much about what I wrote, I simply accumulated words
I simply piled up the words as fast as
                              I could
                         up and down
      `   &
                         sideways

                    erotic narrative archetypes
            (S&M, dominance, being dominated)
            (cross-dressing, gay, transsexuals)
                    erotic character stereotypes
            (blondes, and brunettes and redheads)
(whitewomenblackwomenasian womenmexicanwomenmid-
dleeasternwomen)

    plot elements and motifs invented specifically with their
nerdy English professor neuroses and obsessions and
repressions and in mind: radical feminism, lesbian studies,
deconstruction, slippage, jouissance, sexual harassment,
patriarchy, phallocentricism, anti-Oedipus, queer theory,
post-colonialism,

                 I played with words and metaphors
                 with double meanings &
                      triple meanings &
without any respect (I must confess) for narrative logic
coherency order character development epiphanic conclu-
sions point of view symbolic design voice meaning
            it was just a matter of filling up space
                              PAGES
                                &
                              PAGES

(approximately twenty-five bucks a page I kept
                              telling myself
                              as I would finish
Ah what sprit of creativity I was engaged
in   in those days
                         what inspirations
                              banging every
night on my old beat-up Kaypro

sometimes giving one guy the scenario I was supposed to have given to
another one
sometimes giving a scenario that was supposed to go to the young queer theory dude
to the old fart Victorian or the armchair Marxist guy with the posters of Madonna on his office wall
but who cared
  who gave a shit
    it kept going (full blast) and they loved me for it both
                    the jerks in my department
and all the little cunts in their suburban gated community homes

---

HERE IN FACT LET ME GIVE YOU AN EXAMPLE (AMONG MANY) OF THE TYPE OF SCENARIOS I WROTE IN THOSE DAYS FOR MY COLLEAGUES—OF COURSE I'M ONLY QUOTING THE BEST SEXY PASSAGES—AND I'M SOMEWHAT CORRECTING EDITING EXPURGATING CENSURING (IF I MAY) THE KIND OF ENGLISH I USED IN THOSE DAYS-PURIFYING (IN A SENSE THE KIND OF LANGUAGE I USED IN THOSE DAYS—IMPROVING SOMEWHAT THE TONE THE GRAMMAR SYNTAX—THE PRESENTATION ALSO—WITHOUT HOWEVER ATTEMPTING TO DEFORM THE ORIGINAL

Scenario Created (let us say) on July 4, 1987

Decunstructing Mother Jones

The date is the late 70s, the best of times (for lesbian feminists academics such as yourself, Dr. Eva Jones, Chair of the influential Women's Studies Dept. at Berkeley) and the worst of times (for women with "healthy" hetero instincts like me, Jennie McGrath, red-headed, a brilliant literature graduate students at Berkeley who should have been nearing completion of my degree had it not been for the "C" you gave me on the basis of my extraordinary recuperation of Cather, Stein, Adrienne Rich as several other so-called "gay" writers whom I demonstrated had written fiction which was not at all a disguised version of lesbianism, etc., etc., but actually a disguised disguise which actually masked strong, normal urges that all healthy women have about sex with MEN, coming under (as it were) the wondrous feeling of being dominated and penetrated (yes I know such words are unpolitically correct even during the wild orgiastic late 70s but I use them proudly, knowingly, defiantly, certain as I am of my "position" (as it were) by that remarkable instrument that God placed in a very strategic place on males).

In short, during our graduate seminar (English 725) in Contemporary Feminist Fiction and Theory, it quickly became obvious that you--you with your tweed suits and blonde hair always so neatly placed up in either a bun or one of those more girlish twirls to the side and those huge tits that all the disgusting pimply faced grad student males in the class kept salivating over, while the reaction of the women, all naturally lesbo feminists except me, who came into your class idealistically, hoping to learn more about feminism, which I was naive enough to think was written by and about women rather than just radical separationist lesbian Marxists who hated men and therefore somehow instinctually recognized they should hate me and made me the pariah of the class)--anyway the reaction of the bull dikes around me, their heavy breathing and furtive movements under their skirts or jeans, was both personally disgusting to me and horrifying.

I mean that stuff is unnatural!! And, Prof. Jones, don't think I didn't know your game, the way you liked the effects you got from your students by wearing those tight tweed suit tops that hardly were enough to rein in what all human decency should have demanded that they keep hidden--or how you'd get off leaning over whenever you're lecturing and you've got something on that can lean conveniently open, exposing just enough of the tops of those creamy luscious breasts to get anybody just a little hot. And yes, I'll admit it, maybe it was just being in the same classroom with those horrid lesbians--or maybe it was being more or less forced to witness these so-called "students" involve themselves in lurid sexual fantasies during our study periods together; and of course a couple of times it was impossible for me to just witness, peer pressure forced me into engaging in acts that . . . well, I won't repeat those now).

The main point here, though, is the way you systematically set out to humiliate me and ruin my confidence in my hetereo readings--all this just in some stupid power trip fantasy of forcing me to yield to the strength and vigor of your . . . will. The way you ridiculed my first paper ("Stein's 'Tender Buttons': Towards a Strap-On Approach to Lesbian" Poetics") and even attempted (unsuccessfully) to seduce me in your office. When I resisted, you had it in for me the rest of the semester.

Today, having just received my final grade--a "C"!!--I have decided to take my revenge slowly but fully satisfyingly by arranging to meet you at the lesbian disco bar I know you frequent. My plan is to first win your sympathy, then get you all hot and bothered by flaunting my own gorgeous tits and ass, then talking you into coming back to my apartment, where I have arrange a drink--Quaalude and tonic--in advance that will get you in exactly the mood I wish you to be in. My plan is to get you in a state of total wild desire and then call Husky Hank--my studly gas station attendant lover hunk with the enormous-but-sensitive-slong who's waiting for the right Hollywood director to come along--to come in and give you what you obviously need so badly.

LET ME GIVE YOU NOW (BRIEFLY) A DIFFERENT KIND OF SCE-NARIO, THE SORT I WOULD OCCASIONALLY WRITE FOR THE GRADUATE STUDENTS IN MY DEPARTMENT (AT A REDUCED FEE, I DIDN'T WANT TO EXPLOIT THEIR WEAKNESS BUT OFFER A HELPING HAND, AS IT WERE, TO PUNCH THROUGH THE PASTEBOARD MASK OF REPRESSION AND ANALITY.)
(This example is chosen at random from among a stock of more than four or five hundred.)

Scenario File Created (let us say) 9 December 1988

(Re)Contextualizing the Shattered Venus

You are Cynthia Harrison, Chairperson of the Woman's Studies Department at Vassar College and a noted, if controversial scholar whose recent critical studies--i.e., Reconstructing the Shattered Venus: Reclaimed the Female Body from the Effects of Patriarchy and Out of the Closet: A Semiolgoical Study of Lesbian S&M Styles--have presented passionate feminist arguments about the awful-ness of all men and the beauty, majesty and nurturing features of women. You're also what some redneck men outside the hallowed walls of your Ivory Tower might describe as a "tasty dish"--a blonde bombshell and "blockbuster" with plenty of curves and bulges that seemed very edible indeed. Now in the absolute prime of your sex-uality, you've long since shed the tweed jackets and hair-in-a-bun styles in favor of a provocative new-woman's-studies-prof look-of-the-90s" mode--black leather jackets and boots, lip piercing, etc..

Also shit-canned are the prim manners you had when you arrived at Vassars, married to a dull computer programmer who agreed to move to the East Coast to be with you, but who obvious-ly resented you for taking him away from his nerdy buddies. Long before you won early tenure, your hubby was sulking, drinking, and giving over to occasional rages directed at you. You parried these stupid, drunken histrionics on his part--you knew how to handle yourself in a fight--but when hubby started coming on to your students you decided to toss the jerk out on his ass. Your divorce was granted after you came home one day early to begin work preparing your PDS file for your upcoming promotion to full professor. Your were so engrossed in thoughts of how to best showcase the half-dozen new essays you'd written that at first you didn't notice the moans coming from your back bedroom. When you opened the door, there was Mr. Computer Jerk, pants down around his ankles, his admittedly impressive member thrust deep up into the wet warm mouth of Sarah Johnson--your favorite student in the seminar in Stein you were currently teaching, a woman you had been carefully nurturing for a career in the burgeoning field of Lesbian Studies which you were helping to legitimize at Vassars.

This moment--and the one just afterwards when you witnessed hubby trying to apologize while in the midst of an uncontrollable orgasm in the mouth of the apparently unaware Ms. Johnson--was, of course, indelibly printed in your brain. Once rid of Jerk-Off, you began a new life dedicated to discovering the True Feminine side of yourself that patriarchy had never permitted you to uncover.

Bottom line: you started cruising bars by night, gathering materials for your books, and carrying on with the cutest women students in your grad courses ("Thank God for tenure!" you kept thinking).

I am Jay Blankness-- a sensitive, rather overbearing male graduate student who demanded to be admitted to your most recent seminar which was examining recent tendencies in lesbian porn. Forced to endure your condescending, irrational version of Marxist feminist approach in the seminar, I have further been subjected to repeated harassment by the other students in the class, of whom obviously get wet just waiting for you to show up each week to "whip them into shape" as you jokingly once put it.

Eventually expelled from your class, I began a quick spiral downwards that landed me out on the street, nearly all of my precious books sold to make ends me. Tonight was the final straw. It began with me having to sell my prized possessions--including an autographed copy of Norman Mailer's The Naked and the Dead ("For Jay, a REAL MAN--never let any twat tell you you're not a great guy, Warmest regards, Norm"). Several drinks later, I impulsively went outside the cheap juke joint and began searching for the answers to my pain. I'm not sure if the crystal met I purchased helped supply any answers directly, but it definitely helped propel me out into the next phase of my search.

This phase begins, appropriately enough, in your bedroom, where I've brought you back to help start settling accounts. More specifically my plans are to doing a little reclamation job on the shattered Venus you so obviously identified with--a reCUNTstruction designed to explore possible practical applications of some of the abstract notions about the power of the phallus, collaboration, reader "responses", and border crossings. . . .

****

So there you have it. Other examples of such scenarios are available (at reduced rates) either from the publisher or directly from the author of this tale. Discretion guaranteed. Money back if not completely...satisfied.

Parting Glances

M. Christian

This is a fantasy.

Some of it I know, have experience with, have experienced. But not all—so don't worry: not all of it.

I know what a naked woman looks like, smells like, feels like. So the start I know pretty fully, completely.

The one I'm thinking of doesn't exist, so I haven't felt, smelled ... anythinged her. But I know enough to extrapolate her, build her up out of fragments of other women, other people.

Like this is built up ... extrapolated ... from what I do know.

She has dark hair, as black as soft shadows, like a soft cloud of black powder. She is a little smaller that than I am but I can't tell you if she's short or not. I see her in this fantasy as sitting cross-legged in front of me —also sitting cross-legged. I have never pictured her standing up.

She has finely planed shoulders, with the hard structure of her bones showing through. She is thin, but not a rail; I can see only a few, but not all, of those bones. The ones I see are not a bird's, but rather a woman's. Her belly is slightly round. She is light, thin, but still a very womanly, woman. She is not an ideal, not a poster or a pin-up, she is as real as my experience and my imagination can make her.

Her breasts, for instance, are not perfect. Lovely, but not perfect balls glued to her tanned chest. No, they are small and very pointed,with even a slight curve up towards small-ish, very red nipples. She is excited because of the obvious reason that she is here, in my fantasy, and I wouldn't want her otherwise. Her nipples are smaller than I usually like, but her carriage (and wanting to be here) compensates. Her hair is brown and bobbed fairly low, about shoulder level like a great furry bowl was over her fine face. She has an intensity in her that carries through her posture (shoulder's slightly back, breathing deep and steady) and her eyes.

I forgot to describe her eyes, her face. How like a man. Even in a fantasy.

She has a small face, but not a delicate one. She has a face lit with a kind of wide-eyed enthusiasm. Not a china cup, but rather just a smal and vibrant woman. Despite the pale gleam of her body, her face is slightly tan, perhaps a genetic echo to an ancestry on the shores of the Mediterranean. Her lips are full and rich, her nose a pleasant bulb, her cheeks of grand architecture, her eyes—her eyes mirror my own, sitting across from her. This is important.You wait and see, this is important.

Her eyes are rich brown pools hiding fading mirrors. If I look very, very carefully (and very, very long) I can see myself, bubbled by her corneas, and my own eyes, staring back.

Her legs are runner's lean. I can't see any details of her cunt, her pussy, as she has a small but thick mat of hair. But I know it 'cause I invented her, or at least assembled her from real women. Her lips are dark and plush (a flower metaphor obvious), and her clit is like a candy-red marble.

We are sitting on plastic. Sometimes it's a thick sheet of Plexiglass between us and a raw, hardwood floor. Sometimes, when I'm in that mood, it's a blue plastic tarp. Other times (that mood) it's several black trash bags, taped down to a rough concrete floor—like we're sitting there at the bottom of an empty swimming pool. If I'm really into it(and in that mood), I can all but feel the massive scratchiness of the cement as I shift my ass on the plastic; smell the latent pinch of chlorine; or the insect drone of flickering overhead fluorescents and their distant, flashing inconsistencies.

This is a very vivid fantasy.

I sit across from her.

Me?

This is easy, let me look in the mirror (told you some of this was true): long black hair slightly thinning on top; goatee; sharp nose with a (some say cute) bulb at the end; two piercings in left ear; bad teeth;tall (5/11); thin (145); hairless chest; hairy legs; small tattoos(Japanese for Change, red lightning bolt), and an eight inch cock.

So, we sit: cross-legged, naked, looking into each other's eyes. At some invisible, all but unnoticeable clue that passes between us, glances to glances, we both reach to our right and pick up a scalpel.

This is my fantasy, so I start first.

I touch the blade to her sternum, the gentle depression where her ribs start and bend back around towards her back. Her small breasts make a shallow valley that shows off her bones quite well. Her ribs all but invisible but this tiny plate that is the center of her chest shows clearly, is just a few skin layers deep.

Holding the scalpel carefully, I touch its point to this magical spot. I do not cut, I just touch her, there, at first—just the weight of the knife itself pushing down against her.

A bead of blood forms where surgical, sterile, steel touches skin. The blood is so red it's almost black in its thickness, its richness. It swells up from inside, obscuring completely the tip of the scalpel, the cut it has made with its barely perceptible weight.

I wait, for a moment, till the blood was gathered itself into an almost perfect sphere. Then, with artistic—no—with culinary skill, I pull the blade away and turn it to catch the drop of her blood. With circus balance, I bring it to my lips, open my mouth, and touch it to my tongue.

The scalpel bites the top of my tongue, the pain a flash-bulb through my body as current zaps my spine. I taste metallic salts as I feel something cold and sharp press against my chest.

My eyes have shut against the pain, the revelation of her blood mixing with my own, the tasting of her blood on my tongue. I open them and glance down, being very, very care-ful not to move. I look down just in time to see her pull her own knife away from my chest. On the tip of her own is a tiny drop of myself, a rich, red dot. A tiny spot on my chest burns like a flame is hovering over my sternum.

She takes the knife into her mouth, wraps her lips around the handle then pulls it out. She smiles wide and makes a satisfied yummy noise,then wipes the blood from her cut lips, making them redder than tasteless lipstick. A drop, I see, I watch, forms at one corner and very quickly runs to land almost on her nipple, on the pale slope of a breast.

Carefully, I put my knife aside and lick her blood from her tit. Metal and sweaty salts. Against my bearded chin her nipple wrinkles in excitement and presses harder against me.

I pull away and retrieve my scalpel. We both hold our knives.

I touch mine to her chest again, just a bit above the small red bead that is her blood seeping out from the cut. I take the knife and press gently down, just a little harder, letting more than anything the minuscule weight of the scalpel cut down into her. I don't know if she makes a sound as the knife slices into her skin because my attention is not on her voice but on her skin, parting before me.

She cuts beautifully. The tension of her breasts and the tightness of her skin pulls magnificently at the small incision. An inch, maybe two. No more. Save the best for last. The skin parts and blood starts to flow—first as a parade of dark periods along the fainter white of the cut, but then, as they drop and touch, they flow—sluggishly against the incline of her chest, but then a bit faster. A drop leaves the cut and splashes, thick, on her belly, forming a single Japanese brushstroke. Maybe it has a meaning, somewhere.

For me, it has a clear one: pleasure.

My chest bursts into flame, all the concentrated burning of a sunburn ina single cut from top to bottom along my breastbone. The heat climbs up the ladder of sensation: burn, itch, ache, fire ... a quick succession of feeling as my body samples being parted by her own skin knife. My breath starts to come in quick swallows and my head is full of pressurized helium. I do not speak, so I do not know if my words would come out high and twisted.

Something hot, like molten chocolate lands on my hard cock. A word about my cock: it strains and bobs up and down, the head moving like a buoy in a rough sea. It is a hardness of when you're sixteen and think—anything— about sex. It would be a painful erection, a throbbing one, if I didn't feel the burning of the cutting on my chest more. By being only less painful, my straining cock looses to the blood dripping from my chest, the parting of my skin.

Of course not chocolate. My own thick blood dropping down.

I take my knife and touch it again, just above the red line I have drawn on her skin. This time I press down, I add pressure to the act. My knife drops down through her skin, what seems like miles. I expect, but do not get, bone. The knife drops into the skin, and I pull, gently, downwards.

It parts more of her, reveals more of her body mechanical. I see, as the knife drops down and her skin pulls itself apart along the line, the fainter white of the interior of her skin, the thick red of her insides.The blood flows freely now, but only as free as thick, healthy, blood can. It has to push against its own coagulation. Drops land on her little belly and begin to dot her public hair like black seeds falling from a tree.

I watch her open for me.

The wound is not deep, but my eyes are drawn to the details of it: the red but almost black of her blood as it seeps and trails down, the rainbow of skin types that show as the cut opens up. The richer red of the inner beauty of her, the deepness of her. Watching her bleed, staring at her blood and tissue essence I wonder how far down I'd have to cut to find her, to release the person that must be somewhere inside this bleeding meat.

Waves of pain surge from my own chest. Her knife, her knife—

Pain isn't a word anymore, and it fades from even being a concept. Words like heat, fire, agony drift through my thoughts, sticking for maybe only a moment, with the moment, but then fall aside. I feel my body open. I feel parts of me that have never seen daylight open up and bloom. I see a rose, a blood flower, and think of myself as grow-ing,expanding outward into the sun. The pain is a physical thing, no more transitory or distant like other kinds of pain. The feelings that I receive play with definition just as they play with my consciousness, distorting meanings and expectations. For a moment the wound in my chest is burn-ing, and I see waves of heat flicker past my eyes. Next it is a terrible tightness, my own body tension of being violated by her knife, and my arms feel ready to lock and quake with rigidity. Then it is chilling cold, and my skin feels brittle— cracking up into my heart and lungs. The hurt is a throbbing ache in my chest.

Liquid falls onto my cock—which I can't feel at all. I am only dimly aware of it through the slight temperature dif-ference between it and my blood, falling onto it.

I look through the fog of pain and body crisis and see her, and her wound. I lean forward, and the pain from my chest explodes in a rippling wave of tension and heat, but, still, I do lean forward—till the heat from her own exposed inner self rises in front of my eyes like a boiling pot on a stove. I feel her life streaming up from the cut I have made in her chest, I see her life flowing down from it to fall on her belly and cunt hairs. I smell it, a metallic smell in the air.

I stick my tongue out and rest it on the bottom of the cut. Instantly I am alive with the taste of her—the copper saltiness of fresh, exposed blood. I lick slowly upwards, exploring the thin canyon I have carved into her. I feel her skin part ever so gently as I draw my tongue tip between her breasts, riding the thin line, lubricated by her blood.

As I do this, I rise till I kneel. As I do this, my cock grazes her stomach, slips on the heavy drops of blood that have fallen, are falling, there.

I move back.

Her lips are soft but strong. They glide along the blood slicking my chest, outlining the line she has cut into me in strobing ache. She stops at the bottom and raises herself up. Her lips are painted the red of Aztec princesses. Her kiss is the copper/salt of childhood—the ritual of sucking on cuts to make the pain go away. Her tongue dances with my own as my blood drips lightly, mixed with our saliva, and falls with more fluidity on the head of my cock.

She breaks the kiss. Her lipstick of my blood is smeared. It looks like she'd been eating a cranberry pop or something—

—either that or me.

She returns to the slice in my chest and again traces it, this time from bottom to top, but this time her tongue emerges from her firm lips and pushes, hard, down against the cut. It feels like she is tonguing my heart. I feel my pulse through the blood seeping from the cut, feel the heat in pulsing waves of tension and warmth. It takes her a stabbing,aching eternity to make it from the bottom (a special sharp jab as the skin strains to tear) to the top (an echoing stab, a twinge that straightens me and pops my back).

She pulls back.

I reach out my hand and stroke her delightful belly, painting her with her blood, my blood. I ache to look down at our laps, our stomachs, and see the colors of her and I mixing together to make us. What color do we make, this little woman and I? Is it the same, red, or is it something else, something rare and special. Is our blood purple, shimmering, shining? I save the mystery for later, maybe another time, another fantasy. In this one, I am captured by her eyes.

I lean forward, watching myself approach in her brown pools.

Our kiss is hot, burning. Hot because of our steaming bodies, our roaring genitals. It is burning because our arms entwine with each other and pull us together to touch cut to cut, and deep, hidden, flesh to deep, hidden flesh.

We are connected by our slices. We are together.

My hand falls to her curly hairs, as hers falls to mine. I cup my hand gently and deftly part her puffy, pillow lips to find the hot spot of her clit. It vibrates at a slightly higher rate than my own painful erection. With some of her blood, and my blood, that has fallen through her tangle, I stroke it lovingly.

Her hand has dropped to my cock and she grips it hard, like it is the only thing that is holding her to the earth. It is slippery from our blood, but she manages to get a good grip. At first she just squeezes, hard, and the dull ache rises through me, almost eclipsing the burning from my cut, but then she starts to stroke.

My hand is fine and quick, precise and artful. I paint her clit with her own blood. I try to be careful and cautious. I tickle, stroke, and caress her red (very red) marble.

She-jacks-me-off! With a power normally claimed only by power tools she slams her hand up and down my burning cock! Up! Down! She beats her tunneled fist against the root of my cock, matting and compressing my hairs into a thick swamp of steaming blood! She tries to pull my cock off by squeezing harder as she nears the head! The strain brings tears to my eyes and tries to pull me up off my own legs and into a kneeling position—either that or tear my cock off (more blood! more blood!)!

I push myself down and concentrate on her own pearly clit. I circle it with a gentle finger (no mean act) and fondle it with the plush tip of another. I bathe and wash it in her cunt juice and our blood. I pet her, precisely roam the gentle folds of her, and explore her sex with careful, soft fingers. Beyond my own screaming wound, my tearing cock, I listen to her soft whines and whimpers as I paint her a come with my fingertip, create something out of quick, subtle touches and quick, hard taps that will grow and erupt inside her.

My come—does just that: It is a roaring that falls from somewhere inside my brain and crashes down through my body—leaving twitching muscles and sobbing limbs. It falls like rocks down a great metal pipe, crashing through me with pleasure and more pain than I can stand. I scream into her face, a lion's call of bestial, furious pleasure riding a wave of agony.

My jism paints her little belly, mixing white and red into sticky pink.

She screams as I do, her body twitching and jerking from the currents bolting through her small body. She jumps back and forth, thrashing, shoulders, spine, head this way and that, and whipping my face and chest with her hair.

About this time is when I come, too—thinking me and her, relishing in my fantasy, lost in it.

A fantasy—

Often, very often, when I pull this one out of my inventory, I feel sad that it can't be nothing but one.

But other times, many other times, I am so relieved that it just remains one.

The Game

A.L. Reed

A-D-A-M-A-N-T.

The tiles click into place one by one. The board is set on the carpet between us, so the words slide a little now and then. Your fingers, raw from dish washing and the weather, grip each plasticized square lightly. I am fascinated by your fingernails, chewed down, worn out. You've never worn nail polish, in all the time I've known you. No makeup of any kind. Makes me look like a clown, you say. I can't stand the extra layers.

Which makes sense. You are definitely not about layers. The moment you step in the door, shoes come off, hair comes down. You fight your way out of panty hose, flinging them away, to end up draped on the headboard, or half-hidden under the dresser. Before they're off, a glimpse of flesh constrained, reminding me of times when you have kept me wrapped in nylon ropes, spread wide, dripping onto the bed as your mouth wraps my cunt up just as neatly. After the panty hose, you begin to unzip the skirt.

I am a silent observer to this process; it's understood that I mustn't speak to you for at least half an hour after you get home from work. You're irritable, in need of silence. So I just watch, as the black skirt is stepped out of, the striped blouse carefully hung up, the only item you take care with because, as I know, you hate to iron. Your panties, black and unfrilled, uncomplicated, cling to the curves of your ass, cutting into the skin a bit. I want to slip my fingers under the elastic, pull fabric upwards and taut, press my mouth against one smooth cheek.

These are not appropriate thoughts to be having while you're kicking my ass at Scrabble. I try to focus, laying down my own tiles. I-N-E on the end of your seven-letter triple-word. Paltry. I have never won this game, with you. I wonder if you know why I continue playing it. It is the sound of the tiles, that private snicking. The scratch of the pencil on paper, quiet like a fingernail drawn down my thigh. Your fingers, full of words. I wish to be a small tan tile, picked up, laid down, arranged. By you.

You bend your head over your tile rack, mouth drawn

thoughtfully into a line. This motion again reminds me of the way you come undone at the end of your working day. It is precisely the same look you give me, once you're comfortable. Usually I have situated myself in the corner, by then, head leaning against the wall as I watch. The look is assessing. You know I have missed you all day, skulking around the apartment. You are aware of your own nakedness, and know that I am too, and you are deciding, in that moment, whether to cover it up again or let me explore it. Explore me with it. And in what way.

But first, the undressing. The moments of promise, before. The pursing of your mouth, now, means I have a few more moments to imagine it as you decide what word will bring the game to an end, or near an end. All I can see on my own rack is one tile away from suggestiveness in each case: U,N, T, F, K, L, I. All the C's are already in play. My eyes go unfocused, visualizing.

Your body appears quickly, a magic trick. Skin pale from winter or reddened, in summer, because you know you can't tan but keep trying anyway. I know that skin, I have been allowed access to it, bit by bit, over the last year. At first just your face, and hands. Those strong, worked hands. And then neck, and the feel of a leg. Eventually everything.

The bra vanishes, your small breasts spilling out, and you sigh relief, tossing the slightly frayed scrap away. Your nipples, prominent, the nipples of a larger-breasted woman. Large, dark aureoles. I have felt them scraping over my own body, nudging their way into secret places. Rubbing against my own, smaller nipples. Parting the swollen mouth of my cunt, exploring like fingers, pressed to my clit. Fed teasingly into my sucking opening, while my hips strain upwards, wanting more.

You never give me what I want...too soon.

Clicksnick. Your tiles fall into place, guided by fingers that have probed and poked, scratched and sated every inch of me. You pinch the tiles like you pinch my flesh, sometimes, little sharp motions up my thighs, hips, finally moving to my own breasts to kneed and pull. Your body rests atop mine, in those times, the rough wetness of your pussy grinding against my leg. There is no way I can finish this game. I'm just staring, watching your hands, not daring to look at your face, which will be smug. Shining with knowledge of my thoughts. You do know why I play this game.

Suddenly your hand moves away, last tile down, and the words vanish. You have seized a corner of the board, tipped it up, sending the tiles sliding off. The room is too warm, my eyes are frozen open—colored, naked squares imprinted on them. Like the evenings when you come home from work,the game has officially been declared over for now, words stripped away. A rustling sound, one I know very well, comes from where you are now standing. The sound of clothes, whispering to the floor.

A moment later, the board is no longer empty. Your fingers twist in my hair instead of in letters. My face is guided, mouth urged into place.Your legs spread out to either side, pale arches encompassing me. Suddenly, I know exactly what the sounds the tiles make are, to me. They sound like the word lap, whispered like you whispering a command. There on the floor, reaching to where you are spread out on the board, my wordless tongue obeys.

JFK2
David Cronenbergs Sequel to Oliver Stone's JFK:
an outline in 5 scenes

m.i. blue

SCENE ONE:

BLAM! The bullet erupts from the barrel of the Italian-made rifle and rockets toward its target!

...as John Fitzgerald Kennedy waves to the people of Dallas he's thinking of the soft pale weight of Marilyn's milky white breast in the palm of his hand. Closing his eyes for a moment, the air humid on his face, he feels the brush of her platinum hair across the insides of his thighs, hears her whisper his name, feels the cock stiffen in his pants...

When the steel-sheathed bullet smacks into the back of his head, he comes like World War III.

SCENE TWO:

John Conally, the Governor of Texas, is dreaming that he's swimming across a river of brains. In the basement of the hospital, Kennedy's at the swarming center of a persistent hive of coroners. There's a flurry of steel instruments there: it's amazing that doctors aren't cutting off each others' fingers in there eagerness to get at the dead man. Flecked with small carnage, the sheet is drawn back off the shoulders, then drawn back again over the chest, turned down into the lap, then finally removed altogether, in grisly striptease. Some members of this macabre entourage are glancing surreptitiously at the dead president's massive member. Some of them smirk and whisper rude comments to one another from behind their upraised hands:

"No wonder they called him Big John..."

"That's going to be one bereaved widow, boy..."

In the confusion, the brain is set down, then the heart and lung and kidney; set down, oozing, on porcelain surfaces then forgotten. A voice drones on into a microphone about blue exit wounds and pale bone fragments while a lone high voice tries again to stop chortling, and fails.

SCENE THREE:

"His *brain?!?* What do you mean they lost his brain, Private?!? How the hell do you lose a *brain?!?*" Then, sudden and shocking as Armageddon itself, the general slaps the boy in front of him with a hand as big and smooth as Dean Rusk. The soldier's hand going up to his red cheek in surprise, eyes wild as a caged beast's. The sounds of the general's heavy breathing, that sharp painful intake of breath. Testosterone's musky scent heady in the air. The two frozen caricatures seem to sway toward each other in that electrified atmosphere. For a minute their eyes grow humid with some nebulous intensity...

"Sir! They don't know Sir!" Back stiff again, confused eyes forward again like headlights, but a strange stirring in his loins. Then, quietly: "It's just...lost, Sir. The surgeons said..."

The general leans in as though he were going to kiss the boy, curses "ahh!", then veers away with the prehistoric inscrutability of a shark and impends out of the room. The confounded soldier throws the edge of his hand against his forehead, the sound of the slap still ringing in his ears like a mosquito.

Minutes passing.

Alone in the office.

Arm growing tired waiting for the salute that will release the one still welded to his forehead.

Sweat breaking out now on the boy's rigid body like a rock growing new wet grass.

SCENE FOUR:

In the glow from the light coming through an X-ray of a human skull on the wall... In the empty silent autopsy room... President Kennedy's **BRAIN** crawls out from behind a metal gurney making the slithery squishing sounds of flaccid submarine life!

Already it has begun to regenerate: A snaky spinal cord now propels the brain forward in abrupt, wormy strenuous spurts. A kind of gray foetal hair has sprouted from the cerebrum along the parietal lobe. One blue milky eye, reconstituted, hangs from a stalk and is dragged along glistening behind it. Like some gelatinous mishap, a new penis has begun to bubble dead flesh at the end of those chitinous vertebrae.

Kennedy's brain is leaving a sticky mire of brown-flecked gray goo behind it, the path of some antediluvian snail across yellowed linoleum. It moves in a determinedly straight line, as though it knows where it is going...

SCENE FIVE:

Lightning strikes blue ozone! A crackle of thunder over the night graveyard, the sound of something moving wet dirt. Like tossing the tiny bones of small birds against a windowpane, the wind lashes a moment of unseasonable rain across the headstones: Forest Lawn, cemetery of the stars.

Kennedy's brain burrows into the fecund earth, a gruesome annelid thing, below a monument inscribed with the only name she'd ever really needed, the one they'd chosen for her. The president has been transmogrified, his form that of a wet centipede covered in bony carapace. Quivering pale feelers push it down through the hole it's eaten in the coffin: *"MARILYN...MARILYN... I'M HERE..."* The incipient cartilaginous penis has begun to stiffen in anticipation.

With a sound like a rotten slab of meat being thrown into an oily puddle, the wet husk of the president plops down on the dead actress, twitching...

Blue corpse eyes shatter open like flashbulbs in her dead white face! Green embalming fluid drools from the corners of the infamous, preternaturally-red lips! She speaks!

"BOBBY...BOBBY...IS THAT YOU...?!?"

They kiss...such as they can.

Soundtrack up...fade to black.

San Pedro, 1994

m.i. blue

This is a true story.

Back in March of 1994 I was living in LA, going to school, and trying to make ends meet driving a meatwagon for Mitchell-Meyer Mortuary picking stiffs up at the Coroner's Office or from homes or one of the hospitals, mostly around San Pedro. For houses and places where people expected formal we used the hearse but most pickups at hospitals and the coroner we just used a brown unmarked Dodge Tradesman van it was easier on gas and upkeep and you could pickup more bodies besides. I was making $8 an hour and working graveyard so I could still go to school in the afternoons. I've always had a morbid streak and hell I was a writer. Where do you think you're going to find better material: working for a funeral home or flipping grease at Jack in the Box?

The intern at San Pedro General had smiled at me as I zipped the ugly old dude into the black body bag and put him on the collapsible gurney. All this stuff got old pretty fast when you got right down to it but I preferred what I was doing to this ugly old dead dude to picking up the dead babies. We had a special like suitcase for the babies. You'd come in to collect them at the hospital, set down and open up this case, they'd hand you the dead kid and inside it were these straps you'd strap the dead baby in, close it up and walk out like a salesman or something. The first time I went for a pickup on a dead baby is when I started finding the whole thing ridiculously funny I mean there's only two ways to feel about that kind of thing and crying about it all the time's the other one. Anyway, the intern'd said the name of the corpse twice before I realized he was talking about *that* Bukowski. The writer. *The Notes From A Dirty Old Man* man. I mean Buk. Bukowski. Man, I should have known from that nose of his that huge potato nose. I liked this guy. I mean i'd always wanted to be like that guy he really knew how to write about beer and life and shit. He was drunk all the time. I mean he lived it man.

"Betcha he went out with a beer in his hand," I said to the intern.

"Naw, he died right here," the intern told me. We both looked at his face nodding kind of solemn for a second before I zipped the bag up.

So there I was cruising the streets of San Pedro with Buk's dead body in my van nearly midnight in March you could tell it was March cause you could hear the wind rustling the tops of the palm trees slightly if you hung your head out the window of the van a little. The noise had a hollow brushing sound to it. Eerie, in an 80-degree kind of way.

San Pedro's lower middle class on a harbor. In the day sometimes the sun bakes most of the smell away but at night you can smell the sea and the boats. You can smell the liquor stores and guys sucking shortdogs the bodegas and taco stands and marine shops. Hard work and weak beer. Lots of bars with names like **The Anchor** and **Deep Six**.

Wow. Henry fucking Chinansky in my car. Hank. Buk. I'd never had anybody famous in the back. And I don't know I wanted to memorialize it or something I mean this was Bukowski. The beer poet. So I stopped and got a six-pack of Lucky, popped one and kept it low between my legs as I drove us both back to the mortuary.

Now our embalming room never really smelled too bad. Hospitals had that hospital smell, but even the worst hospital morgue smell was nothing next to the coroner's office it was awful man it smelled like a mix of pinesol, formaldehyde and wet decay something like a cross between burning rubber and the smell of cooking-up heroin. Or so i've heard. The heroin I mean. I tell you it smelled bad all the time, man. Coroner's office had stiffs coming out of their ears all the time and you could always smell em no matter what they did to clean up. And there were always flies buzzing around. Lots of em. Even at night...which I found particularly creepy. But the embalming room at Mitchel-Meyer? They kept it real clean and washed-out. It had a kind of cool and creepy feeling to it.

One night I'd fucked my girlfriend Cecily in there on the slab she'd really got off on it. I thought about calling her up and fucking her with Bukowski here dead in the room with us that'd get her hot. Hell, it would be a kind of memorial to the old dead Barfly guy. Popping another Lucky, I took a swig and unzipped the body bag then rolled him out of there onto the embalming table. It didn't take much to imagine the way Cecily'd giggle and light up all scared and breathe and yell out if I put it to her from behind while she was staring right into his decrepit old dead face. He wasn't heavy but he was kind of stiff and it took me a couple of minutes to finally get him on the table face up. I took off the thin little hospital gown that Buk was still wearing and tossed it toward the big plastic ashcan. Bukowski's flesh had that putty feeling to it. Pliant like a silicon boob, but not warm at all not cold exactly but definitely not warm. Yeh, Cecily, I was saying to myself. Picturing her.

I finished the lucky and crumpled the can in the direction of after the hospital gown. When I dialed Cecily's number I was sort of playing with myself, stroking it through the Levis in time to each ring: one... two... three... four... five... Fuck.

I took my pants and jockeys off and my dick was rock hard from thinking about Cecily. I had a bunch of big rubber bands in my pocket, sometimes you had to use them to stop seepage from the bodies. I wrapped one around the base of my balls and my dick like a cockring and started jacking off, thinking: this is too cool I'm jacking off in the same room with Charles Bukowski's corpse man! I wanted a camera to memorialize this. Like take a picture of me with a big boner with my arms around the shoulders of this dead poet's corpse. That'd make a great cover for my first chapbook!

I imagined Cecily taking the pictures and it really got me off I started laughing.

I took a cool picture of Cecily I have out of my wallet, rolled the poet kind of bending over the edge of the table, and laid her picture on his pale blue back thinking hard about that time we'd made it in here. Spread his old dead butt and hocked a big one on his sphincter, tried to rub it in. Didn't smell too pretty but what the fuck. Staring into Cecily's brown eyes, I tried to stick my dick in Bukowski's ass but it wouldn't give any. Maybe it was rigor mortis or something. And then his center of gravity must have been off he slipped to the floor like a sack, face up again, and I had to jump out of the way. The rubber band was digging into my scrotum and the veins in my dick were as hard as polyurethane, my dick was all engorged and red and all. I chugged down another Lucky looking down at that ugly face and that's what must have given me the idea. I went over to the table and opened a drawer with the surgical instruments in it. Big bone spreaders. Trocars, which are a big metal syringes with a big long needle you stick into the organs to release fluids and gasses and shit. I took a scalpel, went back to Hank fucking Bukowski and slit some cartilage. With his septum cut like, and if I held myself sort of like doing pushups, I could actually stick my dick in his big red potato nose and fuck him that way. When I'd stuck it in as far as I could his eyes like came open in his face then every time my dick thrust in his eyebrows would go up and his clouded-over eyes would pop out. Geeze. I don't know why but it really got me hot I went faster and faster and Buk waggled his eyebrows like Groucho Marx until I came.

That's how much I admired the guy.

I mean, I knew he'd understand.

Someday I want to write just like him.

Robo-Hank

Harold Jaffe

SAFE

Celibacy
Massage * Hugging
Mutual masturbation * Dry kissing
Body-to-body rubbing * Fantasy
Voyeurism * Exhibitionism

RISKY

Anal or vaginal intercourse with condom
Deep-mouth ("French") kissing
Oral sex (if stopped before climax)
External watersports * Cunnilingus

UNSAFE

Anal or vaginal intercourse
without a condom
Semen or urine in mouth
Sharing sex instruments or needles
Blood contact * Fisting * Rimming

After reviewing this flier in the cab of his Toyota truck, Hank folded it and stuck it in his wallet, but then he took it out again and had another look. "Deep-mouth kissing" is risky! What are you supposed to do, put a burlap bag over your face, then kiss? He stuck the flier back in his wallet.

On TV a few nights ago he'd seen part of a flick with Cary Grant and Ingrid Bergman which had a lot of kissing, and Cary Grant had his lips tightly closed the whole time. But that's Hollywood. Besides, Cary Grant was gay, right? Wasn't he living in sin in Beverly Hills with that cow-boy-actor Randolph Scott?

Hank reached around his body for the seat belt, but then

said fuck it. Started his Toyota truck.

The other morning, Sunday, Hank heard one of his neighbors, packed into the cab of his Toyota truck with his wife and two pink little kids, say to another neighbor:

"Burt, I just love my little Toyota truck."

Burt, who is deaf, said "wha?"

"I said I just love my little Toyota truck."

Burt said "wha" a second time, cupping his hand to his ear.

But the neighbor was off to church.

And Hank was off to his assignation. I meant to say date but I've been thinking of Poe lately, who, maybe you remember, wrote a tale called "The Assignation." Safe/risky/unsafe sex would not have been a problem for Poe, hopelessly impotent, but a fabulous obsessive, and one of the most flavorful authors this great nation ever produced.

Hank slipped a cassette into the tape deck: NWA (Niggahs with Attitude), a rap group with sharp teeth. He pulled onto I-5 heading north. Did I say north? I meant south, away from the polluted white 'burbs, toward Chula Vista in the direction of Mexico.

At this juncture you're probably hankering to learn more about the subject of this narrative, Hank. He's 24, OWWA (Off-White With Attitude). He's also horny, subject to depression and rumination, uneasy in Southern California. What else? Nothing else for now.

Hank is courting Luz, a Chicana from Chula Vista, 22-years-old, sharp as a whip, I'm talking head-smarts. She's foxy too, with luminous brown eyes, waist-long black hair and sexy mobile hips. (Confession: I stuck head-smarts before foxy so as not to offend my feminist readers.)

—I thought this was Hank's story. Who the freak is "I"?

—Good question, well-put. The intervening "I" is the narrator. And behind/above the "I" is still another entity which you may call the "implied author." The real author, the Ur-author, squats above the entire proceedings paring his fingernails.

Meanwhile a yellow long-bed Toyota truck on big wheels was bearing down hard on Hank. The driver was an Aryan android: barechested, shoulder-length yellow hair, moronically intent close-together grey eyes, bible and 9mm Colt

Combat Commander in the glove compartment, 12-pack of Bud on the passenger seat.

"Okay, Aryan, it's your freeway," Hank screamed at his windshield, scooting over to the right lane.

Not fast enough for the megafast 'droid, who gave Hank the finger with the same hand he was holding his can of Bud with.

Was it the finger or the *Fuhrer* salute?

Anyway Hank held his fire. His mind turned again to Luz. Smart as she is, Chicana though she is, she believes too much of the bullshit she hears: about safe sex, about virginity being back in style, about Say No to Drugs, about America is still number 1, despite mass murders, serial murders, the homeless, the racists . . . Well, Luz doesn't buy that whole package.

Safe sex is the biggie of course and Hank's been pining. He and Luz have seen each other what? Five times? And he's been shut out. True, Luz's been shut out as well, only she don't see it that way.

What have they actually done? They've kissed (shallow not deep-mouth); hugged of course; rubbed body-to-body, as the flier put it (with clothes on); and there was one back-rub, which Luz interpreted literally, kneading Hank's shoulders with clinical avidity.

—Who's responsible for this Safe/Risky/Unsafe flier anyway?

—Yahweh Himself. Actually the CDC is responsible, that's the Center for Disease Control, in Atlanta, an arm (if that's the right body part) of the federal government.

—What would CDC think of NWA?

—You may be surprised to hear that they prefer celibate middle-class whites who walk without moving their arms to niggers with attitudes.

Oh shit, Hank was in the wrong lane, had to get left, but yet another Aryan-droid in yet another Toyota truck--a customized metallic black 4x4 on big wheels--wasn't about to let him in. The 'droid whipped past with Hank switching lanes just in time.

And now Hank has a (pardon my French) hardon. Driving fast tends to do that to him. Or maybe it was thinking of Luz. Does he affect her in the same way? Does she masturbate thinking of *him?* Heck, Luz is a new-age woman, she sits in front of her PC, adding and subtracting from her database. Have you ever tried to jack off in front of a database?

—*Question: How could the "New Age," white and scrupulous, have metastasized south to Chula Vista, full of brownskins with vivid eyes and nothing-larger-than-a-one in their pockets?*

—*Well, how did AIDS find its way to Texarkana?*
—*Related question: What is Hank doing with Luz in the first place? True, Hank is off-white with attitude, but, hell, he's whiter than her.*
—*Well, your ass is whiter than your face, ain't it? Hank likes her, Hoss. Her luminous black eyes are full of passion, she smiles at him in a way that cuts to his heart, her hair is never not fragrant. Shoot, Hank even likes her restraint, her graceful restraint, because it seems provisional, it guards her powerful passions, which once left unguarded will flood him.*
—*Yeah? When will that be?*

Now NWA was doing "Fuck Tha Police." Hank rolled up his window and slapped his thigh in rhythmic complicity. Not that young Hank had anything against the police, some of his best friends were affiliated with the police: Miss Marple, Sam Spade, Kojak, Colombo . . .
Fuck Tha Police.
If it weren't for the strict copyright protection, Hank'd quote the lyrics, but that's risky, unsafe even. You cross the corporate bigs they make you bleed / stick yo foot in they ass / they make you bleed / There's other ways fuck up the corp / fuck up the bigs / dig / yawl plant a seed / slip it in their martini / grin like they good nig / slip it in their coffee / slip it in their French wine / grin like they good shine / yo / sprinkle it with boolsheeit /

Hank, still on I-5, was passing through National City, famous for its "mile of cars" and about ten minutes due north of Luz, with her fragrant hair (and her head-smarts). Is she primping for her date with Hank, or is she sitting in front of her database thinking Real Estate? Did I say that Luz just got her Real Estate license? She's feels real comfort-able about the prospect of selling Chula Vista.

—Feminist intervention: What's Luz doing with Hank? He's off-white, sure. But he's eccentric/phallocentric, shut him the fuck up, narrator.
—Though I'm the narrator, maybe even the implied author, in accord with poststructuralist protocol I won't presume to speak with authority. Let me say merely that if you muffle/decurve/resect/derail/delete
Hank . . .

It's a moot point, reader/scanner. Hank never got out of National City. Yet another Toyota pickup, metallic blue, long-bed, on big-big wheels, with a bumper sticker that read **RACE WAR, RIOT--TRY IT!**, got him from behind as he was trying to change lanes, totalled his truck, no way that puppy's gonna be glued together after that shit.

And, oh yeah, killed off-white Hank dead.

Actually the killer truck just nicked Hank's bumper, but that was enough to set him spinning onto the shoulder, into the arid hill recently planted with oleanders: yellow, pink, salmon, blue. They resist fuel emissions, smog, most of your industrial pollutants, plus they beautify the landscape, what's left of it.

Yo! Don't go to that refrigerator! It's the next frame, as in a Schwartzenegger flick, and Hank's not dead at all. He's **ROBO-HANK**, an electronic system of organized delirium, with trace elements of Hank's human brain and passions and nausea, but void of sentimentality, which Norman Mailer once said is the "emotional promiscuity of those who lack sentiment."

Unlike Mailer, and Mailer's mega-male-mentor, Hemingway, **ROBO-HANK**'s body is bionic, and he is pledged to hunt down and hamstring not just the Aryan-droids who brutalize others in service to the dominant culture, but their betters in their Beemers and Mercedes and Concordes and executive pews and state-of-the-art golf carts . . .

When he is not jumping all over the digital face of evil, **ROBO-HANK** is travelling the lecture circuit speaking on behalf of sexual abandon. Not just speaking but presenting:

employing the latest electronic-statistical-persuasive strata-
gems to document his case for the body. At first it's an
incongrous sight: this muscular robot with his polytetraflu-
oroethylene skin and Max Headroom stammer contesting
the multi-tiered sexual repression. But you know what? You
get used to it, he grows on you. By the time he's finished
you want to fuck him and his kin and his kin's kin through
every teflon orifice in every alley, valley, freeway, shopping
mall and hog-farm of this great nation.

Bringing Home The Bacon

Thom Metzger

"This is God's country," Carl said, roaring at 75 mph through the petrochemical wasteland. Vast tracts of landfill, junk-yards, chemical sump-holes and slag pits; yes, this part of New Jersey was paradise. He breathed in deep: the stench of chlorine and methane and nameless molecules that ate the paint off of cars and had turned Carl's hair prematurely gray.

Marlie scrunched in closer to Carl, easing his hand up between her thighs. With her other hand she fingered the dashboard idol Carl had bought to scare off car thieves, some Santeria doodad wound round with snake vertebrae. "Mucho Mojo," he'd snarl at the neighborhood kids who eyed the car enviously, "Mucho Macho Mojo."

Marlie pulled his hand out from between her legs and held it under his nose.

"Jay-sus!"

"More?"

He nodded, breathing deeply, as though the aroma came off the cork from a fine French vintage. She'd had her hand between her sweaty thighs for the last ten miles. One whiff made him drunk. A second had him in a trance.

They'd met about half an hour before at the Vince Lombardi Memorial Rest-stop on the Jersey Turnpike. She was sitting at a booth sucking greenish sugary foam through a swollen straw. Not exactly good-looking in the normal sense. But Carl had very little interest in the normal. Her nose was kind of flattened, with wide nostrils. Her skin had a weird pinkish cast to it. Her hair was short and curly. But the thing that got him as he walked by her was her smell: burnt bacon.

Instantly he pictured her naked, slathered in mayo, wrapped in a big wilted lettuce leaf, lolling on a bed made out of toasted white. Marlie was the one: a living BLT.

Yes, she was a porker. Not fat, but full. Not greasy, but slick. Cured to perfection. He knew that if he ran his tongue up between her thighs he'd taste salt and hickory smoke.

He was lucky: there was no free table at the rest-stop. "Mind if I sit down?"

She shrugged, nonchalant.

She understood. She already knew. Apparently there were other men who had a yen for the tangy prime slice. She took it for granted: this wasn't a weirdo, this was a guy who knew when he'd tumbled to a good thing.

They made small talk: he called himself a "chemical salvager." He ran a "redemption center," getting back the precious stuff from sludge. Silver, zinc. Even a trace of gold. She did temp work: whatever was available. A few minutes later they were on the Pike heading for Carl's place.

She took Carl's hand off the wheel again and eased it up herself again. Slightly damp, smooth, parting to let him all the way in. He wriggled two fingers into the prime slice and she slewed her ass back and forth on the hot vinyl car seat, letting out little moans and sighs. He was sure now, just by the sound, the feel of her wetness. Yes, he'd found himself a woman who'd squat and whine like a stuck pig.

Up ahead neon clustered like diseased fruit. Bugs zipped through the air like shrapnel. The noise of the traffic hurt his ears. Swamp land gave way to ranks of gasoline tanks and refinery towers. The petrochemical stink made his eyes sting and his mouth water.

He looked over at Marlie. This time, yes, this time he'd hit pay dirt.

There had been another girl, who had an insatiable desire for Italian sausage. She was a little too much, kind of lump and raw. There was another one who had just a little too much muscle. He wanted them porky, not beefy. She'd had no imagination either. He swore she'd mooed when she came the first time. Then there was the little vegetarian bimbo: too much soybeans and wheatgrass makes a woman bloated. The closest he'd gotten to the real thing was a college girl who he'd picked up after her shift at K. F. C. She stunk—beautifully—of the deep fryer, of grease and gristle and garlic. But she'd taken one look at Carl's basement chamber and bolted. No sense of adventure.

As they roared through the late summer twilight, he knew, he was absolutely sure, that this time he'd found the right one.

The car crunched over the gravel parking lot. Everybody was gone for the night. Carl shut off the engine and let Marlie curl in closer. Body heat cooking the flesh. Late August sun swelter.

She rubbed her hand on his crotch, feeling him get hard, harder, hardest. It wasn't the friction of her fingers, but the sweet animal stink that rose off her body in waves which made him so crazy.

"Here?" she said.

"No. I got something inside I want to show you." They got out, glued to each other like the last survivors from a ship-wreck. Carl fumbled for his keys. Behind this place—not much more than a corrugated steel shed, huge steel stacks rose up like headless giants, blind and idiotic. There was swamp land, a lattice of raised highways through the marsh, the buzz of mutant insects and a steady roar of planes tak-ing off and landing in Newark.

Carl undid the two bolts on the front door and disarms the alarm system. Then he led her down a dingy hallway, past the accounts office, a storeroom full of old manilla folders and discarded computer hardware, deeper into his place. He found the key he used very seldom, undid the last lock and led her down a flight of steps.

At the bottom, he hit the lights. They both winced at the brilliance: two heavy duty spotlamps hanging from the wires. In the pool of light was a huge butcher's block, a half ton of scarred, stained rock maple. A thousand knives had cut into the wood, 10,000s of pounds of raw meat had lain there, while butchers hacked and sawed. Carl had bought the block at an auction three years before and had two of his minimum-wagers haul it back to the shop after hours. "What you gonna do with this thing, Mr. Gans?" one of them said, as they got to the bottom of the steps. "Just put it over there, under the lights," he said.

He fired the men the next day, thinking of all those slaves that got killed after they built the secret passages in the Great Pyramid.

Now he led Marlie to the block. She was naked before she reached it. Pink skin from head to toe: thick hams, fleshy thighs, a heavy heaving chest. And the rank bacon perfume that emitted from between her legs. Jesus, Carl thought, if it gets any stronger in here I'll pass out.

She hoisted herself up on the butcher's block and lay there spread-eagled.

Carl grabbed his butcher's whites off the wall-peg and put them on, shaking. He could barely get the apron strings around himself, and made a crazy knot to secure them.

Then he put on a nice neat paper cap and approached Marlie, mesmerized by the dark divide between her legs. He came at her, licking his lips, smacking his teeth together, sniffing and huffing like a starved dog. She wriggled, waiting for him to make first contact. "Come on, come, Mr. Meat Man," she growled.

Carl fell to his knees at the block, grabbed both of her thighs to steady himself and pushed his rigid tongue into the hot wet jelly-spot. Salty—he was like some wild boar attracted to the salt lick. She was wild and raw. His tongue laid on the healing balm to the wet, wound opening. And the taste hit him: hard and heady. Burnt-meat, smoky, slick like a great slice of bacon. His tongue went up and down, over the oozing cooze and he felt shock waves pass through him. He started to lose consciousness as she clamped her thighs tighter around his head, a vise made of warm flesh. His tongue kept on probing. But he could hear nothing now, see nothing. The air was quickly used up in this meat prison and the darkness closed in on him. The big O hit like a tidal wave and he was dead to the world.

When he woke, Marlie was gone. He had a taste in his mouth like wet charcoal, a sodden pork rind, ash and salt. He rose from the floor and looked closely at the butcher's block. Where Marlie had lain was a puddle of shiny jelly— just the faintest shade of pale pink. He dabbed at the puddle, imagining she'd been cooked down to this human oil slick by the explosion of her orgasm. Yes indeed she'd come. He'd heard it through his thigh-muffled ears. He'd felt the quake, the shuddering, the thrashing, spasming as she came.

But now Carl was alone and soon the puddle would dry to a hard greasy stain.

He flicked off the lights. He ran his tongue around his lips, getting the last of her flavor. I won't brush my teeth, he thought, for a week.

Actually, it was a week and a half. And he only did so then because he had an important meeting with Myra Sandell, who ran a plastics plant in Rahway. If he could cut a deal with her—hauling, disposing, reclaiming her waste—

it would mean another hundred grand a year for Carl's firm.

He showered, put on his best suit, combed his hair and went to meet her at the Apollo Belaire, a pretentious restaurant with fake Greek gods out front and gold-tinted mirrors in the men's room.

Myra was in her early forties, plump, with dyed red hair and nail extensions. As Carl laid out his pick-up schedules, the E.P.A. requirements and which palms needed to be greased at the county offices, as they dickered over pricing, he kept looking at Myra's hands. Pinkish, just this side of pudgy. He wondered what they tasted like. When she off to the ladies room, his eyes were fastened on her ass. For a woman her age, she was well-proportioned below the waist. And encased in the tight business suit, her bottom curves looked about perfect. He could almost picture the trial of fumes she left behind: female hormones, body funk, the seared, slightly-charred breakfast sausage she'd been wolfing down.

He considered asking her out. He liked to think she'd climb willingly onto the butcher's block, maybe fully clothed, legs spread wide while Carl came closer, shining a bright policeman's flash between her thighs. But the contract was too juicy to mess up.

They came to an agreement and shook hands. Carl went back to his car, where he sat a while furtively licking his fingers, getting a faint hint of her breakfast. But much better was the undertaste of her skin.

Later he met a young woman who had a very peculiar odor about her. They were in line at an ATM and Carl sniffed something faintly perfumey, faintly toxic, faintly dead. He figured out quickly where the fumes were coming from: a young woman in a severe, ill-fitting suit. He turned on his charm and soon learned that she was a student at the Heisler School of Mortuary Science: lilies, formaldehyde and corpses. They went to a motel and fell on each other like hungry cannibals while 18 wheelers roared past and the weather channels droned on about low pressure systems and high water marks. When the girl shucked off her ugly polyester suit and boxy too-white panties, she was really quite lovely: with a sumptuous suction sluice that brought tears to his eyes. The sex was great; he pumped her hard and long and she thrashed at the end like a salmon caught on a fisherman's line. But they never saw each other again.

He hung out at a diner near Netcong where the air was always full of char-broiled aromas. One waitress wore she skirt way too short and he positioned himself to see all the way to the flame-red panties when she bent over at the cooler to get more non-dairy creamer. And though he tried to strike it up with her, she figured him for a loser: who else spends that much time drinking mediocre coffee? She'd have nothing to do with him.

The closest he got to Marlie was a woman who worked at the nuclear power plant in Dempster. He drove her out to her place, again late in the evening when the New Jersey stench-dusk was coming down heavy. He took her to the secret basement room and had her stand in the spotlights. She wore her one-piece bright orange boiler suit, so baggy it hid almost everything about her body. But she was game for Carl's set-up and while his boombox played a tape he'd made of a boiler room in overload (gas hissing, valves close to explosion) she slowly peeled off the bulky suit like peeling the stiff plastic wrapper off a perfect piece of fruit. She was beautiful, with well-sculpted legs and nipples hard as arrowheads.

But once he was really on her, in her, lapping at the nether notch, he realized she has absolutely no odor. Whether it was a freak of nature or she'd been sterilized by all the radiation, she was totally smell-free. She hoisted herself up on the block and he joined her. They lay 69ed in the bright arc lights. She was good and she really seemed to like Carl. But afterward, he sniffed his hands and smelled nothing but himself. A near-hit: close but no jackpot.

He kept looking.

It was about a year later, maybe even the exact anniversary of picking Marlie up, when he saw her again.

He was in the supermarket, well after midnight in that weird headachy light that stores use. Bad Muzak, thuggish teenagers wandering the aisles, an idiot janitor mopping the floor with filthy water. Carl was in the meat department looking over the big red slabs, the mountains of ground beef, the Canadian bacon, the sausages lined up like dead soldiers in a mass grave.

He got a whiff of fried pork, but thought nothing of it. This was the butcher shop after all. Then he felt her warmth and looked to his left. There she stood fingering a great wattled turkey neck through the slimy shrinkwrap.

"Hi," she said softly. Did she remember him? How could she forget him, or his butcher's block? Had she ever done it with another guy who wore a white paper cap and latex gloves?

He stammered a greeting and handed her a package of bacon as if it were a bouquet of roses.

She'd put on a little weight in the intervening year. In a tank top and cut-off jean shorts, her body looked fuller. Not fat, just more. Better. He remembered sliding his finger up between her thighs, the taste of wet smoke that lay on his tongue for days afterward.

She had her hair pulled up on top of her head and held in place with what looked like a plastic bone. He almost fell to his knees right there in front of the frozen Swedish meatball display.

They pushed her cart out to the checkout together and in twenty minutes were back in Carl's subterranean meat locker.

She eased her shorts off, wriggling a little to get them down her legs. Then she pulled her halter over her head and law back down on the hard cube of scarred maple. Carl snagged his teeth in the top of her panties and ripped them off. A wave of bacon perfume hit him like tear gas.

His tongue reached, reached further, and touched the wet knot of ginch-flesh. She shivered and raked her fingers through his hair, pulling him deeper into herself.

She almost broke Carl's neck when she came.

He didn't pass out this time, however. And though he knew he wouldn't see her again for another year, he didn't care. As he drove her back to the travel plaza, he worked his hand down inside the front of her shorts one last time. He felt the hot dampness. She moaned and ground her groin against his fingers.

He parked and she disappeared into the travel arcade. Carl sat there for an hour, thinking, remembering. A couple of screaming brats woke him from his trance. He got out his wallet. Then he circled the date on the little plastic calendar and told himself he wouldn't mind waiting another year.

Without Pain, Without Death

Jasmine Sailing

"Everyone knows what happens when you stick a fork into a lit toaster," Annette sneered, rolling turquoise eyes and flipping stringy orange hair to taunt her companion. The gesture went unnoticed.

"Lit? Yeah. Pop, pop, sizzle, and then you fry, and then you die. But I didn't die."

"Sometimes I want to pop you when you talk like that."

They were friends, definitely bonded by pain. Trauma, emotional turmoil, crippled twins of spirit. Sometimes Annette seriously thought Valerie was a nut case. Or more of one than she was, anyway.

Unfazed, Valerie was lovingly caressing the tongs of a fork and, occasionally, dragging their tips across the soft flesh of her wrist. Her emerald eyes had a way of seeming too bugged under contrasting short-cropped black hair when she was focused—they were almost creepy. Eventually, she shrugged. "Sex isn't sex, without pain, without death. Without transcendence above it all."

"If you want death, you'll get it at that rate. Electrocute yourself."

"Pegged it, sweetie. I do want death. I want to be fucked to death without sex. What other way is there to go? Life is filth, and we are the unpure. The contaminated."

Sex, in itself, wasn't unclean. Breeding, yes. The world no longer needed that action and humans were far too unpure for procreation. Lust, yes. Pointless copulation, fucking, nothing but bodies thrust together for physical satisfaction. Sweat, semen, lubrication, saliva (and tears, all too often tears). Wasted moisture for non-lofty goals. Sex could perform higher functions, though, it could be transcendence. Or so Valerie had been trying to convince Annette ever since they'd met in a rape trauma group ages ago. She'd been right about endorphins, anyway, and about burning away the shame.

"If you have the pain," Valerie had confidently stated, "you lose the shame. You don't have that element of sex for physical enjoyment only. And with that pain comes the endorphins, the morphine of the mind. The gateway to true release. You should try it sometime."

Annette hadn't wanted to try *anything* remotely connected to sex. The shame ever burned in her mind, the fear of enjoyment in despicable acts. How could she wittingly take pleasure from something as dirty... something so hateful and cruel... something which could be served only as punishment? Months had passed before she could be coaxed to the point of painful masturbation, and there only as proof that fire can truly burn away shame.

Burning herself was nothing new. Sometimes the mind bled, the mind needed a release for pain. Tears could never leak fast enough, screams could only be smothered by a pillow. At such times it was nothing extraordinary for her to speed up the release by slicing little nicks in her arms. The blood ran freely, pre-coagulation, and she felt some of the emotional pain released. It also worked with burning. Stubbing cigarettes out in her legs, practicing scarification by jamming heated metal rings into her wrists. Of course the latter never really worked, the burn would poof out into a blobular mess rather than the intended pattern. The pain healed her though. It was her own personal version of Jesus.

It was never questioned that Valerie knew about the scars, she had her own batch of them etched across her various limbs. Annette didn't have a habit of bleeding in front of her though. Or at least not until she was asked to.

"Why, do you get a cheap thrill out of watching?"

Valerie smiled sadly. "I don't believe in cheap thrills. Do your thing and I'll do mine. Just trust me, okay?"

Annette shrugged, settled onto her back, pulled up her sleeve, and began lightly pressing her cigarette cherry into random patches of skin. The sizzle was the sound of Heaven, the smell that of purified flesh. She was absorbed enough to ignore her friend's brief exit from the room, and the re-entrance. She was absorbed enough to barely notice Valerie putting on her version of mood music: Cosey Fanni Tutti's *Time to Tell* ("A sexual performance artist, female obviously," she'd been told). She wasn't absorbed enough to ignore it as her skirt was scooted up and her friend's left pointing finger was inserted into her vagina.

"It's cold! It burns!" She shrieked, knowing that didn't bother her so much as the intrusion did. She didn't think she was capable of being physically attracted to anyone. Val? She supposed she admired her physique. Tall, slender, graceful yet tough. It was something to wish for in lieu of her own small and overly stout form. Admiration was one thing, though, she had never looked at Val sexually. She didn't wish to look at anything that way.

"Just keep playing with your cigarette, sweetie."

She tried, but now found herself distracted for different reasons. The flesh of Valerie's finger could have been a frigid icicle, numbingly cold, but it left a trail of fire. Freezing, burning, numbness, pain. She absorbed the feeling, relaxed into it, let go her feelings of degradation. This wasn't sex, this was a friend showing her a new experience. She could feel the bubbling patter in her brain, the chemical reworking, the reputed endorphins, the electricity growing in her body. Eyes closing, body trembling, mind exploding. It was probably (would be definitely, had she the experience to verify it) the first orgasm she'd ever had, and she didn't feel guilty about it. Or not very much so, anyway.

Fire (nothing more extravagant than hot pepper juice—"It soaks into your mucous membranes to make a mild, constant, heat; a feeling of reality against the cold plastic of flesh," Valerie had later explained) burned away the shame. Still, she couldn't quite get into some of the other habits her friend professed to, and later demonstrated. Tying a scarf around your neck, purple in the face and moaning breathlessly, while masturbating seemed dangerous. Perhaps the suffocation could cause brain damage. Hadn't their minds already suffered enough?

And she definitely couldn't swing with the notion that death was connected to sexual transcendence.

"So what happened when you zapped yourself with the toaster?"

"It was a rush, such a rush. You have felt the electricity of endorphins, but this... The endorphins were there, there with a crackling edge. And I could feel something further. My soul was tingling. When my heart sped up I knew it could burst. Rupture into a river of blood, far more pretty than your little razor streams. Can you even begin to imagine the pleasure of orgasmic death exploding your mind while your heart bursts?"

"No and I don't want to. You're a weird girl, Val."

Valerie was still caressing the tongs of her fork. She glanced up for a moment and smiled slyly. "Yes. And you should try it sometime if you really want to touch Heaven."

Annette hadn't been certain of why fire could burn away shame.

"It's the pain, pure and simple. You realize within your core that sex is suffering. As well as you know this you realize that to merely have physical gratification, to take pleasure in a filthy act of copulation, is wrong. If the pain is being forced on you then it is too much. If you have pain with love, with friendship... then the friendship outweighs the force and the pain outweighs the gratification. There is tenderness in a burning touch." Valerie was very lovingly carving the image of a rose into Annette's thigh with a boot knife as she spoke. "You need the trust to give yourself away, and you need the pain to detract from the sinful enjoyment."

"But Ms. Dunright said sex is okay and we have to realize that. We have to know that the men were wrong but some can be right and we can move along and learn how to enjoy ourselves with other people. She said there's no shame in enjoying sex, none in what happened to us."

"Ms. Dunright certainly said that, but do you feel it? Do you *truly* feel that you can move along to enjoying fornication with a man? Being his receptacle? Submitting to him, and to his pleasure, without shame?"

Annette frowned. She couldn't imagine that in the least. It was a soul-shrivelling concept, a fate worse than dreams of toaster-induced death. On the other hand, she could feel the blood pounding in her vagina as her friend's finger dug into the freshly bleeding flower on her thigh. The finger traced new patterns with blood, and crept up to paint the pelvis. Maybe Ms. Dunright needed to quit her day job.

Valerie's toaster experiment was far from being the end of the escalation; she found a much more profound shock to share with her friend a week later.

"I met a man, and I want you to visit his house with me."

"You let a *man* touch you?" Annette gasped. She would have expected anything from Val. She would've expected sex with hot pokers, or checkering the throat with razor blades, or possibly even the amputation of limbs. She would've expected anything but contact with a man.

"No, dearest one, never that. Sex isn't sex with a testosterone mess, after all. I told him I would kill him if he ever tried to plant a single digit upon my flesh."

"And...?"

"And he said he doesn't believe in touching other people. He prefers to watch and touch himself. He also prefers the company of machines. There my interest lies. I want to try his machines. Razors be damned, you should see them. And, maybe, try them as well."

Machines... They sounded enticing, but they were in a man's house. It could be a trap. How much faith could be placed in Val's savvy? Perhaps just enough to take the risk, but this was a situation to think through rather than rush into. Why would a man only want to touch himself?

Pre-toaster, it was still a task to push the concept of transcendence in sex. Learning the emotional impact of pain with trust was a good start, throwing spiritualism on top of the psychology made things a bit more heavy than Annette cared to swallow.

Valerie was the dogged one, though, she never gave up on proving her general rightness. Insecurity? Most definitely.

"Of course you have heard of chakras. I even demonstrated for you, somewhat, that they can be used for releasing pent up energies, for positive sexual stimulation, for general relaxation. There is an eighth chakra that encompasses the entire body; Kundalini, the serpent. If you had ever felt this, if ever it was your will to allow it, you would never doubt the concept of sexual transcendence. The spine is wrenched, the serpent slithers upward, the mind explodes, the world disappears, you are in a daze. Yet your mind is clear and the world feels pure. It actually feels pure. That's a feeling that I doubt you presently have any awareness of."

No. Annette often thought Valerie spoke in a dream-dazed slur, and that nothing was real inside her head. The ultimate escapism, leaving the world for the controlled realms of your own mixed up brain. At the same time she had to admit that the girl often had a point or two mixed in with her ramblings. Purity in the world was an unfathomable feeling.

Post-toaster, it was an impossible task to push the concept of sex, death, and transcendence being crucially linked. Maybe there was validity to the concept of spiritual transcendence through sex. *Maybe.* But death? No. As miserable as the world and life in general were, even given the fact that Annette had absolutely no grasp on the concept of happiness, the time for death was nowhere near her.

It was another week before Annette allowed herself to be coaxed into visiting the machines. And it was only by considering it a visit with machines, and a favour to her dangerously dreamy friend, rather than a venture into the house of a man, that made it possible for her to stomach it. She still wasn't game for trying anything out, but she could at least watch. And, perhaps, share whatever exultation was gained.

"It's okay, he's okay," Valerie had assured her. "A little eccentric he might be, but he's only a performance artist with diverse tastes. I want to *live* his tastes."

She had explained meeting him at an event, the promotional posters showing mechanical contraptions for S/M interaction having been too much for her to pass by. The show itself had been fairly mediocre, nothing more than a few "volunteers" being strapped into an over-sized whipping machine which could be adjusted for varying levels of pain. It was enough to horrify the bulk of the audience, and to leave Valerie wondering how much further the machines' capabilities could be utilized. She'd let the pale and skittish crowds flood the exit behind her and awaited the chance to meet the person behind the machines.

Tall, slender, pale, leather-clad, looking the part of the vogue gentleman with his cropped black hair tucked into a cap and with his billowing jacket tail and lapels, he had introduced himself as "Reddére". Not being one for beating around her point until she lost it, Valerie had promptly expressed her interest in the possibility of volunteering her body for the machines—perhaps even to extremes that his previous volunteers hadn't felt capable of.

Reddére, casual, smiling lightly, had replied, "Finding

people who will tolerate the most simple settings in my machines is never an easy task. Beyond that? No one. I would be willing to discuss your interest." With a sweep of his arms he gestured toward a table and silently awaited her to be seated.

"Ever so polite and...almost distinguished?" Val had later assured Annette.

"Yeah, the quiet of a cat luring a mouse to its paws."

"And, as I've already said, he is aware that if he touches me he will be dead."

Little had the warning felt necessary to her, after an hour in the solitary presence of his aloof demeanor. Pretenses were pretenses, however, and Val preferred keeping hers as stand-offish as possible. The invitation had been made for her to see if she seriously could handle being in his machines. At his house. In the basement.

"If you even *dream* of placing a single digit upon my flesh, I will have you know that I always come armed. Metal alone can approach me if I consent to this."

Reddére had tipped his head back and laughed. "That, my dear, is something we have in common then. I find the cold world of machines far more pleasing than the world of flesh and blood. I will touch no person, and you I will leave to the machines. Any satisfaction gained by me need only be through watching."

Naturally Annette could only assume that her friend was being duped by this man. Buying his lines, confused from feeling only coldness, setting herself up. Ironically, that was ultimately what had convinced her to go along. If Val couldn't be reasonable and keep herself out of trouble, then obviously that chore fell to her only true friend.

"Sounds like a psycho to me Val. Maybe I'm wrong and it'll be a blast."

Reddére's house was a standard grey garden level, generally non-descript. A rock garden and shrubs, low maintenance, filled the front yard. The basement windows were barred and covered with black fabric.

"Looks like he has something to hide," Annette commented.

"Personality inflicts itself in a person's demeanor. I felt safety in him. I felt detachment. This will be perfectly safe."

Val grabbed her hesitant friend's hand and dragged her up the sidewalk to the door. The resonating doorbell was more reminiscent of a gong than a chime. Though the faintest hint of darker shadow flickered through Annette's eyes at the sound, there was no further sign of it distressing her. Both women were considering themselves too conspicuous for noticeable reactions at that point.

Reddére opened the door and bow-gestured them in with his patented light smile. The living room was sparsely decorated; a small black leather couch and an entertainment center with a TV and VCR.

"Would you ladies care for anything to drink? I've just made a pot of tea."

"No!" Annette was adamant. She wouldn't be poisoned or sedated the moment they arrived.

"Yes, please, and thank you," Valerie sighed. "This is my friend Annette. She shares perhaps a few of my feelings about pain and was curious enough about seeing the machines. I share everything with her."

Reddére bowed slightly to Annette, then retreated for the partial round of drinks.

Moments later they were in the basement and even Annette was amazed by the possibilities she saw in the machine before her.

"This is the whipping machine," Val was smiling smugly at her friend's newly awakened interest.

The whipping machine consisted of four chrome-plated metal cones, set in a vertical plane, reminiscent in shape to a St. Andrew's Cross. The whipping portion was made up of two wheels on either side of the x-frame, each of the four wheels having two thin wire cables attached to them. Aircraft cable; nylon coated, thin, extremely strong, with a bit of the bare wire poking out from the end.

Reddére was pointing at the metal cones. "These hold the person spread-eagled. They are largely hollow, with rubber bladders inside. The person would have their arms and legs lubricated before being placed within them. I then fasten the appendages in by squeezing air into the cones. It fills the space between metal and bladder. To release the person, you need only release the air." The latter comment appeared to be aimed at the fidgeting Annette. She quickly noted the method for saving her friend when she turned out to be right about the creep being a psycho.

"It is not at all dangerous, unless the person wishes for it to be," Reddére continued. "The restraint can be very comfortable. And, yes, it can also be tightened enough for pain. Or for amputating limbs or causing internal hemorrhaging." He smiled wryly as Annette cringed and Valerie gaped in near ecstasy. "As I stated before, though, the process is easily stopped and never goes any further than the volunteer wishes. I would most definitely query before proceeding to more painful levels."

He strolled, with his incessantly casual air, to a black leather chair and wooden end table set to the side of the room. Picking up a little box with dials, he waved it at the whipping contraption. "These are the controls. We will leave them here on the table where your friend can seize them from me if need be. With these I can adjust the speed and style of the whipping. The general performance setting is for steady lashes. If you are sincerely interested in taking this further, a higher setting is for irregular lashings with only the wire tips of the cables."

"Okay. Now we know what it does. We can schedule another visit," Annette declared.

Valerie barely even noticed her. "I'm ready to try it now."

"You're crazy, Val."

"Would you mind terribly if I recorded this?"

"Not at all."

"You're crazy, Val. What do you record this for, guy? Do you get off on watching women get tortured?"

Reddére paused. "Yes and no. I, as you so eloquently put it, 'get off' on human interaction with machines. That which we will entrust our flesh to for more than we can naturally attain."

"That's perverse," Annette shuddered, largely unnoticed by the fixated other two, and resolved to stand as close to the console as possible. She wanted to see everything that happened, every minute twitch of a knob, to make absolutely certain that she could stop it.

Reddére opened a tub of Vaseline and handed it to his new volunteer, pointedly heeding the old warning that he should definitely not touch her by applying it himself. After her limbs were properly lubricated he demonstrated how she should slide herself into the contraption. Annette was forced to abandon her console hovering long enough to help her fit her legs in. It was set. A slight twitch of a knob on the console's top panel set the rubber bladders contracting from air pressure—only enough for a comfortable fit.

Briefly setting the console aside, Reddére walked over to a video camera mounted on a tripod directly in front of Valerie's restrained body—set at enough of a distance to also capture the movements of the wheels. Satisfied with the focus, he returned to his seat and placed his left hand on the console.

"Here I can adjust the speed of rotation, the distance, and the angle of presentation for the wheels. This in turn effects the speed and severity of the whipping." As he spoke, he gestured to show Annette which knob was for what.

The wheels rotated slowly on gears, edging the whip cables to the side and allowing them to extend to their full lengths. A portion of the cables slightly higher than the tips began lashing Valerie across the back. A steady rhythm, one set of eight consecutive thwumps and then another.

Valerie smirked. "More, and I'm ever needing something more."

And, this time, her needs were granted. The wheels tilted into more of a slant, bringing the lashes down faster. The length of the cables drew in slightly to sharpen their bite. A knob was turned yet more to set the wheels rotating faster. Valerie gasped and briefly bugged her eyes, then seemed to sink down into her restraints with an expression of dazed pleasure. Her body spasmed without inhibition upon each new set of lashings. It was enough to content her for a short while—and then she was, as before, requesting more pain.

Reddére appeared quietly pleased. Annette was feeling queasy. She couldn't help but cringe as the length of the cables was drawn yet shorter, knowing that would bring the wire tips across her friend's back. The only relief was that the turning speed of the wheels was slowed down considerably. She expected to hear a yelp of pain as the first strokes hit, rather she heard a gasp that was...a sound she had only previously heard during the heights of hot pepper juice masturbation. Uninhibited pleasure. It looked as though the wire tips were drawing a slight trickle of blood each time they fell.

Rather unexpectedly, Reddére stood up to unfasten his pants and then lower them as he sat back down. Annette mentally slammed from shock to fear to protectiveness. She felt for the boot knife at her ankle and scooted closer to the console. Then she just watched as he began masturbating. The synchronicity was incredible. The lashes slowly fell, both Valerie and Reddére gasping with them. Their expressions became steadily more dazed, nearly enraptured, their breathing ever became more sharp. A steady stream of blood grew and trickled down Valerie's back as Reddére sank further into his chair and manically stroked his partial foreskin, causing a steady stream of pre-ejaculate drops for the communal flow of moisture. Neither of them noticed their horrified spectator as they screamed in unison from the agony of full-bodied orgasm.

Inevitably, Annette panicked. She quickly shut the machine down.

"I'd already told him about my toaster experience and my feelings of transcendence," Valerie commented. "I think that was why he wished to try me in the machines. He also has the feel of transcendence and he gets it through metal. You saw how connected we were."

"What I saw was the guy being irresponsible and leaving you in there so he could jack off. I might have saved your ass in more ways than one by shutting it down!"

They couldn't seem to come to an agreement about the experience. It was enlightening, no it was dangerous, that was part of the enlightenment, no that was a risk, risks increase endorphins, and on and on and on.

"You're talking like this prick is a kindred soul when he's just another sleazy man."

"Jealousy, Annette? And where were you before we met? Were you an isolated kindred soul?"

"I wasn't anywhere." And she felt it was true. Before she'd met Valerie she'd felt nothing more than lost, hurt, confused, and isolated. It was partly why she agonized over her friend's extravagantly dangerous habits. Should anything happen to her, should she be taken away, then it would be nothing more than lost isolation again. And jealousy? Maybe. Annette had never come any closer to actually loving someone and she didn't wish to lose the feeling. She didn't want to be left behind, alone, because she didn't have the same goals of transcendence as Val and Reddére appeared to. *Don't take her away from me...*

***

Annette hadn't had an explosive relationship with her family, not like Valerie had. She'd had only coldness, whereas her friend had grown up with violence and eventually run away. It was hard to decide whether the coldness or violence would be worse -- at least the latter evidenced some form of emotion. Perhaps that was where she had gone with her current relationship: Val was definitely intense, a bit crazy, sometimes even frightening. There was feeling there though.

Even their reasons for ending up in the same rape trauma group had been completely different. Annette had been drinking at a party, a lonely seventeen year old wishing to impress her peers, and had been unwillingly pushed into sex in the back yard. At first she'd hoped it would mean something but of course it never did. She was just another cheap piece of trash to use and discard. The situation had been every bit as emotional as her cold childhood development. Valerie, on the other hand, had been jumped in an alley while living on the streets. By three men. She had fought, she had even gotten in a gut shot on one of them with her knife. That had only made the other two beat her all the more severely while they fucked her in the dirt and piled alley trash. She had an attitude about it, that much was clear. No one else could hurt her, she could only hurt *herself.* She'd been the loudest person in the trauma group, the most adamant about always fighting back and trusting no one, and Annette assumed that was what had drawn her to the more quiet and fearful girl in the corner. The one who rarely spoke up and, if she did, always seemed to think everything was her fault and there was nothing to fight. She expected that Val couldn't resist the challenge of teaching her to stand up. Teaching her to hate them more than herself.

Periodic get-togethers for non-group vent sessions had led to Valerie frequenting Annette's apartment. Playing music for her, teaching her feeling through art, eventually teaching her the release of pain. They had never actually decided to live together, though that was likely regretted on both ends, but they became close enough that it was rare for them to be seen apart. Particularly after they began sleeping together. That had been a transition for Annette. That had been taking her life into directions she'd never considered feasible. To be that close to someone, to genuinely allow another person to touch her. At least it wasn't a man.

She would be lost without Valerie. She would have nothing but coldness again.

"Everything in life was pain. Always. I was birthed with pain. My family was pain. Life was constant pain. Sexual fulfillment, gratification, endorphins, it's all pain. When life is physical pain, then you realize that it is at least better than only having emotional pain trapped within your mind. That type of pain is a dark cloud that suffocates you, poisons you, turns you against yourself. And the only true release for it, as you well know, is physical pain. I won't have my head in a cloud. I need to feel and to purge, to externalize. And I need release. I need meaning."

"You're talking about *death* though, Val. That's a far shot from just being pain."

"Is it?" Valerie was bemused. "I told you what I envisioned and felt with the toaster. Said how pretty the red waterfall of an exploded heart, and how intense the rapture of the Kundalini exploding in your mind at the same time, would be. When the wire tips were flaying me, while Reddére was feeling with me, I had that explosion in my mind and I could see more again. I could feel the purity. It was so beautiful... you should try it sometime."

Annette was staring at her friend's back. So many tiny little slices, scabbed over, scarring. Put the puzzle pieces together and you might have a picture of human flesh, you might have nothing more than jagged and sloppy patchwork.

"I know he has other machines. The whipping machine was an experience, most definitely, and I cherished it. He can do more though. He thinks the key to transcendence is through the passing up of flesh and combining in spirit and soul through the grace of machines, of metal. I believe he does have the key to my transcendence."

"Yeah, and I believe he's happily jacking off over that video tape of you."

Val laughed. "Probably. To each their own, it isn't as if you and I don't have our own form of pleasures together." She drew her boot knife and began creating a minimalised mirror of her patchwork back on Annette. Gently pulling her stringy hair aside to kiss her neck as she cut, she whispered into her ear: "I want to go back tomorrow. I need more."

It took every last ounce of Annette's lifelong training in coldness to delay crying and simply enjoy the moment.

Annette grudgingly, feeling defeated, allowed herself to be coaxed back into Reddére's house. She knew he was humouring her fear of him, her mistrust, she expected his kind could smell it. Though she was ever less certain of what exactly "his kind" was. His masturbatory habits disgusted her, yet he had kept to his oath of not touching anyone but himself. At least during the first visit.

This time they bypassed the whipping machine and entered another room in the basement. Valerie had insisted that, while the whipping machine was nice, it wasn't what she needed for transcendence unless he wanted to take it all the way to compressed air bladder limb amputation. The silent smile passing between the two of them at that moment had been creepy. Perhaps a little too wistful on both ends.

Perhaps, though, not as creepy as the second contraption.

"It should relieve you to know that Valerie will actually have more control over what happens to her in this one," Reddére began.

Annette couldn't admit that this actually made her far less comfortable. She wanted to be the one with the control. The other two were far too unstable for knowing when to stop. She forced a relieved smile and allowed him to continue.

"This is called a Stryker frame, used for rotating paralyzed patients in order to reach either end of their body. Obviously I made a few modifications. The straps can be placed loosely, to allow for movement from the confined person. There, on the right side, you see a series of needles and razor blades. I'm sure those are a new experience for neither of you. On the left side you see soldering irons, slightly filed to a sharper point." Reddére paused to flick a switch on the wall, set a few feet in front of the machine. The nine inch old-fashioned irons inverted, and he made a show of lighting a tray full of precisely-spaced alcohol torches—which he then fitted onto a shelf beneath the irons. "The irons will begin heating now, and the heat can be controlled by either inverting the irons into the flames or by leaving them upright long enough to cool."

"So...when they're upright, they won't be hot?" Annette looked hopeful.

A shadow of a smile crossed Reddére's face. "No, not precisely. When they are upright, the base of the irons will settle onto the flames. They will begin cooling off, slowly, but it will prevent the heat from escaping entirely. Now this switch here," and he gestured to one fastened into the Stryker frame, within reach of where the arms would be strapped, "can be used to tilt the wheel to one side or the other. It can even be used, the half position, for setting the person upright again. Valerie can easily access this switch, her levels of pain will be her own pleasure."

Annette was closing her eyes, trying to will her nauseated stomach toward peace. An image of Valerie stroking the tongs of a fork, exclaiming joyously about the transcendence of electrocution, faded into one of her running hot soldering irons through her abdomen. She shook the thought, and helped her disrobed friend mount the contraption.

"Please take this slow at first, for me."

At the least, her earnest was obvious. Valerie merely smiled sadly and nodded.

Reddére had retreated to drag two chairs into the room and set them approximately a foot apart, just to the side of a direct line of view for the machine. The direct line still belonged to the video camera, which he carried in afterward, and set up, before claiming the seat nearest to the soldering iron heating switch.

Valerie was simply hanging in the frame, not trying anything yet. Waiting. Holding Annette's hand and stroking it gently, as if to comfort her. As if to say *do not be afraid for me, dear friend.* Then she was slowly letting go, glancing at the camera, glancing at Reddére, eyeing the switch. The soldering irons, now glowing red, were shifted to the upright position—the flames continuing to tickle their sides.

"We both know fire, don't we?" she asked. "I taught you that fire burns away the shame. You'll know that it can burn away so much more."

Annette nodded, yet again avoiding tears, and slouched over to take her seat.

Good to her word, Val spent a considerable amount of time exploring the two accoutered sides of the frame—delaying actual rotation. The run of a finger tip along the razors and needles, the faint trickle of blood. The light pressing of her left arm into a soldering iron, the smell of burning flesh.

Her spectators sat, silently immersed in her slow curiosities. Tension, the performer baiting the audience.

"What's in this for you? I know why Val does it," Annette finally whispered.

Reddére frowned slightly. "Meaning, I suppose. Finding untinged beauty in the coldness of this world. Trying to share it, trying to present it for others who might learn to feel. Your friend, she knows of beauty. She knows of sharing it. I don't think that is enough for her though. I believe she wants to become it."

"She wants to die."

He snorted, though more sadly than contemptuously. "No. She wants to live. She simply hasn't had the opportunity for *truly* doing so yet."

"What makes you the expert? You barely know her."

"No, but I have felt with her and related to her. Perhaps far more than you have ever even tried to."

Annette considered that possibility. Maybe that was the problem here. Maybe she was so accustomed to coldness, to being closed off, that she had never really been able to open herself up enough in the relationship. She'd tried. She'd partaken in a lifestyle that sometimes made sense to her, sometimes seemed completely insane and deluded. *You're crazy.* Perhaps that type of comment was never meant to be a constant in close relationships. Denial, rather than relation. Perhaps she hadn't ever tried hard enough to understand the other perspective.

Valerie had ceased her toying with the razors and irons. A glance at the positional switch, a slight nod to the audience. The silence was resonant with a hum of tension. She flipped the switch all the way down, keeping her finger pressed firmly against it, and flipped slowly to the left. Just a momentary hiss, a singe as the flesh of her side began settling upon the heated irons, and then she flipped the switch back to the halfway point.

Annette managed to breathe again. She could see the welts already beginning to pucker on Val's side. How could *this* relate to becoming beauty? Not many people would find beauty in massive scarring. She tensed right back up as Val's finger flicked the switch to the full upright position and the wheel began tilting to the right, toward the needles and razors. It appeared to be easy enough for her to balance herself, control which portions of her body would be burned and cut. Initially she let her hip break the descent, a cluster of tips and sharp edges slicing into it, then she began running her leg gingerly across the prickling mass. Tiny rivulets of blood, flowing down steel.

Even Annette could perceive the eroticism of her movements. The arc of her side, trembling slightly away from penetration. The pressure of weight through her hip. The delicate rubbing of her leg against the bloodied needles and razors. Her eyes half-closed, her face contorted with the building of sexual tension. Reddére's face was beginning to mimic hers.

Another half flick of the switch. Upright position. And another, just a brief tinge of fire. Soldering irons scalding already welted flesh. The left hip swollen and black, the side barely scathed, the leg more mildly puckered and blistered than the hip. Not a single cry of pain to match the appearance, only ragged breaths and an expression of absolute pleasure.

"What could she be thinking?" More of a rhetorical question from Annette, nevertheless answered by her fellow spectator -- plucking him from his mesmerized daze.

"She is feeling. Truly free and feeling."

Feeling. No coldness, other than from the razors and needles. No pretenses, no inhibitions, no force. Annette remembered the comments about purity. Could that possibly be part of what Val was feeling? She had claimed to have felt that at the previous session's climax. Annette reflected on it, on the shared ecstasy between Val and Reddére. Neither of them had been aware of anything else, there was only the feeling and the moment. Beauty, purity. And the lone terrified woman hunched by the wall, considering it wrong and putting an end to it. Never believing that perhaps her friend had possessed full cognizance of her actions and that they had somehow held true meaning for her.

"More heat, please." Annette snapped out of her reverie as Reddére acknowledged Valerie's request by inverting the soldering irons.

She *had* been doing a repeat session of lightly rubbing the right side of her body, hip impaled, against the needles and razors. The trickle of blood was flowing faster against metal, and coating her entire side. Tiny dried rivulets striped her front and disappeared into the vastly welted left side. *Now* she began arcing her side down further into the blades and tips, letting her weight settle completely, crawling sidewise to drag metal through her flesh.

Annette thought she could see little snags of skin clinging to the needles. "We have to stop her."

"No. She is only now beginning. And she has the control, the will. Let her live." Reddére was leaning forward in his chair, enraptured, only whispering in distraction.

Live?

"Pegged it, sweetie. I do want death. I want to be fucked to death without sex. What other way is there to go? Life is filth, and we are the unpure. The contaminated."

"Reddére, what do you think purity is?"

The same fixated staring ahead, the same whispering response. "Purity? Purity of emotion, of mind, of soul. Freedom. The world isn't pure. People are not pure. Bred in over-crowded rat cages, lashing out, being taught that nothing matters beyond the self. Reproducing the self for immortality. Building and glorifying the self by belittling everything around it. Losing sight of the self in pursuit of these teachings, these false goals. That is plasticity, falseness, insincerity, the endless manufacture of commodified mannequins. Put them in place and make them look good, they serve no true function. These machines, they do serve a function. They are pure, untainted. Before you, you see freedom. Sheer freedom and pleasure. Attained without tarnishing anyone. Valerie's rapture is pure." As he finished speaking, he once again flicked the wall switch to present the upright, glowing, irons.

Purity. Annette cringed at the next downward flick of the positional switch. The sound was... Initially, the burning sound had been a wet sizzle. Now it was dry, brittle, dull. There was no moisture to be burned from previously charred flesh. She wondered if this was what her friend would consider being fucked to death without sex. There was no human contact, no guilt or shame, no sins of the flesh. Yet there was penetration, and there was definitely pleasure.

The right side again. Valerie was gasping, though not with pain. A red body, one side black, a light sheen of sweat covering her face. She radiated ecstasy. Her body twisted, trailing along stained razor edges and needle tips. Leaving small portions of skin behind, soaked with flowing blood. Side arcing and unarcing, legs grinding together and then separating, eyes closing fully.

Burning away the shame, or cutting it away as well. Annette barely even noticed as Reddére began masturbating again. They were in their world, she was in hers. She was thinking about how fire had been her own salvation, her own personal Jesus. And about the need to touch Heaven with transcendence. Perhaps she could understand it. She could understand feeling unclean, feeling poisoned. She could understand wanting to rend her own flesh to remove the taint of depravity. She could even understand needing to transcend into true beauty for a complete metamorphosis into purity. But hadn't Val been the one to teach her to stick around and keep fighting? She didn't want to lose that strength, to be forced to face the ugliness of life and the world alone.

One moment, both Valerie and Reddére were lost into the same world of rapture. The next moment, Val was upright again and the only sound was the rhythmic scraping of Reddére's hand against his penis. *Misfire?* Val was loosening her straps. She appeared peaceful, radiant, and she smiled at Annette with a look of true joy mixed with fondness. And then she reached up to flick the switch all the way down.

"No!" Annette shrieked, falling out of her chair. She couldn't do anything. She perched on her knees and watched as her friend, her lover, the only person she had ever truly cared for, settled onto the soldering irons one final time. A brief pause, then a flip accompanied by a downward scoot to impale her face, chest, and abdomen onto the heated spikes. Valerie and Reddére both screamed with rapture, two backs convulsing as the Kundalini crept up their spines and exploded in their heads, their cries mixing freely with the wet sizzle of newly exposed flesh. Burning away the shame, transcending into beauty. Salvation.

"Please don't leave me..." Annette nestled her face into the floor and sobbed. Maybe Val had possessed enough courage to pursue her dreams and find transcendence, but she wouldn't be followed. Leaving behind one lonely and frightened friend, one recording video camera, one fellow exulted seeker of beauty, and one metallic lover. It was over.

Valerie was touching Heaven, lost in its embrace. Annette could never again do more than touch herself.

Scratch

Nikki Dillon

The Devil is a lot of things to me and my four house-mates: he's our boyfriend, our employer, and our master. For the rest of the world, he's a fashion photographer known as Scratch—a middle-aged man with deformed eyes and a few unusual physical abnormalities, which may or may not be the product of plastic surgery. His signature appears on the upper right hand corner of each of his photos, in lurid red. It's blood, according to Scratch. He develops only thirteen prints of every picture and, supposedly, burns the negatives in an occult ritual involving goats.

We've never seen a goat around here, though there was a Doberman chained up in the basement—with Gregory—for three or four days last February. Gregory never complains about anything, but the dog whined and barked incessantly. Scratch gave it away to one of the production assistants.

Most people assume that the Devil thing's a gimmick. And it works. One of his early photos sold last week in London, at an auction, for half a million bucks. As usual, Scratch will give a chunk of that money to controversial theater troupes and undiscovered artists. His detractors say he needs the tax break.

Those of us who sleep with him know why he gives away his cash.

Money is what attracts us.

We're his slaves.

Scratch shoots photos for fashion spreads and slick magazine ads. Designer suits. Designer handbags. Designer lingerie. Financial success has ruined his reputation. Last year, before his retrospective at the Whitney, there was an article in the *New York Times* about him. It quoted an anonymous curator who called Scratch "a third-rate photographer turned con-man."

In any case, I believe Scratch is who he claims to be. I've stroked the two stubby hard lumps on his scalp. Covered by his thinning hair, they're located half an inch behind his pointed ears. I've had my neck scratched by his claws and my foot stepped on by one of his cloven hooves. It sure feels real to me.

The five of us live with Scratch here in Milan, Italy, where his photography studio is based. He owns this four-story building—a squat, ochre-colored structure on the water-front by the *navigli*, canals. The neighborhood, once working class, is in vogue with fashion insiders. Gregory thinks it's so hip and so romantic. The rest of us are less convinced. I admit I liked the place when I first arrived here last November. The cobblestoned streets were covered in a thick fog, then, and I couldn't see too clearly. Also, I was more or less delirious.

I had an idea that I was going to get rich.

When it comes to money, I am stupid.

Before Scratch took me to Milan, I'd lived in New York City for nine years. There, I'd led the humbling, wretched existence of an aspiring novelist. I'd been marginally employed as a freelance copywriter for a publishing company that specialized in coloring books. My wages were laughable, so low that I took perverse pride in them. I'd cite the figure to well-dressed, overpaid acquaintances. I enjoyed their stunned reaction.

"How do you survive in New York?" they'd gasp, sounding horrified.

"I guess I have a masochistic streak," I'd say, joking. (It seemed funny, then.) By the time I turned thirty, I'd developed the self-deprecating and slightly paranoid personality of an outsider. My career had showed some early promise, as the saying goes, but was failing to materialize. Mysteriously, one by one, my friends had been absorbed by the middle class. They joined up with that amorphous group, Professionals. I could no longer follow their conversation; it was filled with jargon. As far as I was concerned, they did vague things, in conference rooms, that concerned computers, the law, and television. They owned houses and apartments, furniture, and matching plates. They acquired husbands, wives and children. I saw how they eyed my second-hand clothes, and watched me count out dimes from my change purse to pay for drinks. They'd invite me over to their four-bedroom colonial houses in the suburbs to feed me what I thought of as a "pity dinner." In my apartment, I dined on toast and instant soup.

By the time I met Scratch, I'd written two "literary" novels: *Miracle at the 23rd Street Laundromat* and *Odor of the Swamp.*

Needless to say, I couldn't sell them for my life.

Four days after I hooked up with him, Scratch handed my landlady a check from a Swiss bank and removed me from my roach-infested, one-room apartment on West 121st Street, where drug dealers convened on one street corner and drunken vagrants on another. He hired three handsome moving men to pack up my belongings and ship them to Milan. They called me "Ms. Bellamy," and they handled my chipped coffee mugs and paperbacks as if they were priceless, wrapping every object, including my sneakers, in a sheet of newspaper, cushioned by shreds of white styrofoam which they referred to as "the snow."

The day before we left New York, Scratch took me shopping at Barney's, the trendoid department store. It was cold out, so he bought me a red vinyl baseball cap with fleece-lined earflaps. Now I keep it on the window ledge in the studio, in my office alcove, next to the futon mattress which I unfold at night to sleep on. I don't wear it much, and I never wanted it in the first place.

It cost Scratch $248.00

It's a number I remember, because it was my weekly salary at Dunn and Bradworth Publishing Co.

Fucking price tag. It impressed me.

I work for Scratch eight hours a day, seven days a week. My desk is a card table equipped with a portable computer in an alcove. I'm separated from the photography studio by a wall of rectangular glass bricks. Back in New York, Scratch and I made a deal to produce a book which would wind up on the bestseller list, or even lead to a lucrative Hollywood movie option. In exchange for room, board, a one-way plane ticket and that useless shopping trip to Barney's, Scratch commissioned me to write a book based on his character. I'm supposed to be his first official, authorized biographer, with exclusive access to his correspondence and private papers.

Unfortunately, the book I'm writing sucks.

It's a fictionalized biography, or what Scratch calls "biofic." The working title is *I, Satan*. But Scratch refuses to tell me anything about himself. So I have to take wild guesses and tell lies.

When I objected to doing that, Scratch lost his temper. "Don't be an idiot!" he yelled, stamping the floor with the heel of his motorcycle boot. "Make it up. That's what you're here for, stupid girl." It was one of the few times I've seen him lose control. Usually, he keeps his voice low. Scratch often smiles when he's angry.

My relationship with him is fairly twisted.

I expected that, I guess.

"Candles are in," Scratch told the four of us this morning. He looked up from the latest edition of Italian Vogue. We were all sitting at the long dining table, eating our usual breakfast of bread and water. Some of us—including me—were allowed to have a cup of instant coffee. Katrina, the Austrian dancer, was feasting on scrambled eggs and a slice of toast with butter. The rest of us, half-starving, were trying not to watch her eat. My mouth was watering, and I knew that, when she performed for Scratch last night, he'd liked her choreography, for a change. Probably, she'd gotten laid in some way which was pleasurable instead of humiliating or painful. That's part of the reward when he approves.

By now, most of us prefer the food.

"Children!" Scratch was saying. "We don't *have* any candles, do we?" He was sounding mighty anxious.

None of us looked at him. We all stared down at our plates, like we were fascinated by the geometric pattern on the ceramic pottery, and concentrated on swallowing and chewing.

"Alexandra, dear?" he said.

My heart sinks when he calls my name. I have no idea why he drags me into these discussions. I could care less about what's "hot."

"Yes, sir?" I said, trying to sound interested, instead of scared. I'm scared of Scratch. I wish I weren't. But I am.

"Alex, don't you think we *need* some candles in this house? After all, we're the fashion vanguard. Aren't we?" He looked stricken. The thought of being less than "cutting-edge" terrifies Scratch. At heart, he's a wimp. That doesn't change the power dynamics much.

"Please look at me, Alexandra. I'm tired of the back of your head. That's better, honey. If candles are in a mainstream glossy like *Vogue*...what does that say to you?"

"I dunno, sir. Not my area. I'm arts and letters. Remember, sir?" I tried to sneer at him, to show a grain of irreverence. I do that every now and then, as a mark of self-respect. Usually, I'm as subservient as possible. We all are. That's the job.

"Can't it only mean one thing, Alex? Aren't we a step *behind* the trend? Or, even... Oh, no! Have we *missed* the trend, my slavegirl? Are candles over, do you think?"

I bit my lip. If I said "Yes," he'd punish Gregory.

But if I said, "No," he'd punish me.

I tried to hedge. "*Candles*," I said, in a tone that I hoped was deeply contemplative, as if I were mulling over a Zen koan. "Candles."

That's the way we've all learned to talk to Scratch. We repeat whatever he says. He might walk into the studio and announce, "Platform shoes." And we'll all try to seem surprised and look at one another, frowning and nodding like we'd never heard of platform shoes before. Each of us will say, "*Platforms*," with as much passion as we can muster. After a minute or so, you just hear this chorus of "Platforms, platforms." Or neck scarves, or slave bracelets, or tattoos, or whatever.

It works, sometimes.

Anyway, all he did this morning was to send Gregory out to Dolce and Gabbana's new housewares shop on Via della Spiga to buy four dozen scented candles. Gregory was delighted. Scratch hadn't let him out of the basement for a month. He's been down in there since The Rust Incident.

The studio has a pungent odor at the moment, because Scratch recently bought a year's supply of herbal oils. The house is filled with black ironwork lanterns, floor pillows, pottery, and tiles. Scratch redecorates the whole place twice a year.

This season, the key word is "*Morocco*."

If you're Scratch, *Morocco* means black ironwork lanterns, floor pillows, pottery, and—on the floors and walls—

Moroccan tiles.

If you're Scratch, *Morocco* means blue, yellow and rust. That's the color scheme. It's *Morroco*. *Morroco*'s "in."

The glass inside the lanterns casts splotches of colored light onto the tiled floors.

That light is blue, yellow and red.

Red glass. *Red.* Not rust.

If you're Scratch, that mistake is very bad.

If you're Gregory, it's a disaster.

"Rust," Scratch told us at breakfast one day last month. It was our first Moroccan morning—right after the *Moroccan* redecoration project had been completed. We were eating bread served on handmade Moroccan pottery. In a mood of celebration which turned out to be premature, we were sipping tea from hand painted Moroccan mugs.

Scratch turned to each of us and addressed us, mournfully, in turn. "*Rust*, Matthew," he said. "Katrina, slavegirl, *rust*. Rust, Tomas, my dear young slaveboy. Alex. Sweetslave. Rust?"

"Rust," I answered, in my most consoling tone.

"Rust, rust," we all began to murmur.

The only one who didn't say anything was Gregory. He sat there, biting his lips and getting pale.

Gregory has a degree in architecture. Interior decoration is his area.

We tried saying "rust" for a while, but our voices got softer and softer. It wasn't working, and we knew it.

Gregory got up from the table and went down into the basement. Scratch followed. The rest of us trembled and kept quiet.

Gregory screamed all morning long. I couldn't get a word written. There was no place to hide. He could be heard on every floor. By eleven o'clock, we were all in tears. Even the models and the hairdressers, who don't usually give a shit about anyone. We had to put on our headphones and turn the volume on our CD Walkmans up to ten.

At noon, the screaming stopped. Scratch came upstairs and strolled into the studio. His face was flushed. He threw himself down on the yellow leather couch and began to inspect his claws, which are painted blue. He put one in his mouth and chewed on it, sighing contentedly.

We took our CD Walkmans off and got to work.

Gregory cried for hours afterwards. We each took turns

sneaking down the back stairs to see him. He had a black eye and his chest and back were covered with blood. A piece of his left nipple was missing. Scratch had torn out his nipple ring. Aside from that, he looked all right. It wasn't half as bad as the time Gregory stuck his nose into the fashion end of things and advised Scratch to shave off his goatee.

I untied Gregory's hands and tried to put some disinfectant on his tit, but he wouldn't let me.

"Don't worry," he reassured me. "I'll be okay."

I handed him a tissue and he blew his nose.

"I wish I hadn't let him down like that," he said. "His approval means a lot to me, Alex. I respect him."

I left him to himself, since I had half a chapter to finish before sunset—and I was still recovering from the night before, when I hadn't met my deadline. We all gave up on Gregory a long time ago. Getting punished can be confusing, but Gregory actually likes Scratch. That's what's so pathetic.

Then again, Gregory's under more pressure than some of us. Architecture and design are more important to Scratch than anything in print. I never get more than bruises and bloody welts. Tomas, the Brazillian painter who lives on the ground floor, gets whipped regularly, too. Katrina, the dancer from Vienna, claims she gets a sharpened stick up her ass, but we doubt the veracity of that. Even Scratch has limits.

Matthew, an American sculptor who lives on the top floor, in the penthouse, has had his arms and face cut up with razor blades half a dozen times. Apparently, he was letting people do that to him before he got here. Out of all of us, I'd say Matthew gets along best with Scratch. Not counting the fashion people, obviously. They don't live with us. They're only at the studio during the day, from ten to six.

No one knows what Scratch does to *them*. Whatever it is, it doesn't happen on the premises. The models and the make-up artists, the production assistants and the stylists have all got their own apartments. When it comes to fashion, Scratch makes house calls.

I was an easy mark for Scratch. Since adolescence, I've had a weakness for melodrama and bad men: guys who everyone knows will be unfaithful, the ones who radiate danger, talk you into selling heroin, or ask you to sleep with their best friends so they can watch.

I got interested in Scratch's grainy old black and white photographs long before I ever knew him personally, around the time I moved to New York City from Pittsburgh after college. I loved the crooked camera angles. I loved the sweat stains and the smeared mascara. I loved the hint of perversion and decay. In the old days, Scratch wasn't selling anything. Aside from that, his work's unchanged. What he's best known for now are the magazine ads which, as he puts it, "push the buttons, just so far." Like the series he did for Ferragosto shoes, with the cop, the nun, and a pair of sling back sandals. He won an award for that one.

About Scratch himself, I'd only heard rumors. I'd been told that he was wanted by the F.B.I. for pandering, and that he had Mafia connections. What intrigued me, though, were the reports that he gave money to the arts. Stories floated around about artists and writers who'd had chance encounters with Scratch. They'd described their projects to him. He'd given them money, based on the "concept," in advance.

I met Scratch in SoHo the night after my thirtieth birthday. I was in a crowded bar on Prince Street. I saw him from across the room and didn't recognize him. The newspapers keep running a retouched photo of him, so I didn't know exactly what he looked like. Even though he was wearing dark glasses, and he was wrinkled and balding, some part of me must have understood that it was him. An excited shiver ran through me when I looked in his direction. I walked across the room and stood a few paces away from him, at the bar. He was flanked by a tall, suntanned couple, dressed identically in velvet. They were too gorgeous to be considered human.

When I heard the gorgeous woman call the older guy "Scratch," I knew what I had to do. I was ready for it. I took three long strides—as slinkily as possibly—in the direction of the Devil.

I undid a couple of my shirt buttons.

No results. He kept on talking to the Gorgeous Creatures.

I propped one high-heeled boot on the rung of a bar stool.

Still, nothing.

I hiked my skirt up and ran my hand along my thigh.

Scratch glanced in my direction.

Suggestively, I ran the tip of my tongue across my upper

lip.

Bingo.

A moment later, he moved to the empty bar stool right beside me, making that Darth Vador wheezing sound I'd read about. He huddled over his beer, hunching his shoulders with his head down, so that I couldn't see his face. He searched his pockets, took out a velvet ski cap, and put it on, pulling it down low over his forehead.

He was acting like he didn't want to be recognized. It's the same game Scratch always plays.

"Excuse me, sir," I said, coming up behind him. "May I ask you something?"

He pushed his sunglasses down on his nose.

"Yes, dear?" he said. "Ask."

I looked straight into those eyes, the long-lashed eyes that resemble a cow's—dark brown, without a pupil or an iris. I'd read descriptions of them in *People* magazine.

I leaned forward and whispered in his hairy pointed ear. "Are you Scratch, the fashion photographer?"

"Why do you ask that, darling?" he whispered back, so that I felt his breath on my neck. "If I were, what difference would it make?"

"Well, sir, you'd get a decent blow job out of it, for one thing."

He smiled, wanly. "In that case, my dear, old Scratch would be inclined to answer yes."

I grabbed him by the arm and led him to the men's room. A guy was pissing in there. He nodded "hi" at us. We nodded back while we walked into a stall. I sat down on the lid of the toilet. Scratch undid his pants and pulled out a flaccid dick. I licked its shaft twice, slowly.

Limp.

I gave his head a tongue kiss.

Nothing.

I slurped his whole worm down my throat.

Bingo. An erection.

I proceeded to treat Scratch to a lengthy session of deepthroating. I nearly gagged twice, but both times I kept it to myself, recovered quickly, and bounced right back in there. By the time Scratch started to whimper, tears were running down my face and my chin was full of drool. I slugged back a teaspoonful of cum.

For the record, Scratch's cock is a hammerhead, bulbous

at the end, and I'd say about five inches when erect.

"Haven't I seen you on TV?" Scratch asked me, when I stood up. He was zipping up his fly. "You're an *actress*, aren't you?"

I rolled my eyes at this old line. Scratch didn't notice, luckily. "No, sir, I'm not an actress."

"What a shame. You could be one, you know. You belong among the world's young beauties."

What he meant was, he liked the way I sucked his cock.

"Thank you, sir. You're exaggerating."

"No, dear. Beauty has nothing to do with what you look like. It's all lighting and cosmetics."

"*Oh.*" Full of flattery, Scratch is. What a guy.

"Are you a dancer, then? A video artist? Let me guess."

"I'm an emerging writer, sir."

"An unknown author," he sighed. "How pitiful. Most unfortunate. Not much money in that these days."

"You said it, sir," I agreed. I unlatched the stall door and walked over to the sink. Scratch stood beside me, while I washed my hands and face. At the urinals across the room, two guys pretended to ignore us.

"Unless, of course, you have a marketable concept." He held the door open for me. "Do you, child? What's your name?"

"Alexandra Bellamy. Call me Alex if you want, sir."

"Do you have a marketable concept, young Alex who sucks off strangers in the men's room?"

"You bet I have a concept. And, sir, I'm anxious to sell out."

"I thought you might be. Shall we go someplace quiet to discuss it?"

"Sure thing, sir. Thanks."

"It's my pleasure." Scratch came to a stop in the middle of the hallway and extended his hand, formally. I shook it, checking to see if his fingers were covered with fur, like I'd read, but he was wearing velvet gloves.

("Velvet! Sad news, young friends. It's history. I'm thinking nylon. Aren't you, my little sweetslaves?")

He looked down at his heavy silver wristwatch. "My club should be open for another hour or two. Shall we?"

We made our way past the tables. I felt totally at ease. It was as if I'd just jumped out of an airplane and discovered

I could fly.

I wasn't scared of Scratch. Not yet.

As we approached the exit, I turned towards the bar and saw the tall couple in dark sunglasses watching us, a crestfallen expression on their perfect faces.

"Go to hell, Gorgeous Creatures," I thought. Scratch would rather fuck *me*.

"Hey, old dude. Are you who I think you are?" said a voice when we stepped outside into the crisp November air. Three guys in tattered overcoats were gathered together, looking hopeful.

Scratch narrowed his eyes. "That depends. Who do you think?"

One, who seemed to be their spokesperson, stepped forward. "You're the most innovative cultural force in the Western world," he said. He had bleached blonde hair which fell into his eyes. His face was partially hidden by black beard stubble.

Scratch took off his sunglasses. He gave the supplicant a thorough looking-over. It took him all of two seconds. Then he put his sunglasses back on.

"Dude, my name is Sand Dune," said the doomed young man, hurriedly. A stream of words poured forth as he pitched his concept to the Devil. "I'm a performance artist from L.A. and I've got a devoted cult following and now I'd like to compromise myself and whatever artistic values I have left. I don't want to shake the establishment up anymore because I'm tired and I'm hungry and more importantly I want a car, so I'd rather be fistfucked and eat shit in exchange for money. Hey, dude? You listening? Lemme introduce my company to you. This hunky little dude to my right is Nathan Smoke of the Smoke Brothers acrobatic team. He's got a washboard stomach, see that? The fox on my left is Jimmy Bob, a transvestite clown from Louisiana. He never insults anyone, anymore. Guys n' gals both love him. You'll find the three of us can be very, very entertaining. We're cutting edge, but not offensive. We push the buttons just so far. You read me, old dude? Our act is up your alley. It's a circus act, featuring the simulated crucifixion of audience members. I thought it, uh, it might, um, you know..." Here, Sand Dune faltered. Scratch was ignoring him.

He'd taken out a portable telephone from his briefcase, and was speaking into the receiver.

"158 Prince Street," he said into the phone.

"Dude, you interested?" finished Sand Dune, unhappily.

"Not today," he said dismissively, as if poor Sand Dune were a street vendor trying to sell him a plastic watch. Scratch put his hand on the small of my back, guiding me to the corner.

A limousine, painted violet and with its windows darkened, pulled up at the curb. An overweight, middle-aged man in violet jeans and a matching jacket got out of the driver's seat and opened the back door. Scratch ushered me in, and I slid gracefully on to violet seats, with a lot of leg room. A violet carpet lined the floor.

("Matthew, Katrina! Oh, Tomas, honey, do come up here, I implore you. Forget that ghastly painting, this is urgent. I need input. Violet? Finished. Yes or no? Answer me, someone! Today, please. Style marches on!")

As the driver closed the door to the limo, Sand Dune and company rushed towards the car. Sand Dune managed to stuff a xeroxed flyer in Scratch's gloved hands before the door slammed.

"Please step back from the curb," the driver ordered, gruffly.

Sand Dune had no chance. I didn't know how long I could keep him but, for the moment, Scratch was mine.

I was proud of myself. I'd been servile, and I'd seduced him. I thought I'd beaten out the competition.

I was so naive in those days.

As if Scratch were selective, and didn't chose his slaves by chance.

The door to Scratch's private club, on Tenth Avenue, was unmarked. Inside, it was almost completely dark. A single spotlight was set into the shiny marble floor. Black candles shaped like lilies floated in oval pools of water, set into shiny marble table tops. In the dim light, I felt invisible: loose, carefree, and ready to take chances.

A waiter in a white jacket led us to a corner table. He wheeled over a tray with an ice bucket on it, uncorked a bottle of champagne and filled our long stemmed glasses.

"So tell me, pet," Scratch said. "What's your proposal?"

"Well, sir. I'd like to write a book that would sell. Nonfiction. A biography. Yours."

As I was talking, it occurred to me that maybe I should have made my proposal first, and offered him a blow job afterwards. I had never prostituted myself before. I wasn't sure how it worked.

Scratch seemed to sense my insecurity. He covered my hand with his, and patted it reassuringly. He had removed his gloves. Coarse fur, like the hair on a horse's mane, scraped my skin. He began to scratch my forearm, lightly, with one of his thick hooked claws. He lifted my hand to his mouth, and kissed it. Suddenly, he bit my knuckles, hard.

I winced.

He gripped my hand with both his hairy paws and bore down with his sharp front teeth.

Groaning in protest, I tried to pull my hand away. I stood up, knocking over my champagne glass. It shattered on the floor. Alerted by the sound, a waiter turned towards us. When he saw who it was, he looked away.

"Let go!" I said.

He relaxed his grip.

I pulled my hand back and rubbed it. It was numb and bumpy, covered with his teeth marks.

"Pain," said Scratch. "Alexandra, pain."

"Pain," I repeated.

I understood immediately.

I'm smart about some things. I sat back down.

Scratch studied me a moment. "It's a job requirement." The artists whom I sponsor all know pain. Don't you, Alex?"

I didn't answer.

"And if not, dear," he said tenderly. "Would you like to? Alex who shows off her slender thighs in bar rooms? Alex who eats rice and beans? Alex whose telephone has been shut off? Pretty Alex, who is a disappointment to her parents? Talented Alex, who pulls out her gray hairs? Lovely Alex, who—much to her surprise—is over thirty? Cocksucking Alex, who is so charming and such a failure? In some sense, haven't you been seeking pain and degradation all your life?"

I couldn't answer. He knew things about me which I'd

never told anyone. It was as if he'd held up a mirror and shown me a reflection of myself. Had he set some kind of trap, devised specially for me? For the first time, I was frightened.

"Shit," I said, weakly. "Sir. You hit a nerve."

"Does that surprise you?" Scratch turned a cigarette slowly between his shaggy thumb and index finger.

"Well, sir. Yes."

"Scare you?"

"I admit it does, sir."

"You feel manipulated? Humiliated? Exposed?"

"Uh, yeah. I do."

Scratch rubbed his hands together, gleefully. "How nice for you, darling. And darling, how nice for me! I'm touching nerves and pushing buttons! That's my area, you see."

"But do you know *me*, somehow, sir? Me? Alexandra Bellamy?"

Scratch chuckled. "What a question! Cocksucking Alexandra! I'm ashamed!"

"Have we met before? What...what's going on? Please tell me, Scratch."

"Have we *met*? Do I know *you*? As if you were different, or original or important! Is there some scrap of dignity left to protect inside the young whore's body, after all?"

"I'm...I'm confused."

"I can see that," murmured Scratch. "I find your innocence most arousing." He leaned back in his chair.
"I want to hurt you, Alexandra Bellamy. Think it over."

I sat, smoking, and watching a metal clock above our table as its violet hands moved, in quivering spasms, counting seconds.

At around four o'clock that morning, I had my skirt pulled up and the Devil's well-greased dick inside my ass. He kept pulling it all the way out and shoving it all the way back in me. I'd had a virgin asshole until that morning and, frankly, the first time wasn't fun. I'd spent an abortive twenty minutes screaming "Stop, please stop!" until I got the hang of it.

Ah, pain.

One pleasant aspect about having my anus split in two was that I barely noticed that I was being beaten. Scratch hit me, repeatedly, with a patent leather belt from Donna Karan's spring menswear collection. I didn't give a shit about that, or anything else. All I could think of was my asshole.

That's the trick to pain, really. It helps you break things down into essentials.

"Well?" said Scratch, stretching out on the rumpled velvet quilt in his hotel room and switching the channel to MTV.

I took a deep breath.

"Hello, Alex! Are you with me?" He snapped his fingers.

"Um, sir," I said. I couldn't speak. I couldn't move. I would have liked to call a doctor.

"Are you with me? Yes or no? You've had your trial run, whore. Now I need a final answer."

I looked up at the violet ceiling and closed my eyes. "Sir," I said. "I'm in. Do whatever the fuck to me you want."

"That's nice, Alex. I'm so glad you feel that way. That's what I like to hear."

I dragged myself into the bathroom and shut the door. I didn't want Scratch to hear me crying. I wasn't happy. My initiation had been traumatic. I climbed inside the bathtub and, tearfully, examined my rear end.

I turned the tap on.

Water hurt.

I wondered what my ex-girlfriend, Becca, would have thought if she could have seen me that way, with my back covered with red marks, cleaning out my shitsmeared butthole. She would have kissed my forehead and made me some herbal tea. Perhaps we would have discussed our three favorite old topics: commitment, intimacy, and communication.

Those were the things which Becca had wanted our relationship to be based on.

What was the basis of my relationship to Scratch?

Submission, sex and money.

Three real words in exchange for three small loads of crap.

The second floor of Scratch's house in Milan serves as his photo studio. With its bright overhead lights and sense of emptiness, it reminds me of a high school gym. It's minimally furnished, with metal desks, a leather couch, a table, and a row of cabinets to hold our "toys" and magazines. Outside the darkroom, rolls of film hang from a clothesline, drying. There are five floor-to-ceiling windows, with thirty square panels of glass inside each one. I tend to count the panels of glass, from one to 150, over and over again while I'm being punished.

Tonight is like every other night. It's six o'clock. The models, the hairdressers, the stylists, the production assistants and the lighting technicians have gone home. We're all alone with Scratch inside his building—it's just me and the four artists. Every night, he comes to us, looks over what we did, and gives us his review.

Right now, he's reading the chapter I wrote for him today. He's lying on the yellow couch. He looks morose. I can already tell he doesn't like it. Why should he? It's such bullshit. The book's supposed to be about him, but I don't know what I'm talking about. I have no facts, not even basic information like where Scratch was born, or where he went to school, or when he began to use a camera. Aside from "candles," and "platforms," I have nothing.

"Oh, Alex," says Scratch, sadly. He puts down the sheaf of papers on the Moroccan tile floor. His hand dangles languidly off the couch. "Who or what is this about? You've come up with a crude caricature of me. Surely, you don't see me like this, do you, pet? As a silly, self-involved, egotistic fashion person? Surely, darling, you've failed to convey the nature of my...power." He strokes the pages with his furry fingertips, tracing circles with his blue claws.

"Maybe so, sir," I concede. In fact, my take on Scratch gets more and more vague as time goes on. My opinions, my beliefs—everything is getting weaker. Living with Scratch, I'm disconnected from the outside world. He pays our rent and provides our meals. Usually, they consist of bread and water, but, if you're being rewarded, the spread can be lavish. Four times a year—winter, fall, spring and summer—he gives us each a stack of mail order catalogues. We check off the books and magazines we want to read, the CDs we want to hear, the clothing we want to wear. Deliveries arrive from the United States, six weeks later, in shapeless brown packages which we tear open eagerly, like presents on Christmas morning.

Scratch pushes up the sleeve of his blue and rust stripped T-shirt and runs his thumb across his dragon tatoo (a leftover from last spring, when "dragon" was the word). For a moment he's absorbed in thought.

"Honesty!" Scratch pronounces, suddenly. He hands me back the sheaf of pages.

"Sir?"

"Alexandra, honesty."

"Yes, sir. Honesty."

"This wasn't honest, Alex. Was it?"

"No, sir. It was not."

"Wicked slavegirl. You're a liar."

Annoyed, I forget myself—and lose my fear. "Fuck it, Scratch," I blurt out, recklessly. "I'm just doing what you told me to. You said to make it up! I asked for facts and information and you..."

A terrible, angry smile appears on Scratch's time-worn face. My moment of rebellion vanishes.

"Sorry, sir. Forgive me. Can I take that back, sir, please?"

"Impudent, dishonest Alex," he hisses. "You shall regret those words! Undress."

I unzip my shirtjacket (Shirtjacket, yes? Yes!) and shrug it off. I unsnap my rust bra. I slip out of my yellow panties and my yellow maxiskirt. (Maxiskirt? Indeed!) I pull off my boots of soft, blue suede. (Suede! The Eternal Return!)

Naked, I walk through the empty room. As I pass the window, a group of male models from the agency across the street glances up at me with passing curiosity. They've seen the routine at Scratch's studio, many times.

When I reach the round wooden conference table in the center of the room, I clamber on to it, using a chair as a footstep, and lie down. I rest my forehead against the smooth surface of polished wood.

"Head up!" Scratch wheezes.

Lifting my chin, I began to count the 150 glass panels in the windows. One, two, three, four... I hear Scratch's motorcycle boots click against the tile floor. He walks to the file cabinet and opens the drawer where we keep our five tubes of lubricant, and our shared instruments of torture.

I hear him riffle through the contents of the drawer. I count faster. Twelve, thirteen, fourteen...

He shuts the drawer, crosses the room, and stops behind me. Fifteen, sixteen...

"Hands behind back, slave. Must I remind you every time?"

I start to shiver.

"Slavegirl," says Scratch, "have you been dishonest?"

"Yes, sir. Right, sir. Oh, yes, sir. Yes, I have."

"Dishonest Alex! Repeat after me. I, Alexandra Bellamy, am a lazy parasite who contributes nothing to society."

"I, Alexandra Bellamy, am a lazy parasite," I repeat.

Seventeen, eighteen, nineteen...

Before he hurts me, Scratch keeps me waiting. I don't know what's going on behind my back. I don't know what he's holding in his hands.

Twenty, twenty-one, twenty-two...

I count, to help the time pass more quickly while I'm waiting for my pain.

I need it, now.

We all do.

Our nerves and buttons work the same.

Her Secret Pleasure

Tsaurah Litzky

I.

She had always liked to play with it. Her mother would yell into the closed bathroom door: "What's taking you so long?" She would yell out: "Just finishing, mom, it's a number two."

She loved to roll it into balls; she loved the smell, although she knew she wasn't supposed to. It was supposed to smell bad, but she loved it so; maybe there was something wrong with her. It reminded her of somewhere else, a long time ago, a hot place: maybe a tropical jungle with big palm trees hairy with vines and spiders, where the earth was moist and warm, seething with sweaty, crawly creepy bugs, little beetles everywhere, shining like diamonds. The smell was sweet like molasses but deeper, a dark smell, pungent, roses covered with mud.

Sometimes she liked to fashion little flowers out of her shit, daises or buttercups. She could play with it all day, but when her mother yelled in the bathroom a second time with that little shapr edge of concern in her voice, "What the matter, did you fall through the hole to China?" that's when she knew it was time to stop. She'd scrape the sweet shit off her hands, put it back into the bowl, wipe herself off, pull up her pants, and wash her hands. She had to wash them good; it took a long time to get the smell off.

II.

She loved to rim him. He used to call her "my little rim queen."

"My rim queen," he would say, smiling at her suddenly when they were eating linguine and clam sauce, or when they were waiting in line at the movies. Sometimes he would call her up from work. "Hello, rim queen," he'd say, and in the background she could hear the sounds of the wood shop; hammers and the whirring of electric saws. She would be happy then because it meant she was thinking about it too, wanting her to do it again.

Of course, there were other things they did: she sucked him and he sucked her, but less often. When they first got together he always used to suck her, but time had made him more passive. Maybe she had created the situation with her eagerness for rimming.

Turn over, turn over, please, she would beg, and he would roll over on his belly and stretch for her. He had a small, tight ass, hardly an ass at all, but when she parted him with her tongue he was a whole empire of sweetness. The downy corona of blonde hairs that grew above his lovely pink, puckered anus were spun sugar in her mouth; the smell was heady and intoixicating. Sometimes as she was rimming him she would feel one her hands travel south to her little nubbin; she would rub it with her middle finger, up and down, to match the rhythm of her thrusting tongue. She would take her other hand, and, bringing it around in front and making a magic circle of her fingers, would pull his cock, tonguing his sweet ass all the while. Meanwhile, she would rub herself harder and harder. Usually they came together. He didn't like it too much when she put two fingers and a thumb up there, but after he had come, he would sometimes let her do that, and she would fuck him gently until he was hard again.

After they broke up, she was bouncing off the walls. No matter how hard she rubbed herself, she could not bring herself off; she walked around with a raw, sore ache in her center. One night in a bar she picked up a guy; he liked sixty-nine, but he was rim-shy. Another time she went home with the step instructor from the health club; he let her rim him, but she couldn't detect even the faintest stink of it; maybe he lived on liquid vitamin pills and didn't shit. She pretended to come in order to get it over with and get out of there.

After that she started to play with it again. With no mother to call her out of the bathroom she rubbed it in her palms, sniffed it for what seemed like hours. It was heaven. She remembered reading somewhere that playing with your own shit was one of the symptoms of schizophrenia, but one day she decided: If being schitz was wanting to bask in smells of a lush and fecund jungle, so be it. She would crown herself Shit Queen, the great and schitzy Shit Queen, and her empire of feces-flowers would scrape and bow before her.

Shot Rocket Hotel

L.A. Rocco

The root of my problems lies not in my vagina, but in my intestines. It's the first time I've ever purchased antacid, and I hadn't eaten yogurt in over a year because I ate so much yogurt the last time I could ever remember eating yogurt, it'd taken a whole year for me to even walk by the yogurt section again in the super-market.

Now it's all I eat, and the antacid, this week. If there's one thing I know, food'll either give you heart disease, or cancer, or it'll make you crap your brains out, but not yogurt; not yogurt. Pupil influenced by the masses, and the masses of my intestines, shit on televisions everywhere in every room trying to soothe, hypnotize with flashing, and non-fat yogurt commercials telling you you can live forever.

I get a burning, a swelling in the middle. The M.D. says antacid will do me some good. I am a piece in the assembly line. I have the day job, like most of the masses, the job at the place that ate their innards away.

Eat or be eaten; eaten by your own stomach. Get up, go to work and eat up my antacid tablets. Knowing I'm not living forever. So why take an antacid? Eat a yogurt? Do a job that's gonna eat me up?

Usually I get onions. Mostly onions, and any of the other turnip-types and vegetables that are on sale. I eat several onions a day. People say onions good. I used to take onions out of the food I ate, but now they're most of what I eat, just like the antacids. And I don't sleep much at night; I do it to myself sometimes twenty times, and sometimes with vegetables, but never tried pickles. No, I don't sleep a wink all night, maybe - all I do is come and pass gas, fuck and fart, listening carefully. That's when I'm alone, and have eaten many onions. When I'm not alone. I fart silently.

My farts seep out so slowly when another is there, in bed and under the covers hoping to god it will dissipate before it floats out into the open air beyond the blanket's borders.

That is life; food and tv, sex, sex, and work. And dying is doing what you have to, not what you do do. And you would think I'm the kind of girl who would just let 'em rip without a mention because it takes so much effort to silence a fart.

You'd think I could buy these designer condoms I wanted on my own, proud and perverse like my underwear which hangs on the wall. But like the fart, I have some girl I know purchase the novelty electronically-tested condoms because I don't have the guts. I give her the money and stand with her on line casually pretending I am preoccupied with my hair. After the merchandise is bagged and we're not even out of the store, I say "thanks"—how silly of me—and take the change from her.

My boyfriend would fart silently as well, unless he was not farting at all (but I knew that he was). Whether it be consideration or shame - except when I might be laughing and a laugh might spontaneously come out the bottom of my ass; we did not subject the other to the sound of flatulence. Such excretes and refuse were already being offered to not another in the form of verbiage.

And He doesn't like it when I use His name in my writing. IT'S AN UNFAIR REPRESENTATION. He says. I don't understand, so I call Him nothing. My boyfriend is nothing but a pronoun.

"You did the most disgusting vile thing imaginable," He said to me. "Finding sexual pleasures in another," I did, while I was at the day job, as a rocket scientist I had moved away for the job which ate at my innards.

I begged Him to return to me. But I never understood why He didn't leave me before that. Shouldn't He have been just as displeased with me finding sexual pleasures in my finger and my smelly underwear? Or the cucumber, or the carrots. or the turnip-type objects? Or when I mentioned the conventional sex with food I'd been doing? He never said anything then. He must have thought I was doing it for exercise, because I told Him once. I do it 'til my cellulite hurts. When the relationship gets bad I should let Him be finding carrots in me, and more and more. He would be competing with the vegetables for my attention; I wonder what He would say about finding carrots in there. I'd go skipping back to him from my trip to the toilet to say, "Hey, did you even notice I had a pickle in me!? I didn't!"

He doesn't want me to have desire. There is a biological need to live and a biological need to die. So you bring yourself closer, you do what you have to. And that's what's most important, getting remarkably exceedingly closer and real-

izing how close you are, important because all of everybody's life is mostly going to be spent dead. Six yogurts sit
at the bottom of my belly. And do not exceed 16 tablets in a
24 hour period. Antacids in assorted flavors, and sometimes
I just need more.

Maybe we have to stop eating the onions.

"You trying to get one of these off," He told me, when we
used the designer unlubricated condom I went through a
foolish ordeal to obtain. He says He doesn't like it and it
makes me feel ashamed somehow. The condom in my
garbage pail is wet now and heavy heavy in my mind.

Just as I was unable to masturbate freely with my
boyfriend in the room for a long time, I was unable to sleep
around people as a child. It was because I didn't want anyone thinking I was dead. I had a fear of scaring them like I
did when my mother found me this on time floating belly
down in the bathtub. She took hold of my hair and ripped
me out of the water thinking I'd drowned, and I had merely
been playing. What a scream she let out as she embraced my
dear wet body

One night, He asked me why I was having such a hard
time sleeping. I told him I was horny as hell. I wanted the
straight and narrow in my behind, a penis, a stiff finger. I
wanted to extend the nausea I feel a great deal of my life, a
nausea I thought might be caused by life but might be diet
related; and I always felt remarkably good after a good pass,
so why the hell not.

"I want it in the ass."

I wanted it in the ass and now I'm writing about my
bloody asshole. I don't know if I went off the birth-control
because I wanted it in the ass more, or if I wanted it in the
ass only after the horrid abrasive novelty-rubber incident
that rendered traumatic fear of all condoms in me, and
because there are no eggs in your asses - as long as you
don't eat them or put them in there intentionally from
below. I'd not have to be humiliated by rubber again. I got it
with a finger and a soapy dick in the shower. He surprised
me, it happened fast and it hurt really bad. I had a vision of
Mom ripping me from the water as I ripped his dick right
out of me in immense pain.I grabbed onto the wall and the
hot water beat down onto me. When my behind couldn't
bear it again, I took His penis by my hand and put it in for
some more. He enjoyed it more than me, I think, except for

afterward when my clit felt like it'd been through an earth-quake.

He couldn't believe I couldn't buy condoms when that girl I asked to buy them made jokes about the fuss I made. Yet I'll blab on about my BLOODY ass amongst friends 'til they turn green hearing about it. I bet I could go purchase a bloody ass in any convenience store; I'd have no reluctance there.

All day since I shitted out of my sorry ass and wiped blood onto toilet paper, I've b een talking about ass-fucking.

Before I left my room to go see HIm one night very late afterward, I unloaded my garbage because I wanted to find the fucking condom, because I had to remind myself of my humiliation. At first I couldn't find it—it showed up, of course it was there. I had to do some digging for the rubbery thing. I even touched it, picked it up with my bare fingers, its potent old sex stench reeked so sweetly, like rotten fruit, like over-sexed-masturbated-upon-underwear; I couldn't believe it. I dropped it back into the trash and heard it recoil dully, as sticky latex will.

And then I was having a frustrating time in HIs bed, and He asked, "Don't you want me inside you?""

And I said, "Yes."

"Then why don't you take me?" meaning fuck sex, not the hand job and oral finagling. I told Him I was stupid and con-fused. and the humiliation rose to a cataclysmic blush.

"Why didn't you go off the birthcontrol?" He asked.

I had watched the white fish body become and become and come and come, and lose itself in tender- infertility. But one my form was once again rejuvenated and its own, sore in the onion, but it was interned.

"I don't know!...But I'm going back on it." I said

"Do you want to be in it?" He asked.

"No, I do hate it, pills are scary." (I don't know if it's true for aspirin and antacids, and some medications, but it's surely true for birthcontrol: a necessity to eat every day like food.) Pills are attachments, you put them in your mouth and they become you, part of you, making you bigger, mak-ing more of yourself but you are less of yourself, "I hate the pills, but how else am I gonna keep the eggs from coming, from breaking out of my onion?"

All I could think about were the stupid nonlubricated designer condoms, each individually cased in a colored gold-circle coin, how cute I thought they were packaged. Oh you can't trust these, He said.

But they're electronically tested, I assured Him.

How hellish, Him saying to me, you, trying getting it off. I only feel embarrassed by the fucking rubbers now, buying them and fucking with them and Him not liking it because it stuck, Him not liking it. Yet, I make Him finger my ass and I know He doesn't like it.

It's a shame because rain coats used to turn me on, the snap and the smell, similar to that of Band-Aids releasing warm scabby-knee memories...and the sweet smelling moment of getting to inspect it later, alone me and the trash. But right then I was too embarrassed to break out with my disgraced raincoat. Pinky-finger assfucking, because I told Him to. I offered my saliva as a lubricant, using spittle to his cuntly penis, but he reached over for the bottle of Oil of Olay on my bureau; now my ass looks and feels younger.

The Assholes

Ronald Sukenick

1958. If you want to see what America is like, go to Paris. Paris is like a petri dish for Americans, it isolates the germ and lets it grow.You take a few Americans fresh from the States, drop them into the medium of the dish and wait a few months, sometimes just a few weeks, then examine the resulting growth.

When Ron first drops into that petri dish he's living in a series of fleabags on Rue Monsieur le Prince. The Beats, already famous and with whom he has incidental contact, are living in the Beat Hotel on Rue Git-le-coeur.

One night Ron sneaks a woman into his room on Monsieur le Prince, a good looking girl named Daisy Shane, just out of Sarah Lawrence, because she gives every indication of wanting to get it on. But when they get into bed--and it's a tiny single bed too—she tells Ron she doesn't do that kind of thing with boys. She isn't kidding either. Daisy is American as apple pie, and that's what apple pie is like in those days. Frozen.

Ron is frozen himself. But he's frozen stiff and she's just frozen. Stiff or not, Ron finally realizes he's not going to get anywhere. By three A.M. Ron is so pissed and frustrated and sleepless that he kicks her out.

"But where am I going to go?" whines Daisy.

"Your problem, sweet heart."

But for days afterward Ron worries, where did she go, a young, inexperienced girl with no French in a strange, tough city? Even more though, Ron is worried about himself, like that wasn't a nice thing to do. Because at the time Ron's thing is being a nice guy. Is it possible, he wonders, that he's not really a nice guy?

The fertile isolation of the petri dish is already having its effect.

The germ is germinating.

Next time Ron sees Daisy she's with Gregory Corso. They're all sitting around a table on the terrasse Aux Deux Magots. Those days you can still go to the Deux Magots with a straight face, though it's already starting to fill with American tourists inflamed with the romance of

Existentialism, who refer to it as "the Aux Deux Magots."

Corso or no, Daisy is as frozen as ever. She says she's staying with Corso in the Beat Hotel. She confides to Ron that the toilet is so filthy in the Beat Hotel she cries every time she goes to the john.

There are many Americans who come to Paris planning to stay till their money runs out and then when it runs out decide they don't want to go back to the States. Young men and women with no careers, they usually blunder around a few months on a few emergency checks from home and then they go back anyway. Those who stick with it settle into a lazy,pleasant, marginal life which is either admittedly aimless or which they often call something like "painting" or "writing." Now and then it actually is. They develop a variety of petty hustles to beat the impossibility of getting a work permit, and the women always have an additional option as a last resort.

A few months after meeting Daisy with Corso, Ron sees her sitting in a cheap café on Carrefour d'Odeon with Art and Strop. He sits down and says hello to Daisy. She's got a long pony tail that emphasizes her youth, and wears one of those yellow t-shirts that says Herald Tribune. Art is dressed in full establishment Ivy with tie and tweed jacket, khaki slacks and white bucks. Strop is wearing a leather jacket and dark glasses and seems to be assuming the role of a rebel, which of course is a traditional American way of working into the establishment. He refers to middle class American tourists generically as "the assholes."

As in, "Why don't we go over to St. Germain des Près and watch the assholes."

Daisy is going on about her financial difficulties, and how she doesn't know where her next franc is coming from.

"I'm living on the money for my ticket home," she says. "Now I don't know what to do."

"I thought you were hustling money from one of the assholes," says Strop.

"He wasn't an asshole, he was my boyfriend."

"That doesn't mean he wasn't an asshole," says Art.

"Who are the assholes?" Ron asks innocently.

"Who are the assholes," repeats Art. "You know who the assholes are."

But it's a question Ron continues to ask himself.

"I don't know where to turn," Daisy says.

"Maybe it's time to use that number I gave you," says Strop.

Daisy bursts into tears.

Ron suddenly has an appointment and leaves. He knows what the number is. It's the number Strop gives women when they're down to their last asset.

Some months later Ron bumps into Daisy at Shakespeare & Co., mingling with the middle class derelicts attending a poetry reading. He didn't know she liked poetry but he knows she's interested in Art, who is reading some Ogden Nash style doggerel. The book store is not the same Shakespeare & Co. that was a center for literary exiles of the Lost Generation, but what the hell, it's something else. The indescribable miscellany of strays who hang out there look like the center of the Lost and Found Generation.

Daisy is upset. She just left a guy she was going out with. "I'm just, I don't know, shook up."

"How long were you going out with him?"

"Three days."

"Three days, so what's the big deal?"

"We had a bad fight. Actually, I thought he was going to beat me up."

"How come?"

"Well I told him I'd go to Geneva with him, but I didn't tell him I'd stay there. When I asked for some money I guess he thought I was going to go shopping or something. After he found out I was taking the train back to Paris he got furious. I mean what does he want, I just met him."

"Anyone I know?"

"No, he's a much older man."

One thing you have to hand to Daisy, in the Paris wars she's an intrepid soldier. She's got guts and somehow she sticks it out in the sometimes somber City of Light.

Many months later Ron meets Daisy again at a big American party in the seizième, in a quartier that's sort of the equivalent of Park Avenue, and she doesn't look any the worse for wear.

This is a party involving the early *Paris Review* gang. Through Art, Ron has acquired a passing friendship with a Rockefeller scion who invites him. They go over together on the Metro. The trip is confusing because the pretty Radcliffe grad his friend is with keeps rubbing up against Ron like she wants to get it on. Ron would have willingly obliged since he doesn't have a girl at the time and is horny to the point of death. But as soon as they get to this bash they all immediately lose themselves in the mob and the martinis and Ron never sees either of them again.

When after several hours of martinis Ron comes out the other side of the tobacco smoke and alcohol fumes, he's for some reason leaving the party with Art, Daisy and several drunk and raucous young American guys of a kind with which he does not normally hang out. They all wear jackets and ties, now rather askew, and seem to be having something like a prep school reunion. Aside from being stinking drunk, they show all the signs of good breeding.

Much as Ron dislikes this type he finds something attractive about them. They seem happy. Happy-go-lucky. Why shouldn't they be? Golden children of the Golden Calf. Carefree Canaanites. The ring leader, Guy Lobe, is from New Canaan, Conn. Lobe is slightly older and works in Paris. They head for his apartment on the Ile St. Louis, where there is the promise of yet more booze and possibly other, unspecified goodies.

They end up in Lobe's apartment, which is well furnished with oriental rugs, antiques and whisky, and he even has a little pot, which is very exciting in those days. I mean, you could blow some pot and it was like so far out you could tell yourself that all your inhibitions were off on a walk around the block.

Not counting Lobe there are three of these guys besides Art and Ron. They're on their summer vacations from various business and law schools. After a while it becomes obvious that Daisy has been to bed with Lobe, and maybe also with Art. She doesn't even bother denying the heavy handed innuendos of these two.

Daisy's new sexual license makes Ron a little jealous, but it's not too surprising at this stage of her growth in the petri dish. And really he's less jealous than envious of these guys who had whatever it took to make her acquiesce.

But now maybe because of these vibes a joke starts where they begin saying since she's already got it on with two of them she might as well make it with the others. Daisy just laughs at them and tells them to stop being jerks.

Ron figures she might be a little uneasy by this time, the only woman with all these drunks, and he offers to leave with her. But the other guys boo and hiss and accuse him of trying to hog her for himself, and Daisy just tells Ron to stop being a jerk.

They joke and badger her for a while about sex but naturally they don't get anywhere though she's reasonably good natured about it.

Finally Lobe says, jokingly Ron presumes, "All right, we'll pay you."

"I don't do that kind of thing," says Daisy with a smug little smile.

"Bull shit," says Art. He puts his hand on her ass and says, "Twenty-five bucks." She knocks his hand away.

"Each," he adds.

Daisy sort of giggles. She's as drunk as the rest of them and her laugh sounds slightly hysterical now.

"What the shit, make it fifty," says another guy as he starts pawing her.

"Cut the crap," she snaps. The guys are more focussed now and she's treating it less like a joke. "And get your dirty hands off."

The place goes quiet for about a minute.

Then Guy Lobe says, "How much do you want?"

She gives him a long, hard look and then she just shrugs her shoulders.

"All right," says Lobe. "A hundred." He looks around. "Is that okay with everyone? A hundred a piece."

"I don't have any money," Ron says.

"He doesn't have any money," someone repeats.

"Fuck him. He can watch," says Art.

Daisy's eyes are beginning to look glazed, like she's about to go catatonic. "Let's see the money," she says.

"A hundred bucks. One shot a piece," says Lobe.

They start pulling out their wallets, Art goes around collecting the bills.

"Going once, going twice," he says. "Okay." Art puts the money on the table, big bills, Ron sees at least two hundreds, some fifties.

Lobe starts unzipping her dress. She doesn't resist. They hoot as he takes her clothes off, applauding and whistling as Lobe drops each item to the floor.

Ron already knows she has a beautiful body but he doesn't realize how beautiful. She's got a body worth a million bucks and Ron can understand why she's decided to cash in on it. The guys can see they're going to get their money's worth. It shuts them up for a minute anyway.

"Shit, a hundred bucks a piece," says one of them finally with a forced laugh. "Which piece is mine?"

"I want a breast," snickers another.

"Interesting what money can buy," says Lobe.

"Or what you can sell for it," says Art.

What they do is get her on her hands and knees on the table and play with her for a while. Ron gets a look at her face and she's staring into space. The best way Ron can describe her expression to himself is she looks like she's taking a shit.

The guys around the table are still laughing some but it doesn't sound like laughter anymore. It sounds like their throats have gone dry, like Ron's. The sounds that come out are like the coughing of an old drunk stumbling along an empty street on a winter night.

Finally they put her on her back with her legs off the edge of the table. Art takes out his cock, grabs her ass and goes in. The others watch like animals watching a stud mounting the female in heat. "Hung like a stallion!" one of them says with unconvincing bravado.

It doesn't take very long, it seems like maybe thirty seconds before Art groans, twitches and flops out.

For Ron what's going on is a certain loss of innocence, even though he's just watching. If I ever thought I was a nice guy, forget it, he thinks. All he wishes is that he had a hundred bucks.

The third guy comes in her mouth. After that they give her a bottle of whisky and she takes a long drink.

Lobe goes last. He turns her over and penetrates her from behind, then pulls out and carefully separates her cheeks to expose her asshole.With a look on his face that might best be described as devout, he bends down and starts licking her asshole, working his tongue all around and then in. You can actually see the point of his tongue flicking in and out of her hole. After a short time the tip of his tongue starts turning yellow-brown, she's probably been eating in those student restaurants.

"Good god," says one of the guys. "Holy shit," says another. Treyf, Ron thinks, and is immediately surprised at thinking it.

Lobe straightens up and starts drilling his cock up her ass. "Wait,"she says, "that's not . . ." She gives a little cry and then takes it.

Soon Lobe is up to the hilt and moving like a piston. He comes with aloud yell that could be of triumph or despair, Ron can't tell which. After he pulls out he takes a mouthful of whisky, swishes it around, and spits it on the Persian rug.

When he's done with it they offer her the bottle. She shakes her head. "The money," she says numbly.

"The money," Art repeats. He picks it up and counts it out in front of her nose. Then he rolls the bills lengthwise in a tight cone. "Hold her," he says.

But it's not necessary. She just lays there as he carefully works the cone into her ass. She starts wriggling to accommodate his thrust, the first sign of animation she's shown. With one last, hard push the bills disappear.

At that moment her body stiffens, she screams and her head rolls so Ron can see her face, eyes closed, mouth gaping, bearing an expression that could be pain or bliss.

"Yeck," says one of the guys.

Now evidently disgusted with her, and maybe with themselves, they get her dress on quickly, hustle her out the door and down to the street. "Oink, oink, oink," says Art as she stumbles out the court yard door. Ron follows quickly after her but must have turned in the opposite direction. She seems to have disappeared in the dark streets. At this point her ass is literally worth five hundred dollars.

It's two a.m. and everything is closed, including of course the Metro. Ron can't find a taxi, he hopes she can. If not he figures she's going to have to walk carefully because they didn't even give her time to get her underwear on.

When Ron remembers this episode it gives laundered money a new meaning.

APPENDIX A

Selected Reading List of Books by Some of the Contributors—Certainly Not Comprehensive, but Fairly Representational

Don Webb
Uncle Ovid's Excercise Book (FC2)
A Spell for the Fullfillment of Desire (Black Ice Books)
Stealing My Rules (Cyberpsychos AOD Press)
The Double (St. Martin's Press)

Robert Coover
Spanking the Maid (Grove)
The Public Burning (Grove)
Gerald's Wife (Simon & Schuster)
Pricksongs and Descants (Dutton)

Ian Grey
Sex Stupidity and Greed: Inside the
    American Film Industry (Juno Books)

William T. Vollmann
Whores for Gloria (Pantheon)
The Butterfly Stories (Grove)
The Rainbow Stories (Penguin)
The Atlas (Penguin)
The Royal Family (Penguin)

Kim Addonizio
In the Box Called Pleasure (FC2)
Tell Me (BOA Editions)

Jimmy Jazz
The Sub (Incommunicado)
The Symphony of Urban Decay (Incommunicado)

Michael Hemmingson
The Naughty Yard (Permeable Press)
Nice Little Stories Jam-Packed with Depraved
    Sex & Violence (Cyberpsychos AOD Press)

The Mammoth Book of Short Erotic Novels (Carroll & Graf)
Wild Turkey (Tor/Forge Books)

Larry McCaffery
Avant-Pop: Fiction for a Daydream Nation (Black Ice)
After Yesterday's Crash: The Avant-Pop Anthology (Penguin)
Some Other Frequency: Interviews (Univ. of
    Pennslyvania Press)

M. Christian
Dirty Words (Alyson Publications)
Guilty Pleasures (Black Books)
Eros ex Machina (Masquerade)

Thom Metzger
This is Your Final Warning! (Autonomedia)
Blood & Volts: Edison, Tesla, & the Eleectric Chair
    (Autonomedia)

Harold Jaffe
Eros/Antieros (City Lights)
Straight Razor (Black Ice)
Sex for the Millenium (Black Ice)

L.A. Ruocco
Document: Zippo (Soft Skull Press)

Ronald Sukenick
98.6 (FC2)
Doggy Bag (Black Ice)
Mosaic Man (FC2)
Narralogues (SUNY Press)

APPENDIX B

Some Final Quotes to Leave You With

" . . . *pornography is not sure.*"
  —Roland Barthes, The Pleasure of the Text

"Abstinence sows sand all over
The ruddy limbs & flaming hair,
But Desire Gratified
Plants fruits of life and beauty"
  —William Blake, Songs and Ballads

"It was a good thing that I raised egoistic masturbation to the
dignity of a cult."
  —Jean Genet, A Thief's Journal